Albany County
Public Library

**Sources of
Library Materials
FY 11**

16.8%

46.8%

4.6%

5.6%

23.1%

0.4%

2.7%

- Donated Items
- Individual Cash Gifts
- Replacement Fees
- ACPLF
- City Sales Tax
- County Sales Tax
- Friends of the Library

GUARDIAN
OF THE
GREEN HILL

GUARDIAN
OF THE
GREEN HILL

Laura L. Sullivan

Henry Holt and Company
New York

Henry Holt and Company, LLC
Publishers since 1866
175 Fifth Avenue
New York, New York 10010
mackids.com

Library of Congress Cataloging-in-Publication Data
Sullivan, Laura L.
Guardian of the Green Hill / Laura L. Sullivan ; [illustrations by David Wyatt].—1st ed.
        p.   cm.
Sequel to: Under the Green Hill.
ISBN 978-0-8050-8985-1
[1. Supernatural—Fiction.   2. Fairies—Fiction.   3. Brothers and sisters—Fiction.
4. Superstition—Fiction.   5. England—Fiction.]   I. Wyatt, David, ill.   II. Title.
PZ7.S9527Gu 2011   [Fic]—dc22   2010029231

First Edition—2011
Book designed by Elizabeth Tardiff
Printed in September 2011 in the United States of America by
R. R. Donnelley & Sons Company, Harrisonburg, Virginia

1 3 5 7 9 10 8 6 4 2

For Buster
and
for you

GUARDIAN
OF THE
GREEN HILL

She Will Be My Creature

MORE SKIN THAN FLESH, more bones than skin, the artist hunched over his easel. He added shading under the eyes and thickened the hair, then growled in disgust. It was still nothing like her, nothing like what he wanted her to be. The eyes were only wistful, not yet weak and sorrowful. The round chin looked too strong. . . . It would never tremble. Even the short curling silver hair looked too tidy, nothing like the unkempt locks of one given up to despair. And that is how he needed Phyllida Ash—hopeless, self-pitying, cringing, and powerless.

He tore the paper off with a flourish and fed it to his goat.

"I am only half the artist my father was," he said bitterly, sketching out new lines on a fresh sheet.

"True," said the goat, "but you are twice the magician." He munched on the paper contemplatively. "Perhaps if you switched to charcoal."

"You just don't like the taste of ink, Pazhan," the man said.

"Be glad I don't use oils. I will, though, just as soon as I can worm my way in. Into the house, into her confidence . . . and into her place at last. One good sketch, and I'll have a hold on her, enough to create an opening. Then when she sits for me, when I can do a proper portrait, she will be my creature."

"Will she really do as you say, Gwidion? She'll give it up, just like that?"

"You've seen what I can do."

"Sketches to make the innkeeper give you a free night and a full flagon. Portraits to charm some gullible young woman into leaving her loved ones to follow you . . . till you've had your fill. I've seen that, sure enough. But this is something else entirely. Phyllida Ash is a strong woman, bred to her role for generations, and she has powerful protectors. She may keep the fairies in check, but do you think they don't love her?"

"What of you, Pazhan? Do you love her?"

He shrugged his goat shoulders. "That is neither here nor there. I am part of your family. So long as there are Thomas men, I am yours, not hers, till such time as you strike me thrice in three days."

Which didn't quite answer the question, but Gwidion nodded. "My only inheritance. My father's only inheritance, and his father's before him, when it could have all been ours. All mine."

"Have I been such a bad bargain?" the goat asked archly, but Gwidion ignored him.

"Soon I will come into my own. No more wandering, a penniless rover. No more living by my wits, day to day, town to town. Here is where I belong, Pazhan, here at the Rookery, at the Green Hill. Whether they like it or not, I am home."

They Came to Me

MEG MORGAN PLUCKED a last plump jade-green berry from the thorny hedge just before the Gooseberry Wife could lurch her corpulent body close enough to nip. She gnashed her small, grinding teeth in pique as Meg escaped with her prize.

"You shouldn't tease her," Phyllida chided from across the lawn. "She takes her job very seriously."

The Gooseberry Wife was a lumbering, bloated caterpillar as long as Meg's arm. She haunted berry shrubs, guarding them from the marauding hands of youngsters, preserving the fruits for the cook's tarts and fools. Meg looked into her squinty eyes from a safe distance, but found herself compelled to look instead at the large black false eyespots on the top of her pale-green head.

"I'm sorry," Meg told her. "I want them for Bran."

The Gooseberry Wife shivered her segmented body in annoyance, making each spiny witch-wart hair along her back stand on end.

Meg carried her handful of berries back to Bran. He lounged on a chaise, scowling. Every few minutes he tried to rise, muttering something about wood to chop or rents to collect, but his family shoved him down again. He was restless, furious at his imposed sloth, but too weak to protest. After all, he'd died only two weeks ago.

It was teatime, a custom the children wished had followed the colonists to America. Here in England they realized how welcome a fourth meal is to someone who spends the better part of the day tramping through the woods, running, playing, and fighting. The more sedate adults, Phyllida and Lysander Ash, contented themselves with tea and thin, floating lemon slices and a few McVitie's digestive biscuits. The children—Rowan, Meg, Silly, and James Morgan, Finn Fachan, and Dickie Rhys—gorged themselves on scones and clotted cream, sardines on toast, eggs, seedcakes, nut cakes, and fruitcakes. To Phyllida's horror, they insisted their tea be served cold and sickeningly sweetened, and though they consented to lemons, they looked at them suspiciously if they weren't cut into wedges.

Now the carnage of crumbs lay scattered across the tables, and the children (save James, who was studying a small civilization of black ants) were playing croquet on the manicured lawn, making up rules as they went along. At times they seemed to confuse croquet and cricket.

"Out of bounds!" Silly shouted.

"No such thing," said Rowan, who really had no idea.

"Ow, my shin!" Dickie wailed.

"Sorry, no depth perception," Finn said, in a tone that sounded far from apologetic. "My point," he added, stopping to pull his black silk eyepatch into place. The game had degenerated into something like violent polo without the horses. Silly compensated somewhat for their lack with her raucous neighing laugh.

Dickie dropped out, joining Meg, while the others continued in deadly earnest. Rowan and Finn, antagonistic as ever, might have caused each other some serious harm if not for Silly getting between them, not as peacemaker but with her own keen desire to beat the boys. Legs were struck, feet trampled, turfs uprooted as they pounded across the lawn. Soon the rifle crack of mallet upon ball faded into the distance and peace reigned, more or less, in the English countryside.

Meg and Dickie drifted to the hedgerow and looked across the sunken wall of the ha-ha to the sheep-strewn meadow. The sheep, white with black faces, were echoed in the sky, deep lapis dotted with small white clouds barely tinged with a darkness that hinted at a distant storm. They grazed contentedly, unaware of the little men in green who methodically sheared the softest wool from their bellies.

"They're like chipmunks," Meg said absently, much to Dickie's bafflement.

"The sheep?" he asked, perplexed.

Meg gave a little laugh. "Oh, I forgot you can't see them. The Weavers are out among the sheep."

"And they look like chipmunks?"

"No, no, I didn't even realize I was talking out loud. I meant fairies are getting to be like chipmunks were back at Arcadia." Arcadia, sylvan seat of learning in upstate New York, was where all their parents taught. "They were pretty common, but they didn't let themselves be seen. Then when you saw one, it was always a little thrill. The fairies are getting to be like that. Commonplace somehow, not surprising anymore, but still extraordinary." She didn't think she had expressed herself very well, but Dickie understood.

"There seem to be more of them than usual," Meg went on. "Maybe it's just easier to see them for some reason. On the grounds, too. Phyllida told me, back before the war, that fairies don't generally come on the Rookery property, except for a few, like the brownie or the Gooseberry Wife. But I see other ones here every day now. The Weavers and flower fairies, and I even stepped on a stray sod yesterday, right here on the lawn."

"I wish I could see them," Dickie said.

"You can stand on my foot if you like. You said that's one way, stand on the foot of someone who can see fairies."

He sighed longingly but shook his head. "And end up like Finn, with a hazel stick in my eye? No, thank you. They don't like spies. Anyway, I *have* seen fairies, the ones who wanted to be seen, and for the most part I didn't enjoy it much." Despite his words, Meg noticed something like pride on Dickie's face. She remembered that evening when she was racing to the Green Hill as Seelie champion in Rowan's place. Every horror of the Unseelie Court had tried to stop her. The worst was the skinless Nuckelavee.

How brave Dickie had been that night, luring it away and foiling it with its nemesis, fresh water. He'd pooh-poohed her praise later, saying, "Nothing's so bad if you know what its weaknesses are." But Meg was still impressed by his valor. Even in bright, unthreatening daylight, when he was his pale, pudgy, sniffling self again, he possessed, in her eyes at least, the air of a hero.

"I wonder why we can all see them . . . Rowan and Silly and James, I mean."

"You're related to Phyllida. It must be in the blood. Meg . . ." He hesitated, not sure how to go on. "Phyllida doesn't have any children, you know."

Meg just looked at him.

"I mean, you four are it. And from what she says, it's always a woman of her bloodline who's the Guardian of the Green Hill. So that's just you and Silly. You two are the only ones left. I was just wondering if someday—it's not a nice thing to think about, but she is awfully old, and someday . . ."

Meg's eyes widened in alarm. Oddly enough, it had never really occurred to her that she might be next in line. "No!" With all the chaos of the Midsummer War, she had been too preoccupied to carry things to their natural conclusion. The present was enough to fill her head, and though she had some vague idea that she had an obligation to learn about fairies, this suggestion of being Guardian was shocking.

"Phyllida will live a long time . . . a very long time." Oh, how she hoped so, for love of the old woman and, now, for newer selfish reasons.

"Hasn't she said anything to you about it?"

"No, nothing." Come to think of it, there had been vague hints, mentions of her birthright, of the duties and obligations that come with gifts, of her family's heritage. But she thought it was just history, nothing to do with her own future.

Seeing how uncomfortable Meg was, Dickie wisely let it drop.

He was just wondering if asking Meg to point out which particular sheep were being sheared would count as an eye-losing offense when they were interrupted by hooves clattering on the cobblestone path that led to the croquet lawn.

A big roan horse skidded to a halt inches from Phyllida and Lysander, panting and lathered in sweat. His rider tumbled off and made the barest bow before gasping out, "Please, Lady, you must come quickly!"

Phyllida got to her feet, dusting the crumbs from her lavender frock and anchoring her rose-bedecked straw hat more firmly on her head. "What is it, Cain? What's amiss?"

"I don't know, ma'am. Young Evan came running to the stables and said whoever was fastest on a horse should go for the Lady. Jim said he was, but by the time he was finished bragging, I was on Lightfoot and away."

"Evan didn't give you any clue what it was about?" Phyllida asked even as Lysander hailed a servant and gave instructions that their carriage be readied.

"It's at Moll's house, is all I know. You're to go to Moll's house."

"Is it the baby? Oh, dear, has the doctor been sent for? I don't know why folk will still call me before the doctor for scalds and chicken pox. Cain, if your horse isn't done in, please ride for Dr. Homunculus and send him after us, just in case. Lysander, the coach—"

"Nearly ready, my dear," he said calmly. These little emergencies cropped up all the time and might be anything from a broken leg to a cow gone dry. If a pretty daughter stayed out all night, Phyllida was called, on the certainty that the fairies had snatched her. If a man went astray, they looked to her for a charm to win him back from what was undoubtedly a glamour of some sort. If dishes broke a bit too often, it was surely the result of mischievous bogies who had to be banished. Phyllida had some serious duties to perform as Guardian of the fairy sanctuary, the Green Hill, but more often she played a role somewhere between patron and witch doctor for her tenants and the villagers of Gladysmere.

Bran tried to push himself up, but Phyllida was instantly at his side. "Stay, Bran dear. You'll open your wound again." She might be his daughter, grown old in the real world while he was trapped by the fairies under the Green Hill, but sometimes she had to scold him like a mother. The arrow hole in his chest—mark of his great sacrifice in the Midsummer War—had nearly closed, but any vigorous movement still caused him great pain. If he wasn't very careful, the injury seeped thin pink-red blood through the bandage.

"But if it's the fairies—"

"If it's the fairies, I can handle it myself," Phyllida snapped. "I did it for seventy years without you."

Bran flinched, and Phyllida looked abashed. She hadn't meant to remind him how he had abandoned his wife and children for the twilight world under the Green Hill.

"It's likely nothing. You stay here and heal. Let May bring you some more tea."

Bran mumbled something about tea coming out of his ears,

and that he'd had enough mollycoddling, but he settled back into the chaise.

"Can we go with you?" Meg asked as her great-great-aunt and -uncle made their way to the circular drive at the front of the Rookery.

"I don't see why not," Phyllida said. "It will be good for you. You can see a bit more of the countryside, meet some of the tenants. It's best to know the ins and outs of those who live and work on your land. Makes everything run so much more smoothly."

But it's not my land, Meg thought.

"Can James come too?"

Phyllida assented, but when Meg asked if he wanted to go, he told her with great brevity that he was still delving into ant culture and couldn't be disturbed in his scientific and anthropological endeavors. He explained this all with the word "no." At four years old, he was exquisitely single-minded.

"He'll be fine there," Lysander said. "May and June will look after him." May and June were maids, twin sisters born an hour apart, but in two different months.

Meg, less trusting, called out to her brother and sister in the distance where they still sported in their frenzied game with Finn. "Rowan! Silly! We're going on a drive with Phyllida." They answered with shouts and screams. "Did you hear me? Watch James, will you?"

Rowan waved and called something that sounded like an affirmative, so Meg ran back to the drive where the carriage, driven by a liveried coachman, was just rolling up. The two dapple-gray horses stomped and flicked their tails, annoyed at having been taken from their oats on such short notice.

With the wind whipping her hair and the bright July sun browning her neck and freckling her nose, it felt like a festival day. Though she loved the Rookery, and the grounds (and the house itself) were vast and varied enough to entertain almost without end, it was good to get away and catch a glimpse of the rest of the world. The Rookery was nestled against the deep woods, but as they went east, they came to more open country, rolling fields of high golden hay. They passed houses that seemed to be from another time, half-timbered cottages with dormer windows, flowers trailing over the sills, pear trees climbing the walls. Where the river ran parallel to the road, she saw a mill with a great wooden wheel turning eternally in the flow. Fields were divided by hedgerows or by dry stone walls made with rocks removed in the first plowing centuries before, stacked without a drop of mortar to hold them in place. From some of the fields rose little hills, like the Green Hill in miniature, some the size of giant tortoises, some as big as cars, some oblong, as large as a bus. Meg pointed them out to Dickie.

"They're tumuluses, I think. Tumuli? I'll have to ask the Wyrm." That learned but forgetful beast had fallen asleep in the sun-warmed carp pond back at the Rookery. "Graves, in any case, or barrows, as they call them here. They could be from the Neolithic. That's the Stone Age," he added, seeing that she didn't know but wouldn't ask. "They were probably a lot bigger, but have been worn down."

"You mean there are . . . bodies . . . under all of those mounds?" Fairies were ceasing to scare her, but she shivered at the thought of ghosts.

Lysander, overhearing, said, "Don't be silly, girl. There are bodies all around us." Meg looked, half expecting to see a field of corpses. "People have been treading this earth, and falling on it, for centuries . . . millennia! Our tiny lives are but an ant's step along the long road of human history. Every man who has ever lived in this green and pleasant land, save those alive now, is dead and buried. Only think how they outnumber us! Makes our troubles seem wee, doesn't it?"

"I don't like to think about it," Meg said in a little voice.

"Lysander, leave her alone," Phyllida chided.

The sun was as warm as ever on Meg's shoulders, but beneath it blew the first breeze of impending evening, and Meg felt suddenly chilled. She made herself look at the barrows again, trying to dispel the feeling of doom. You're just being silly, she told herself. Dead people . . . ghosts . . . bosh! There, that's just a hill with sheep-cropped stubble on it, nothing more.

She gave a little shriek, quickly stifled with her hand. A form rose from the tumulus like a corpse from the grave. A dust-colored man in loose clothes, as though his flesh had shrunken away from them, sat, then stood, then looked directly at the carriage. Directly, Meg would have sworn, at her.

"Who is that?" she asked.

They all looked, but none could identify him. Her relatives didn't seem concerned. "Probably an artist," Phyllida concluded, dismissing it. "They like to gather around here to paint the old church up on the rise, or the remnants of the hill fort. He'll probably wander to the Rookery eventually."

"And like as not try to sell you his sketches," Lysander added.

"I can't tell you how many pen-and-inks and charcoals and watercolors I have filed away, just waiting for one of 'em to be worth something when the artist becomes famous. Or dies. Hasn't happened yet."

Meg stared back at the form shrinking rapidly into the distance. Sure enough, he had a contraption beside him that looked like a folding easel. Only an artist out to capture the hazy golden hues of the declining sun. And he had not been staring at her in particular. Why, they rode in such an outlandish contraption, who could help but stare? While there were many farmers who still used horse-drawn carts, they were big, practical things with modern rubber tires. Sometimes she even saw tractors and mechanical threshers being pulled by a team of drafthorses. But the Ashes' conveyance was straight out of the Victorian beau monde, a barouche on high, red wooden wheels. The carriage itself looked like an old-fashioned perambulator, seating four passengers face-to-face. It might have rolled down the streets of Victoria's London unremarked. Of course anyone new to the area would stare.

The dust-colored man was forgotten when they pulled up to the little brick farmhouse half surrounded by unmown hay mixed with wildflowers. Rusted cans, snippets of curling wire, and planks studded with nails lay scattered along with other rubbish. The front was cleared, probably by the peregrinations of a large Yorkshire sow and her farrow. White geese raised their sinuous necks in alarm as the barouche rolled to a stop, then arched them downward, hissing threats.

Without warning, Meg felt dizzy, a throbbing rush of blood to her head. For a moment, her vision dimmed and she was aware of a sorrow so terrible it was like an uncontrolled fear, swallowing her up, leaving her shaking and irrational. She grabbed for Phyllida's hand and squeezed the old woman's fingers until she cried out, "Mercy, Meg, what's wrong?"

"I don't know . . . I don't know! Something terrible has happened here. Can you feel it? We should have come quicker. I should have known before. Oh! It's too late!" She collapsed into sobs, much to Dickie's consternation. He took her other hand awkwardly while Phyllida disengaged herself from Meg's viselike grip and, alarmed, scurried into Moll's house.

"Meg, what is it?" Dickie asked when they were left alone.

"I don't know," she said again, calming, though convulsive aftershocks of sobs still echoed through her. "I just felt, all of a sudden, a sadness so great. . . . Dickie, what's wrong? What's wrong with me?"

"I don't feel anything," he said. "Something to do with the fairies, maybe? The house does look dour, though." Little sooted-over windows glared balefully at them from the ramshackle dwelling. It was obvious that no one had cared for it in quite some time.

They waited in awful silence until suddenly a keening wail rose, an unearthly sound that made the very windows rattle. A woman with eyes glassy-red from weeping burst from the shack, looking wildly around.

"Colin!" she cried. "Colin, love, where are you? Come back to me, my darling!" She disappeared into the greenwood, her hair streaming behind her.

Phyllida tried to follow, but though she was hardly frail, a person of eighty-odd years can't catch a woman of twenty-five. She rested against a linden, panting. "Moll! Come back!"

"She's looking for the Green Hill," Lysander said, coming up behind her. He leaned heavily on his gnarled cane. "She thinks she'll find him there."

"We must go after her. She'll do herself harm."

While Lysander mustered some villagers to go after the crazed Moll, Phyllida sat Meg down on a bench at the edge of the pig wallow.

"They came to me," Phyllida said, speaking with her eyes closed. "When Bran was healing in his ash tree, Moll's mother came and tried to speak with me. They never call the doctor, if they can help it. I refused to see her. I was so worried about Bran. Then Moll's brother came, just two days ago, and I turned him away with a wave. I said I'd be by soon. Oh, not soon enough!" She hid her face in her hands and fell to her knees in the muck. "Such a happy little man Moll's baby was! I was there for his birth, and I swear he smiled to see the world for the first time. Not yet a year beneath the sun . . ."

"Her son died? Phyllida, it's not your fault."

"Yes, yes, it is! I was so caught up in my own life, my own fears, I neglected my duties. The Green Hill, the people who live nearby, my people, my tenants, are more important than me or my own blood. I should have come at the first call, even if it was nothing, only some petty problem. That is my obligation. Better Bran had died than that poor wee laddie. Better I had died."

"Can't we do something?" Meg asked. "We brought Bran back to life. Isn't there something we can do for the baby?"

Phyllida shook her head. "That kind of thing happens once in a thousand years. Bran was dead, but his life was trapped elsewhere. And Bran had an ash tree bound to him. The babe doesn't. It is a custom that has fallen out of fashion. Ah, another failing! I should plant a tree for every one of them. I haven't kept the old ways as I should. Oh, Meg, I am so old, so useless." She bowed her head until she was almost lying in the pig filth.

Meg didn't know what to do. The poor baby, and now her great-great-aunt, font of wisdom and pillar of strength, collapsing into helplessness and despair like this. She took Phyllida by the shoulders and pulled her up almost roughly. "Tell me what to do," she said earnestly.

By the time the doctor arrived in his little red convertible, Phyllida and Meg had laid out the tiny body, a time-honored female chore. They had cleaned and dressed Colin as well as they could. The best of his clothes were hardly fitting—rough and twice-mended, with food stains on the collar—so Phyllida had improvised a shroud with her petticoat and covered his face with a lace handkerchief embroidered with bluebells and foxgloves.

Dr. Homunculus assured Phyllida there was nothing she could have done—nothing even he could have done. "He had a trouble with his heart since birth. Some illnesses are past mending," he told her.

His words meant little to her. She was Guardian of the Green Hill and of her people, not he. Ignoring him, she told Meg, "Poor Moll has lost her mind for a time, but the fairies look after the mad. We'll find her soon enough and do what we can to give her peace."

And You After Her, My Pretty Pet?

"Dickie," Meg asked a few minutes later as they strolled along the dusty unpaved road to the Rookery, "do you think I should help Phyllida look for Moll? Or maybe try to find Gul Ghillie and ask him to help?"

"Speak of the devil," cried a merry little voice, "and he will come!"

A brown, freckled boy stepped out from behind the Rookery gates to meet them. He cut a little caper. Then, too full of high spirits to simply walk, he turned into a great gray lumpy toad and hopped the intervening distance. A tongue thick as a cow's flicked out and lapped up a snail. He turned into a boy again, still crunching the gastropod.

"Gul!" Meg cried. "Nice to see you."

"Oh? I thought perhaps you never wanted to see me again." He spit the snail's horny operculum onto the turf and crushed it with his heel.

"That was a long time ago," she said, referring to the war of two weeks past.

"What are you doing here?" Dickie asked rather rudely, and Meg looked sidelong at him. This was the Seelie prince, albeit in disguise! Didn't he have any idea how to treat royalty?

"Oh, just taking the air," Gul said nonchalantly. "I heard about the trouble yonder. Bad business." He shook his head. "He was a fine child. Any fairy mother would be glad to have such a bonnie laddie."

"You're not supposed to be here," Dickie insisted. "None of the fairies are supposed to be at the Rookery unless invited, especially you."

This was strictly speaking true, but a fairy who had risen from the earth as soon as the molten magma cooled enough that there *was* earth certainly wouldn't be stopped by any silly rules. It usually took a fair amount of Phyllida's skill and fairy lore to keep fairies safe from humans and humans safe from fairies. Lately she had been neglecting her duties. Iron nails driven into the sod had rusted away, never to be replaced. Crows stole the bells that tinkled in the wind at the gatepost. There hadn't been a four-leaf clover hunt for weeks. None of these things alone can keep out a determined fairy, but collectively they create a general feeling that fairies are unwelcome, and usually that suffices to keep them at bay.

"You know more than a lad of your age should," Gul told Dickie, giving him that intense stare a border collie gives a straying sheep, then bolted for the tall grass, where he was soon lost among the cowslips and yarrow.

"I wonder what he was here for," Dickie mused.

"Well, he would have stayed if you hadn't been so rude," Meg countered. "I haven't seen him since—"

"Since you killed Bran for him," Dickie finished for her. "You're getting as bad as Silly, thinking the fairies are safe. If he was here, he was up to no good. Prince or no prince, he's a fairy, and that means trouble. We should check with the others."

They found Rowan, Silly, and Finn in their rooms performing perfunctory ablutions in preparation for dinner. Rowan's hands were pristine below the wrists, filthy above. Finn had a streak of grime behind each ear as if his face was a clean mask slipped on over permanent dirt.

"Did you see Gul?" Meg asked from the hall.

"Was he here?" Silly asked, jumping up and down on her bed in glee. "Oh, I can't believe he didn't come to see me. I wanted to show him what I've learned. I've been practicing my fencing with a pair of swords I found in the old armory." The Rookery was filled with arms and relics from every generation that inhabited it, from sabers and arquebuses to modern fowling shotguns. "They're not the same as Hen and Brychan, but I'm getting used to them." Much to her dismay, her fairy weapons had been taken from her after the Midsummer War.

"He doesn't care what you've learned," Meg said sharply. Dickie was right. Fairies were dangerous, selfish. How had she forgotten? She rubbed her eyes. She felt a little hazy all of a sudden, confused. They *were* dangerous, weren't they? She didn't feel like herself. I'm just tired, she thought. Tired and upset by what I saw today. She shook herself like an agitated bluebird puffing her feathers.

"He trained us for the war, that was all. He doesn't need us for anything now. I'm sorry, Silly, but he's not our friend. You can't trust him."

Silly stuck her tongue out and called Meg an old stick-in-the-mud.

Meg ignored her. "If he didn't come to see us, what was he here for? Phyllida and Lysander weren't around. Did he visit Bran?"

"Bran came to play croquet with us," Silly said. "We would have seen if he was talking to Gul."

"Bran got out of his chair? He . . . played?" He was too weak to run around. Trust that stubborn lout to put himself in danger as soon as her back was turned. The others wouldn't think to make him lie back down. Things seemed to fall all to pieces when she or Phyllida was gone from the Rookery.

She looked around, aware of an empty space. "Where's James?" she asked her brother.

Rowan shrugged.

"But you said you'd watch him."

"I did? I don't remember."

"When we were leaving. He was watching the ants and you said . . . Oh, Rowan, you're useless!" Meg stomped off to take care of things herself.

She wasn't really worried. The Rookery was swarming with servants, and Phyllida was so loved and respected there was no one in the village who would do her or hers any harm. But what if James broke his leg, or got stuck in a tree? What if he fell into an abandoned well? It didn't matter that she didn't know of any wells on the property. In fact, that made it all the more likely, because who would fall into a well they knew about? Maybe little James had been poking around the old summerhouse, and when he pushed aside the brambles in search of some novel bug, he crashed through the forgotten well to his doom. . . .

Oh, no, there he was, still playing with ants on the croquet lawn.

"James," she called, running up to him and hugging him, relieved as if she'd just dragged him dripping from the well. He felt unnaturally cold. "Are you all right?" she asked, laying the back of her hand on his forehead.

He shook her off and stared at her unblinking. "Your eyes are red and puffy. You look ugly!"

She gasped. Gentle, loving, self-contained little James hardly ever had anything but hugs and caresses and praise for his adored eldest sister. Before bed every night, he would crawl into her lap and stroke her dark brown hair while she told him a story. *Surround me with your armies*, she'd say, and he'd throw his plump little arms around her neck, squeezing with all his love until she cried, *I surrender!* He'd never said an unkind thing to her in his life. She gulped and tried to dismiss it. Maybe it was just a phase.

"Come in and get washed up for dinner," she said.

"Dinner? Hooray!" He jumped up and did a little dance. Well, at least he was cheerful, if not his typical sedate self.

"Look out, James. You're stepping on the ants."

"I know," he said serenely, continuing his jig.

She grabbed his arm and pulled him off the mound. "James! I'm ashamed of you! You know you don't kill bugs. It's not right." And it's not like you at all, she thought. "Especially ants here at the Rookery. You know what Bran said. They might be very old fairies."

He struggled against her grip, snaking out one leg to stomp a few more. "These aren't fairies," he said. "I checked. They're just crunchy ants." He wiped his mouth, and she thought she saw a tiny black leg flick off his cheek.

"You didn't . . . eat . . . an ant, did you?"

"I'm hungry!" was all he said, and he broke free and ran inside.

Phyllida failing, James rude and cruel . . . What's happening? Meg thought.

Phyllida and Lysander still weren't home by the time the children gathered for supper. Meg looked worriedly at James, but as far as she could tell, he was his old self—he focused on his food with single-minded determination and hardly seemed aware of the others, unless they tried to snag some last morsel he'd set his heart on.

Though she knew it wasn't exactly a polite topic for the dinner table, she told them about Moll, sparing them a detailed description.

"I think we should look for her," Meg said.

Rowan, stuffed and sleepy after an afternoon of turning croquet into a blood sport, said, "Sounds like Phyllida will take care of it. That's what she does, isn't it?"

"But I'm supposed to . . . I should help. Come on. Silly? Will you go?"

"Well . . ."

"We'll go to the Green Hill."

"I'll go!" Finn chimed in.

"Already a cyclops," James said, not looking up from stuffing buttered boiled new potatoes into his mouth. "Wanna be blind?"

"James!" Meg admonished. But it was true. Finn had been

punished for spying on the fairies, and even if he went under her aegis, he wasn't likely to be welcomed. "I'm sorry, Finn. I can't take you to the Green Hill."

"Go on, take him," James said, spewing crumbs. "Maybe he'll fall in love with you like you want."

A wave of crimson climbed from Meg's neck up to her cheeks.

"And if he's blinded," James added, "he won't care how you look!" He chortled while the others looked on, aghast.

Meg reddened the rest of the way, until even the part in her hair was a line of scarlet. She stared straight ahead so there wasn't the slightest chance of making eye contact with Finn and said, "James, go to your room this instant!"

He ignored her.

"I said—"

"I heard you," James said, grabbing half a leftover roll from Dickie's plate. "Don't have to do what you say."

She was sorely tempted to throw a fit, if only so she could yell away some of her embarrassment, or failing that, to grab James by whatever arms and legs she could catch and haul him off to his room. But she thought he would probably ignore her ranting lectures, and no doubt struggle against apprehension. Successfully wrestling a determined four-year-old without hurting him is a difficult undertaking, and just at that moment Meg really didn't feel up to it. She had to get away, from her family, from the Rookery. She had to get out into the woods.

She bolted from her chair and ran out the door, only breathing easily when she reached the edge of the forest. She heard steps behind her and turned to find Finn.

He regarded her with one dark blue eye . . . one beautiful blue eye . . . Stop that this instant, Meg Morgan! He fingered the black silk patch that covered the other eye, and Meg shuddered to think what might be beneath it.

"It's okay. You can stare," Finn said casually, and it took her a moment to realize he meant stare at his eyepatch, not the rest of him. She usually only did that when she was absolutely sure no one was watching. How in the world had James known she had the smallest, tiniest, ever-so-insignificant crush on Finn? Perhaps she hadn't taken the trouble to guard her feelings from him as she had the others, since he was only four. Evidently growing up, though, to judge from today's outbursts.

"Do you want to see it?" he asked.

"Your . . . eye? No, no thank you."

She thought, hoped, it was an attempt at friendship, but realized that being Finn, he was probably just trying to make her feel sick and squeamish.

"It's not bad. It doesn't ooze much anymore."

Meg turned abruptly away, vague, hopeful visions shattered by revulsion. Yes, it was Finn, after all.

"I know you can't take me to the Green Hill, but we can go looking for Moll together, if you like."

She stammered out something negative and dashed away like a hare. She couldn't bear to have him look at her. She had to be in the woods.

When the boughs closed over her head, she calmed again, and as her skin dappled with golden evening light filtered through the oak leaves she actually became capable of coherent thought. She thought—she couldn't help herself—about Finn.

He was vile. Selfish. Conceited. Arrogant. If she hadn't taken him to the Green Hill once, he would never have given up the eggs that held Rowan's and Bran's life forces, and they would have died. That made him practically a murderer. No, she amended, that wasn't fair to Finn. She herself was the only one of them who had actually proved capable of murder.

All right, she thought, Finn was all things wretched and contemptible. Then why did she feel compelled to look at him all the time? Why did he creep into her thoughts when she least expected it? True, he had blue eyes (well, eye) and silky black hair. He was tall and confident and practically as handsome as the Seelie prince. But what was that compared with the myriad faults in his character?

He didn't even like her. Why would he? She was plain and awkward. That was how she saw herself anyway. If you looked at her, you would be charmed by her clear, bright, compassionate hazel eyes. You would admire the dark brown glossiness of her hair even when, as now, it was tied in a knot at the nape of her neck and had bits of fern fronds in it. She was slim and graceful, and weeks of tramping through the woods and practicing archery had made her strong. She always knew the right thing to do, even if she didn't do it or it took her a while to work up enough courage. She was really quite remarkable. But all she saw when she pictured herself was a gawky tongue-tied indecisive girl with freckles.

She sighed, and turned toward the Green Hill. Probably Phyllida had already found Moll and was even now making up a bed for her in one of the guest rooms, feeding her broth and tea with whiskey. The sun would be down soon, and the wind was picking up. It would rain any minute, and she would be soaked before she could get home. What was she doing out here? Then that dizzy, vaguely disoriented feeling returned and she rubbed her eyes. When she set out again, she was heading not back to the Rookery but deeper into the woods.

The wind was whipping now, tossing the treetops in a vigorous, swaying dance. At the forest floor it was more sheltered, but the wind still plucked strands of hair loose from their knot and lashed them across her eyes. She heard a faint sound beneath the rustling roar overhead—a small hollow ringing, like bamboo bells. A moment later she came to a glen that had caught the day's last sunlight. She thought it was a pond at first, an azure field that rippled and tinkled a melodious tune. But no, it was not water but masses of bluebells carpeting the hollow so thickly she could hardly see the green beneath them. And in the middle of that sea, a hunched, bobbing form like a coracle—a man on a folding stool. She gasped, and he turned at the sound. It was the man she'd seen on the way to Moll's, and there was an easel before him. A large reddish goat lounged at his side, chewing thoughtfully on a sprig of bluebells.

Meg didn't know, and Phyllida hadn't thought to tell her, that no good can come of a bluebell wood. Phyllida, thorough in all things (until recently) hadn't bothered to warn Meg and the others away from bluebells for the very simple reason that they were supposed to have finished blooming in April, before the children arrived in England. From late March onward, in the mottled shade under scattered beeches just putting on their spring finery after shivering naked through the winter, bluebells sprout their nodding clusters and call the fairies to play. Humans, too, are tempted to sport among blue petals and pollen, but many's the young couple who spend an evening, or a night, in a bluebell wood and find their lives changed evermore.

Woe to he who hears the bluebells ring! You may run joyously to their sweet clarion call, but remember, if you can hear the bells, so can other things, and they are coming just as eagerly. Never trust anyone you meet among the bluebells.

Poor Meg didn't know this, but as a properly brought-up American girl, she automatically distrusted strangers. Odd then— isn't it?—that she didn't feel the least desire to flee upon seeing this man.

"Hello," he said, smiling pleasantly. "Look what I have for you." He leaned his cadaverous body to the side, revealing a water-color portrait of a girl. She was lovely, her eyes large and melancholy, looking as though she yearned for something but didn't quite know what. Meg stared at it for a long time before she realized it was a picture of her.

"Who are you?" she asked.

"Oh, just myself." He laughed. "That's what you say in these parts, isn't it? Well, you don't look like a fairy, lass . . . or perhaps you do . . . but I'll tell you my name anyway." He stood and made a little obeisance. "I am Gwidion Thomas, master painter, artist extraordinaire, scholar of sketches and doctor of daubs, at your service!" He held out a hand that was all knuckles and nails, and she shook it, thinking in the back of her mind that there was something she should be doing. Running away, perhaps? Yes, that was it, but why? Oh well, she thought, it must not be important, and she turned her attention to the picture of her, quite literally mesmerized.

All around her the bluebells were ringing in hushed murmurs, tossing their heads in the stiffening breeze. Meg felt like she was in a fog as she stared into her own eyes.

"You are Phyllida's relation," Gwidion said, or asked, as she stared at herself.

"Yes," Meg said. "She's my great-great-aunt." Her voice in her own ears sounded like it was coming from very far away, an echo of something she had once heard.

"And she is the Guardian."

"Yes."

"And you after her, my pretty pet?"

"Yes, I think so."

"Ah, so not declared yet. I had hopes when I saw the two of you out on your errand today that you'd already been declared her successor, declared and freely accepted. It would have been easy for me then, pretty. Look how you stare at yourself. This is only a quick portrait to lure you out here, and already it has almost consumed you. You cannot tear your eyes away, can you, pretty? I have you tonight, you are mine, if I want you." A shudder rattled his bones. "No, Phyllida is my target. She must either abdicate in my favor or declare me her successor. She must return what is mine, by right, by blood. I can control you easily enough with my art, but she will be a tougher nut to crack. You are just my tool to pry her open."

Meg listened to all of this absently, without concern. Look at me, she mused, staring into her watercolor eyes. That is me. Then who am I? She felt like she was the portrait, fixed and still, and the painting was the living, feeling thing. She was pleasantly powerless, waiting for the hand of some artist to tell her who she was, what she should feel.

"Go home now, my pet," Gwidion said. "Run home, little faun, and forget about this night. Tomorrow I will come to your door, and you will not know me. But you will let me in and do everything in your power to keep me there. You will get Phyllida to sit for me. She will let me paint her portrait. And then, when the final stroke of color is on the canvas, she will do my bidding, and the Rookery, the riches, the Green Hill itself, will be mine. At last, a Thomas man will get what is due him."

He turned Meg around by the shoulders, his bony fingers pressing her soft flesh, and gave her a little shove out of the bluebell woods. She moved off as if in a dream. When she was far enough away that her footfalls were lost in the wind's rush, Gwidion stuffed her portrait into a leather portfolio.

"A shame the magic doesn't last longer," Pazhan said as he chewed bitter bluebells.

"It is not a question of time, but of purpose," Gwidion replied. "Each picture can be for one precise end, to force one particular emotion, to convince someone of one exact thing. Meg's picture was to lure her out to the woods. Phyllida's portrait, my magnum opus, will be to force her to give up the Guardianship. Perhaps there is some magic that would let me seize full control of a person's entire being, but I have not learned it yet."

"Or perhaps if you were a good enough artist to truly capture your subject's soul . . ."

Gwidion twisted his long thin lips into a scowl. "My father could have done it."

"Your father had tales and dreams. He put his dreams on paper, on canvas. You try to paint your dreams into the world."

"My father had no ambition," Gwidion said shortly. "He talked every night about the inheritance he should have had, but did nothing to get it back."

"The stories made him happy," Pazhan said, licking petals off his lips with a blue tongue. "The dream and longing were enough, maybe better than any realization. You want the waking dream. Will it make you happy?"

"As happy as a king!" Gwidion cried.

"However much that is," Pazhan mumbled under his breath.

Have you ever walked to school, or to a friend's house, someplace very familiar, and suddenly looked up to have no idea how you got there? Cars, dogs, ladies in gardening hats and gloves, all passed you by while you walked on autopilot, in a daze, blinded by your own thoughts. Only, when Meg looked around and found herself in the forest, she couldn't even remember what she'd been thinking about. The residue of magic just made her shrug, get her bearings, and head back for the Rookery, but she was left with a feeling of a gap. It was almost full dark now. Where had the time gone? Or was it only that the clouds had moved in to beat back the sun's last light? Daydreams, daydreams, she thought as the first raindrop landed on her nose. She broke into a run, and the heavens let loose with a flash and a deep, earth-shaking rumble of thunder.

She had never felt a storm like this. It wasn't the fury—she'd seen thunderstorms in her upstate New York home snap birches in two. No, it was the intimacy. The rain when it struck her face seemed a playful slap aimed at her; the wind wrapped itself around her arms and pulled her this way and that. And the thunder! It got inside her belly and shook her from within, an inquisitive spirit roughly invading her body. She wasn't particularly alarmed until a bolt of lightning struck the deer path directly in front of her.

She shrieked (and was immediately ashamed of herself for shrieking) and jumped back, the hairs along her forearms tingling with the electricity in the air. A creature stood before her, as high as her waist and made of light, arcing and sparking.

She made a little motion with the fingers of her left hand, a gesture of dubious efficacy Phyllida had taught her to ward off evil, which any Italian grandmother can show you. The creature, which was slowly evolving eyes in a semblance of a face, looked at the gesture quizzically, then formed a hand of sorts and made it back at her, taking it for a greeting.

"We are the Ani Yuntikwalaski," it said. "We thank you for waking us."

"I . . . I woke you?"

"You shed the blood. You ended the life and returned the life. It is a big thing, as big as the earth, as big as the sky. We slept in the clouds, but you have awakened us."

"I don't understand," Meg said, backing away as the electrical charge became more pronounced and she smelled singed hair.

"We go now. You are not particularly flammable, but you

conduct electricity too well for us to stay. We leave you a gift and our thanks."

The glowing figure of light beamed upward in a blinding flash, a fractal pattern of reverse lightning from the ground to the sky.

Something glinted on the grass where the creature had stood. Meg picked it up gingerly, a little afraid of electric shock, but it was only a cool, hard, translucent stone, dark milky blue and charcoal, like gathering thunderheads, with veins of red and gold fire. It vibrated in her palm, and when she held it to her ear, she heard a low, growling rumble from within.

She got home well after dark. No one had noticed her absence, and no one had waited up for her, except the somewhat disheveled butler, Wooster, who scurried out to meet her with an umbrella, which he dropped in a puddle. He took her muddy shoes and made her stand on a towel in the hall until the worst of the rain had dripped off her. Still clutching her gift from the Ani Yuntikwalaski, she dragged herself upstairs to bed. She fell asleep quickly—few people know how wearying it is to be controlled by a magic spell—but before she did, she had time to wonder just who the lightning creature was and what on earth it meant by thanking her for waking it up.

There's Something Stirring in the Earth

MEG STAGGERED DOWN late for breakfast. Finn was arguing with Phyllida about why he couldn't have any coffee.

"You let us have tea, and that's the same thing."

"No, it isn't. Coffee will stunt your growth. Tea is healthy, full of antioxidants."

"But I always drink coffee at home." It was true. His parents hardly paid attention to anything he did, and the revolving staff of maids and nannies charged with his upbringing would yield to almost any demand to keep him quiet. All things considered, it was surprising Finn hadn't turned out even worse.

Meg put her stone in the center of the table, where it was promptly grabbed by Silly, then Rowan, and almost dropped in the struggle. This morning the stone was sapphire blue with milky swirls.

"What is it?"

"Where'd you get it?"

"May I see it?" This last was from Dickie, who was too polite to snatch the stone himself. Lysander plucked it out of Rowan's hands, examined it through his half spectacles, and handed it to Dickie.

"Do you know what it is?" Meg asked her great-great-uncle.

"I know precisely what it is," he said, looking very wise. They waited, on tenterhooks. "It is a rock. A pretty one at that."

They groaned and growled, then a sinuous form uncoiled itself from Dickie's shoulder and hissed inquisitively.

"I have seen such a stone before," the Wyrm said. "But not for many years. It was in my travels to the colonies."

"The colonies?" Meg asked.

"Your homeland. I believe it became known as Amerigo, or something of the sort." He scratched his head with the tip of his scaly tail, much as an old professor might scratch his skull in bafflement. "Dear me, I seem to remember nothing of the recent history of Amerigo. All forgotten, all gone. How delightful!" The Wyrm had spent a lifetime learning everything there was to know, then, bored, set about forgetting it. He could tell you all about the Etruscans, but every detail of the exotic lives of Cyprians had escaped him. He could speak sparrow, but not wren. He could teach you how to make a Napoleon pastry, but hadn't a clue what happened at Waterloo.

"This is a weatherstone. An interesting oddity, though not particularly useful. It tells you what the weather is."

"Like a forecast?" Rowan asked.

"No, nothing so practical. More like looking out the window. Today it is sunny, so the stone is clear blue like the sky, with a few high clouds. I imagine last night it was murky and full of lightning sparks. If a tornado came by, you would see it, in miniature, in the weatherstone. So you see, more a conversation piece than anything truly handy. Now, the Phoenicians had a stone that told you what the weather would be like tomorrow—very practical for a seafaring race."

"Where did you get it?" Phyllida asked.

Meg told them about her excursion the night before. She didn't mention Gwidion—she had no memory of him.

"What was it the thing called itself?"

"Ani something-or-other," Meg said.

Phyllida and Lysander exchanged puzzled looks. "Haven't heard of it either," Lysander said. "Ani? Well, there's Black Annis, but she's ferocious, so if it didn't try to eat you, it wasn't her. I'll ask Bran, but I thought between the two of us we knew every fairy in these parts. Some kind of lightning fairy?"

"Ani Yuntikwalaski," Dickie said.

"That's it, that's what it called itself," Meg said. "What is it?"

"A Cherokee spirit of lightning and thunder. I read about them last summer when I was at camp in North Carolina." He spoke as though excusing himself. He was always a little ashamed of his knowledge—the more obscure and esoteric it was, the more abashed he felt. He also didn't mention that his father sent him to camp to try to "make a man out of him" (which he had overheard quite accidentally). Who can say if it is more manly to play flag football and fish and swim in frigid lakes with unknown muddy depths, than to immerse yourself in a new culture and set about meeting its representatives? Sports made Dickie wheeze, and something in the North Carolina air had aggravated his allergies, so he spent all his time with the old Cherokee woman who cooked and mended for the campers, hearing the tales of her ancestors. His only hikes were to the library to check out books on Cherokee history.

"What on earth is a Cherokee spirit doing in England?" Phyllida wondered.

"And what did it mean about waking him up?" Meg asked. "I don't think I woke anyone up."

"Ye killed me," a rough voice said. Bran stood in the doorway, half in vivid sun from the garden, half shadowed from the kitchen. He had an uncanny knack for hearing everything that was discussed on the Rookery grounds and appearing without warning.

Meg hung her head. It didn't matter that she had entered the Midsummer War to save Rowan or that Bran would have killed her (or would he?) if she hadn't loosed that temporarily fatal arrow. And it hardly mattered that they had all brought Bran back to life afterward. She had taken a life, and what's more, had found it surprisingly easy. She still remembered her sense of resolution when she marched up the Green Hill, the certainty of her fingers when they released the bowstring, the sureness of her aim, the power she held within her that night . . . and she fought those memories. It wasn't right that there should be any feelings other than sorrow and shame associated with the Midsummer War.

"Ye killed me," Bran said again, "and brought me back to life. I was the Midsummer sacrifice of the seventh year. I was supposed to die, for the land." Or I was, thought Meg. "That's what it's all about, ye know. Since the hand of man first set a seed in the earth, blood has been shed to keep the earth fertile."

"That's crazy," Silly said.

"That's what fertilizers are for," Finn said with contempt. Bran looked at him like he didn't belong in the conversation.

"What d'ye think makes the best fertilizers? Bones, ground up . . . blood meal . . . manure . . . all things from the body of a living beastie. Man or beast, life must be given to the soil, or it will not give life back. Every seven years a man is slain on the Green Hill so that things will stay the same—the corn will grow, the hops will sprout, the apples pip. But it didn't happen that way this time . . . and things will not stay the same."

"I messed it up, didn't I?" Meg asked, miserably. "You mean, now things won't grow?"

"The barley's high, and you ate gooseberries yourself yesterday. Of course things are growing, ye daft girl. The blood was shed, the sacrifice made. That part was taken care of. But ye did something else too. Ye brought the dead back to life. That doesn't happen, or if it does, so rarely it becomes the stuff of legends. If killing can bring life for seven years, what have you wrought with resurrection?"

Meg had no idea, but felt a little shiver of trepidation at the thought.

"Bran," Phyllida said severely, "tell us clearly what you mean, please. What has happened?"

"Daughter, I don't know."

"But you said—"

"I don't know, I only feel. There's something stirring in the earth." Meg had visions of worms writhing under her soles. "I thought at first it was only me, that I wasn't quite used to the world yet, the world above the fairy lands, or the world beyond my own death. I've had this feeling, like something waking up, something moving and stretching for the first time in centuries. And Meg's the one who changed everything."

Meg didn't know if she liked this and was just as happy when Rowan asked, "Why didn't the Ani-thingummy thank you, Bran? You're the one who came back to life. If something happened because of that, shouldn't you get the credit?"

"And not our dumb old sister," James added under his breath, just loud enough for Meg to hear.

"Och, it's just luck it happened to me. Could have been any one of you brought back to life—that's not what matters. I was the fiddle, Meg the fiddler. It wasn't any of my doing."

"You volunteered to fight for the Unseelie Court," Meg pointed out. "You volunteered to *die*. If you hadn't done that, none of the rest would have happened."

"Ah, weel, men die willingly every day. Not so much in that."

"The truth is we don't know," Phyllida interrupted, tired of competing possibilities. It made her head hurt a bit, rather like when Lysander tried to argue politics with her. "The Cherokee spirit went away, right? Well, I say unless it comes back, we don't have to trouble ourselves with it."

"But what if that's not all that woke up?" Bran asked. No one had an answer they were willing to speak aloud.

"Well," said Silly at last, "if we don't know for sure the weather-stone was meant for Meg, can I have it?"

Of course Meg wanted to keep it for herself, but of course she said yes, and Silly grabbed her treasure and took it to the doorway, comparing the cloud puffs to the floating specks of white in the stone. They were an exact match.

"Did you find Moll?" Meg asked, willing to bring up that unpleasant subject if it took some of the attention off her.

Phyllida shook her head. "They had search parties out all night, and not a trace of her. Cain's uncle has a hound that's supposed to be a prime tracker, but he's in Penzance, so it will be a while before they can have a try. I know she's looking for the Green Hill to ask the fairies for a boon, but it does us no good to look there, since she doesn't know where it is." She turned to Dickie and Finn. "You can't find the Green Hill unless it wants to be found. Only my family can find it whenever they like." Which Finn already knew from experience, Dickie from research and conjecture. "I called on the Seelie Court for help, but they wouldn't answer my summons." That wasn't unusual. The fairies, capricious and only rarely concerned with human matters, couldn't be controlled even by their own Guardian.

"We'll help," Rowan said authoritatively. Meg managed to hide her annoyance. Last night when she asked for his help he preferred to eat and sleep than comb the woods. Now, in front of Phyllida and Lysander and Bran, he looked all good and noble for volunteering to help in the search. No one seemed to care that she was the only one to brave darkfall and storms and Cherokee spirits and . . . wasn't there some other danger too? It seemed there was, but—funny—she couldn't recall.

Now Rowan was mustering the forces like a general and

bossing everyone. No, she had to admit it wasn't really bossing. Her brother had a knack for leadership which Meg entirely lacked. It wasn't that she was a follower by nature, only that she couldn't rouse and inspire people to her own way of thinking. She frequently had good ideas, but it was up to the others to decide whether they should follow them. If not, she either had to pursue them herself or follow someone else against her better judgment, giving ominous warnings like poor mad Cassandra.

They were clearing the breakfast dishes and discussing their search strategy (with Meg muttering *I was going to go anyway, you know*) when Wooster came in and announced, "There is a, ahem, *gentleman* here to see you, my lady." Even the children, who as egalitarian Americans did not recognize the British class distinction of gentleman, could tell from Wooster's tone that he thought the visitor was anything but.

Phyllida raised her eyebrows. "A tenant? Someone from the village?"

"No, my lady. An artist." He paused a moment to let this sink in. "And a goat."

James, who had heretofore been busy drinking cream directly from the pitcher, gave a sputtering chortle. "Perfect," was all he said. "Just perfect."

They filed to the stately front door. As a rule, guests were admitted into a special parlor near the entrance hall that served as a receiving room. It was pretty, but not furnished as delicately as the family's main parlor. After all, Phyllida said, so many of her visitors had mud on their boots. This time, however, she intended to be just polite enough to maintain her reputation for benevolence, then promptly shoo the interloper away. They had enough sketches of their own manse and neighboring ruins. She would probably buy one without even looking at it, on the theory that this would both make her visitor happy and get rid of him all the more quickly. Such business was best performed at the threshold, where a *thank you very much* could be immediately followed by a firm *good-bye* and a slam, if need be.

Meg trailed behind with some trepidation. She didn't remember her second encounter with the artist, but she was still faintly unnerved by the first, when she had seen him rise like a mummy, or a zombie, dead and not dead, from the hill tomb . . . for surely it must be the same artist.

"Now, don't act interested," Phyllida said under her breath as Wooster was about to open the door. "If he thinks you're an easy mark, he'll never go away."

Wooster flung open the door, and before he could announce the visitor, the cadaverous man eased his way inside, holding before him a piece of parchment like a shield. To Meg's surprise, Phyllida said, "Oh, please come in, right this way," and led him not to the rough reception room but to the rosy, cozy family parlor. Before the front door closed again, she glimpsed a large reddish-brown goat with a dark manelike cape of fur on his shoulders, eating pink foxglove flowers.

The train snaked behind Phyllida, and they gathered around the man as he set up his wares. Meg could see now why Phyllida let him in. On the creamy piece of paper was Phyllida's face, looking warm and welcoming. It was obviously a quick sketch, almost eastern in its understatement and fluid simplicity, but it captured Phyllida's essence. It was more than good enough to work a charm as simple as getting invited inside.

"Oh, lovely! How delightful!" Phyllida said, going into raptures over each sketch and watercolor drawing the man laid out. Meg, craning her neck around the shoulders of the others, had to admit there was a certain vim to the paintings, a lifelike quality that was something more than mere realism. There was the ruined church, evidently done the night before in the setting sun's red haze. Washes of color dominated form—the tumbled stones and crumbling walls themselves were only suggested, while the air around them looked heavy with light. Like the others, it seemed to have been done quickly, capturing a moment, a fleeting impression. She didn't know if it was good—it was certainly nothing like the Old Masters she'd seen in books or the modern art in New York City—but it made an impression on her. There was an ink drawing of the line of cedars that led to the Rookery and a charming charcoal of the little bridge that arched over the stream. The water rippled exactly as if a pike had brushed the surface with his dorsal fin a moment before.

There were a few faces she didn't recognize, and then ... oh! An intent little countenance gazing out of an antique carriage window. Meg saw herself in soft pencil lines. It wasn't a very magical portrait, but few can resist a compelling and flattering portrayal of themselves. Then, too, some of the artist's last spell lingered on her, so she felt drawn to the picture and, thus, to its creator.

"Do you like it, little one?" he asked. "I saw you and your illustrious relations in that charming equipage, and I couldn't resist a quick drawing. I hope I have not been presumptuous." He made a peculiar crouching movement evidently meant to be a bow.

"It is so like me," Meg said. "I saw you on the roadside. It couldn't have been for more than a second or two. How did you do it?"

"Oh, I have a knack for such things," he said lightly. "Take it if you like it." Meg held it reverently.

"We must pay you for it," Phyllida insisted.

"No, no, wouldn't hear of it." He stretched his long thin lips into an ingratiating smile. "Tell you what you can do, my lady. I'd like to paint your portrait." He held up the sketch of Phyllida. "I took this from the *Gladysmere Gazette*. I saw a photo of you at some festival, and I thought, What a kind face, what a gracious lady she must be." He slid the sketch across the table toward Phyllida, who took it up automatically. "But that hardly does you justice. There's only so much I can do from a flat picture in the paper, a copy of a copy of a copy, without the zest of the living woman."

Yes, only so much, but that was enough to have made her weak and uncertain, confused about her duty and careless of her obligations, for the two weeks he'd been executing trial sketches. Not quite enough to make her give up altogether and hand over the Guardianship to him. It would take a masterpiece, perhaps the work of weeks, to accomplish that. "Now I see you in the flesh, I know what a paltry thing this daub is, and I hope, I dream, I yearn to be permitted to pay your lovely face the honor it deserves." He crunched himself into that bow again, a flattering, charming courtier.

"Well, I don't know," Phyllida demurred, but he could tell she was only protesting for form's sake. She was entranced at the idea of being immortalized.

The artist whipped out a fresh sheet of paper and pulled a charcoal stick from a worn leather satchel slung over his shoulder. "Here, let me try from life." Under the gaze of the audience young and old, he shifted his keen eyes from Phyllida to the paper and back again, making quick, light strokes. His lips moved as he drew, but he didn't make a sound. He was of course casting a spell to make Phyllida assent to this, the first step in her overthrow. There was no particular ritual, no magic words, just the unyielding will and determination to bend her, to make his creation on paper and the living woman one and the same thing, blank and featureless save for what he chose to bestow on them. As the lines and shading appeared on the page, he concentrated his thoughts, his power hard-won in the East, on one very small thing: Phyllida must agree to have her portrait painted.

He sealed the spell with his scrawled signature in the corner and passed it to Phyllida.

Lysander leaned over her shoulder. "It is you! Exactly you!"

"Yes," Phyllida said, frowning slightly. "Exactly."

Poor Gwidion. For all his artistic talent, for all his Persian magic, he was only a man, and, like every man, occasionally clueless about what will please, or more importantly, displease, a woman. It is true that this new portrait was much more accurate than the one taken from the grainy black-and-white photograph. This one captured every line of her face, *every* line. It caught the slackness in the flesh of her cheeks, the sagging of her once-firm jawline, the lengthening of her earlobes (a sign of enlightenment in a Buddha, but only of gravity in the rest of us), and the age spots that dotted her neck. Yes, it was exactly like her, and that is a thing very few women are happy to see.

Phyllida was a beautiful eighty-four-year-old woman, but she was still eighty-four. When she pictured herself in her mind's eye she was twenty, or thirty, or perhaps even a hale and vital forty. She never quite remembered she was old until she looked in the mirror, and then she could compensate somewhat by holding her head just so, looking up slightly, dimming the lights. This stark reminder worked a spell on her far stronger than any of Gwidion's conjurings. She stood abruptly, pushing the parchment away.

"You are a very fine artist, I'm sure," she said coldly, "but I do not need any such frivolity as a portrait. I'll buy this"—if only so she could destroy it—"but then you must be on your way. Perhaps the historical society would like your picture of the church. Good day."

Gwidion's jaw dropped in his skull-like face. What a powerful woman! What resistance! He hadn't thought it possible she could defy that spell. He concentrated for a moment, focusing his efforts on Meg and the ideas he'd planted the night before in the bluebell wood.

"Oh, please, Phyllida," Meg said, leaning against her arm affectionately. "I would so love to see a portrait of you."

But Phyllida, her pride piqued, was steadfast.

"Can't he paint one of us, then?" Meg asked.

"We don't need such fripperies." She wasn't inclined to reward the man who reminded her she was no longer young.

"But he paints so beautifully," Meg persisted, appealing as a kitten. "I only wish I could paint so well."

Gwidion pounced on the opening.

"I give lessons too, m'lady. That is in fact my specialty. For the children, or for you." He kept his attention on Phyllida, not realizing she was already a lost cause. Vanity would keep her safer than a legion of bodyguards.

"Please, Phyllida," Meg said.

"Oh, please!" chimed Silly.

"We'd like to very much," Rowan said more soberly.

Finn didn't say anything. He was looking at the sketch of Meg, thinking it was really rather good.

"It may be pleasant for the children," Lysander said. "Give them some distraction from . . ." He had been about to say from wars and danger and death, then remembered there was an outsider among them and let the sentence trail off. "What do you say, old girl?" He put his arm around her.

Old girl? It was really too much. Lysander had used that term of endearment for his wife since their early calf-eyed courting, and it always made her smile, but not today. She stalked out of the room with a backward wave of her hand, saying, "Do whatever you like."

You'll Pay for That

AND SO THEY DID. It was arranged that Gwidion should stay in an empty keeper's cottage on the grounds and give the children art lessons each morning. No time was fixed for his departure.

"Can we start right away?" Meg asked.

"Why not?" Gwidion said. What did it matter if Phyllida refused to be painted? He was now a member of the household and would have the leisure to study her even without her consent. In the meantime, here were the children of her bloodline. Perhaps some use could be made of them.

He declared that they would paint al fresco, and when Silly asked, "Who's he?" Gwidion explained it meant outside in the fresh air.

Finn snorted (though he hadn't known who al fresco was either) and said snidely, "The ignorant children can fingerpaint."

Carried away by this new, unexpected diversion, they forgot about searching for Moll (which was mostly an excuse for adventure to everyone but Meg) and fluttered about like titmice, gathering folding tables and bits of broken pencils. Dickie remembered a bottle of India ink in his sanctuary, the library. When he finally found it and shook the bottle, half of it spilled down his shirt, and he saw that the other half was dried into a cake. Meg ran off to Phyllida to ask if she had any proper paints for them to use.

She found her in the little sitting room that adjoined her bedroom. She was perched at an aptly named vanity, staring into a silver-filigreed mirror. Phyllida's back was to the door, but Meg could see her great-great-aunt's reflection, distant and autumnal, looking at some far-off place, or time. Phyllida started when Meg called her name softly.

"Oh, Meg dear, come in, come in." She smiled and patted the plush seat beside her.

"Are you okay?"

"Of course. Just indulging myself in a bit of sentimentality. Did that artist fellow stay? Well, it may be good for you, as Lysander says. You'll never want for beauty if you can make your own. I've done a bit of painting myself." She gestured to the wall at a postcard-sized painting of violets with a slug crawling up the stem. "Without much success, as you can see. My tutor told me, 'If you can't paint but must paint, stick to flowers.' Even the ugly ones are pretty; if you do them badly, people will know what they are, and as a last resort, you can always say they are abstract."

"I think it's nice," Meg said honestly. "You did the slime on the antennae perfectly. I came to ask, do you have any paint we can use, or brushes, or pencils? The artist has some, but not enough for everyone."

"I think I do. Yes, it's been years, but they should be in the third room on the left from the stairs, on the top floor. I had a studio of sorts for a few months. The late afternoon light there is just right. Like mirrors in very good boutiques, it makes everything look much better than it really is. Perhaps I should live up there." She said this last to herself.

Meg was turning to go after the paints when Phyllida called her back. "Meg dear, I wanted to talk with you about something. Whenever you have a moment. Yes, go, go learn to paint. You'll enjoy that. But when you're done, come find me, there's a good girl. Oh, wait, one more thing." She rose and went to a wardrobe. After pulling the hangers back and forth, she came out with a large linen shirt. It was the weathered white of many washings, but so finely made it had only just begun to fray at the cuffs. It was soft as dandelion fluff and crinkled into fine wrinkles in Meg's damp palm. As she laid it over her arm, it caught the light, and she saw that the tiny, precise stitches were wrought in silver thread instead of white, a subtle glint at the seams and collar. Little splashes of color dotted the shirtfront—cyan, cinnabar, rose madder.

"You don't want to get that pretty shirt all covered with paint," Phyllida said. Meg looked down at her own gauzy blouse, a bright, blotchy print that was supposed to be reminiscent of India, in green and fuchsia and orange (which are more harmonious than you might think). She thought it was nice, but it was mass-produced in a factory, and when she compared it to Phyllida's shirt, which had been woven on a nearby cottager's loom from flax locally grown, and cut and sewed by skilled hands, not machine, her own seemed a paltry, cheap thing.

"I wore this as a smock when I was painting," Phyllida went on. "It's big enough to cover you to your knees, so you don't have to worry about paint splashing on you. The most entertaining things are so often the messiest, at your age anyway."

Meg scurried away, promising to return after her art lesson. She found the others grouped on the croquet lawn in various poses. Rowan had a proper easel, borrowed from Gwidion, and Meg brought another from Phyllida's studio. Finn and Dickie had folding tea tables. Silly had commandeered the milking stool and sat on the ground cross-legged with her paper hanging over the round edges.

Gwidion walked among them. "Today you will draw by instinct, without detailed instruction, so that I may gauge your natural talent." He had never given a lesson in his life and had learned his trade in a haphazard way from his father, so he really didn't know where to begin. Still, he looked impressive as he wandered from student to student, looking over their shoulders, giving them tips on shadow and perspective, speaking in his rather grandiose way with words like *cinquecento* and *chiaroscuro*. They didn't understand half of what he said, which was exactly what he intended.

He told them to draw what they saw. Meg chose a vista of the sheep meadow beyond the ha-ha, following Phyllida's theory that, like flowers, it would look pretty and be recognizable even if poorly executed. Her sheep were nebulous balls, and her field nothing more than the white unmarked paper. Gwidion looked over her shoulder, made a noise like he had just stepped in something unpleasant, and walked away without further comment.

Silly, working with her tongue poking out and head bent so far over to the side she was almost lying on the paper, drafted an ambitious battle scene with croquet mallets as weapons and balls flying willy-nilly. When Gwidion reminded her rather sharply that she was supposed to be drawing what she saw, she replied that she did see it, in her head, and after that he mostly left her alone.

Dickie, with whispered advice from the Wyrm curled invisibly on his shoulder, was drawing an amazingly accurate representation of a cooperative snail who crawled slowly across his table. "If you decide to eat him afterward," the Wyrm said, "soak him in milk first. It will plump him up and take away any taste of mud. Unpalatable little beasts at best, but the Gauls always had strange tastes. Garlic and butter, that's the ticket. Hmm, an odd phrase, that. What ticket, I wonder? A train ticket? A carnival ticket? A lottery ticket? I knew once, but thank goodness I have forgotten." Dickie's pencil traced the lines with a draughtsman's precision and a naturalist's eye for detail.

"The snail to surpass all snails!" Gwidion said, making Dickie bow his head to hide his pleasure.

He went to Finn. "Ah, what have we here? A still life of a melon? A dirigible?" He made a show of looking around for either of these objects. "No, a face. I see it now. Who can it be?"

Finn mumbled something.

"Speak up, lad! Art knows no shame, talent no modesty."

"It's her," he said, indicating Meg with a jerk of his head. Meg looked up, and her face instantly reddened, which she fervently hoped no one would notice.

Her hopes were dashed. "Not a melon, then, but a beet!" Gwidion said, looking over at her with a laugh. He took the page from Finn and handed him a fresh sheet. "No people yet, lad. Look about for a better subject." He tore the paper into bits and flung them up over his head so they scattered in the gentle breeze. One landed at Meg's feet. When no one was looking, she picked it up. It appeared to be her nose, though as Gwidion said, it looked more vegetable than animal, bulbous and spotted like a rotting potato.

Is that what I look like? she wondered. Is that how he sees me, a misshapen thing covered in freckles? She pressed her lips together and felt angry tears come to her eyes, a strange kind of anger that was so many other things too.

You might as well know, though Meg didn't, that wasn't how Finn thought of her. He simply didn't have a drop of artistic skill. He was trying for something entirely unlike a rotting potato.

Meg furiously scribbled her sheep's wool as Gwidion wandered to Rowan's side.

"The masterpiece!" she heard him say.

Rowan really did have a talent for drawing, though he had never ventured into any medium other than pencils, pens, crayons, and sidewalk chalk. Knowing his limitations, he did not try to do a face from the front like Finn, but chose instead a rear view. On his sheet of paper were a set of shoulders and a head of sleek hair done in black ink with faint streaks of blue. Just at the nape perched a fat, dusty black and gold bumblebee, its pollen sacs full, cleaning its antennae. Over the shoulder, just beginning to be sketched out, came a hand apparently ready to smack the bee. It was abundantly evident what would happen next.

Gwidion leaned forward with real interest. Though this was certainly not the masterpiece he called it, there was evident skill in the boy's fingers, a facility for translating thought to paper, idea to form. He had glanced discreetly over at Finn, who was absorbed in starting a new drawing. Yes, this Rowan had drawn the Finn boy. His brother? He had assumed all the children were relatives and descendants of Phyllida in one way or another, but he had gotten the impression from Finn's choice of subject that he wasn't Meg's brother, after all.

Gwidion traced back his family history. These must be descendants of Chlorinda, Phyllida's elder sister, who had fled to the States rather than inherit the Guardianship. Gwidion's own lineage traced from Phyllida and Chlorinda's mother's brother, their uncle, Llewellwn Thomas. He tried to figure out exactly how he was related to these children, but the litany of greats and removeds was too daunting. No matter, he thought. The inheritance is rightfully mine, not theirs. When I have done what I came to do, they may go back safely to their dull little homes and forget all about me. Safely, that is, so long as they don't cross me.

All the same, he found himself considering this young Rowan chap. He was in the same position Gwidion's grandfather had been in—eldest male, by all traditions of every land destined to inherit everything, yet being usurped by that little chit of a girl, Meg. It might have been self-interest that motivated Gwidion, but he felt a sympathy for these other males who were swindled out of their inheritance. While he was here, perhaps he would cultivate the friendship of these boys, these distant relatives of his. If he gained their allegiance, they might be of some help, and in any event it would cause more disruption and unrest in Phyllida's line.

But what was the relationship between Rowan and Finn? There

must be some malice there, because Rowan had put his heart and soul into this drawing of Finn about to experience a terrible pain. He drew with conviction, and he drew with relish. He evidently wanted Finn to be hurt, and with more than mere boyish mischief. Still, he didn't quite want it enough to make it come true.

Gwidion was loud in his praise of the boys (utterly ignoring the girls), telling them that, as members of such a proud and noble family, was it any wonder they should have such prodigious talent? He buttered them up, and all the while, he studied them. At last he settled behind Rowan again and took up his pencil.

"Here, my boy, let me help," he said, and settled himself into the trancelike state required to draw a picture so compelling it forced one to do his bidding. This one was tricky, partially because it had been begun by another hand than his, partly because there were two subjects to control, the bee and the boy. With a stroke or two of the lead, he added agitation to the bee, a sense of danger and insulted pride that made the bee ready for attack. Turning to the boy (all the more difficult because he must give will to a hand, not a face), he made the fingers seem to twitch in irritability, created an almost palpable sensation of tickle and itch in the skin of his nape. He focused all his energy on this scene, picturing it on the page, in his mind, in life, thinking, *Let this come to pass.*

Then he watched.

It took no more than a minute for a bee to appear. Had it already been there, irritated by some inner vexation? Or was it a creation that had not existed before it was brought to life with pencil and paper and skill? In any event, it buzzed angrily and made a beeline for Finn. It circled him tauntingly and then settled at the back of his neck. Gwidion watched, trembling in anticipation, and Rowan, noticing his interest, followed his gaze in time to see his picture come true.

The bee landed, Finn swatted, and the inevitable conclusion was heralded with a howling wail of agony and anguish. (No one but the bee paid any mind to the bee's anguish, for of course a honeybee dies after stinging.)

Finn ran around in circles, screaming, and even Meg, who rushed to him in consternation and figured he must have cut a finger off at least, to judge by the noise, thought he was overdoing it a bit. He grabbed and clawed at the stinger, breaking the poison sac and making the pain much worse as a new surge of toxin made its way into his flesh. Finally Meg calmed him down enough to look at the wound, and she used a flat, dull paint knife to scrape away the remains of the stinger. He rubbed and scratched the wound with one hand and scrubbed at his face with the other.

Everyone but Meg erupted in laughter. Finn, eye bright with wiped-away tears, turned on them with fury.

Gwidion chuckled. "Oh ho, don't take it so hard, little man! What is a tiny prick compared with the tribulations life throws at us? Would your ancestor Llyr make such a bellow, or his father before him, Llewellwn?" Mentioning the names was risky, but there was little chance these children had heard tales of their family's black sheep. He clapped Rowan on the shoulder. "Why, I bet your brother, or cousin, or whatever it is here, wouldn't hardly flinch if a dozen bees stung him. I thought this family was made of sterner stuff."

Finn found his voice at last. "I'm not a member of this stupid family! Rowan's not related to me. I'd jump off a cliff if he were! I hate all of you!"

Gwidion's face hardened and, quick as a shot, he crossed the distance to Finn and boxed his ears smartly.

"Impudent, lying imp, how dare you try to trick me? Get out! Not part of the family? Why waste my time?"

Meg tried to tell him that Finn had never said he was related to them, that Gwidion had never asked. She was stunned. She'd never seen an adult strike a child before, and though she'd read about children getting spanked or whipped or slapped, it was the stuff of novels, not real life.

Dickie gave a gasp, but Rowan, almost as shocked as Meg, shushed him with a meaningful look. I'll keep your secret, Dickie, the look said. You are more one of us than Finn is. It was one thing for the hated Finn to be struck, quite another for friendly, shy, innocuous little Dickie.

Finn's face was all shades of red—his cheeks flushed with anger and mortification, his eye scarlet with tears, his ears the brightest of all, crimson from the blow. He stood stock-still for a moment, his breath coming in pants. Then his jaw tightened and he looked at Gwidion with a fixed concentration that nearly made the man quail, for it was the same focused look he knew he had when he willed one of his paintings to come true.

"You'll pay for that," Finn said, evenly and coldly. He looked like he was going to hit Gwidion back. He took a step forward, but as he did so, the great goat who had been kneeling nearby rose. His bleat was like a roar, and he lowered his massive curved horns at Finn.

Finn looked from goat to master and didn't like the odds. "You'll pay," he whispered again, stern and resolute like a man. Then his strength collapsed and he ran away like a boy. Meg could tell he was crying as he ran.

She wanted to go after Finn. She wanted to run for Phyllida and tell her that they had made a mistake letting this violent man teach them. She wanted to cry herself. Then all at once, her resolution vanished. The children gathered around Gwidion with trusting little faces as his pencil flew. He drew, and the faces became even more trusting.

"What a foolish boy," Gwidion said condescendingly. "He thinks I hit him—how silly! Don't you agree?"

"Oh yes," they all said.

"I could never hit anyone, could I?"

"Oh no," came the chorus.

"Finn is a liar, isn't he?"

That one was easy, even without Gwidion's picture of them all credulously clustered around him.

"Yes, Finn is a liar," they echoed.

Gwidion nodded and tucked the pictures into his vest. His controlling spell over the children didn't have to be very powerful. You don't have to get someone to believe something forever—you only have to convince them of it once. After that, however strong the evidence to the contrary, most people will cling to a belief out of sheer stubbornness.

Meg was left with the idea that something unpleasant had happened, but she couldn't quite recall what. They resumed drawing, but the joy of her art lesson was gone. Gwidion was all charm and praise once again, but it was evident he was only interested in the boys' work. Any compliments to her drawing were barbed, and her confidence fell ever lower. When they took a break for lunch, she handed Rowan her smock.

"Here, take this. You're getting charcoal smudges all over your clothes."

"Don't you need it?" he asked as he slipped the lightweight long-sleeved shirt over his arms.

"No . . . I don't think I feel like drawing anymore. I'm not very good at it."

This was Rowan's cue to say she was good and to ask her to stay, but he was too full of Gwidion's praise and thoughts of his own talent to pay her any mind.

Meg finished her treacle tart and headed morosely upstairs to find Phyllida, a little guilty she hadn't gone sooner. When she was halfway up, a large cat scampered down to meet her, coiling its sinuous body around her ankles so she tripped and caught herself on all fours. She sat on the steps and had started to scold the cat when she realized it wasn't one of the Rookery felines. There was Old Tom, the fat kitchen tabby who kept the mice in constant terror, and several dairy cats, but she could tell at a glance this wasn't any of them. For one thing, it had two tails.

For another, it spoke to her.

"I do like a nap," he said, licking his paw and looking away from her, as cats will when they are really interested in you. "But even I think four centuries is a bit much. Thank you for waking me from my long slumber, pink one."

He stopped licking his paw just long enough to touch her knee with his nose.

"Who are you?"

He looked at her, surprised. "You did the great magic, did you not? Surely that was all for me, lovely me? I imagine you heard of my great beauty and unsurpassed softness and decided you must stop at nothing to do me this favor. And I, in return, allow you a glimpse of me."

"I'm ever so sorry, and you are certainly beautiful, but I don't know who you are, and I didn't mean to wake you up."

The cat squinted his moon eyes at her. "Truly? Then you are indeed a barbarian, as my people have long averred. I am Bake-Neko, and I come from the land where the sun is daily born. Nippon, it is called."

"Do you mean Japan?"

"Perhaps you call it that, but I do not, or I would have said so." He looked away again and licked a part of himself that made Meg look away too. His double tails twitched and coiled together like a caduceus. When he had forgiven her, he lifted his front paw and revealed what looked like a dead mouse.

Meg recoiled and said, "Ewwww."

Bake-Neko took this for a sound of awe and praise, which only goes to show that good things can sometimes come of cultural misunderstandings.

"You won't throw it away, will you? Or bury it?"

"Um, no, of course not," she said, though she intended to do just that.

"I will tell you something, since you freely confess that you are an ignorant savage. Do not dispose of this mouse. We cats, even demon cats of heavenly beauty such as myself, wrap all our presents in dead rodents. Or dead birds, depending on the season.

You cannot get to the present inside unless you let the wrapping rot and decompose. Inside will be a treasure beyond value. If you attempt a dissection, it will vanish, and of course if you throw it on the dustheap, someone else—probably a burying beetle or stray cur—will make off with your gift."

"I never knew," Meg said wonderingly, recalling how many dead lizards and mice and pigeons her own cat back in Arcadia had left for her. Had they all contained presents?

"You humans are all ignorant barbarians, methinks," the two-tailed cat said with a twitch of his whiskers. "I return to my home now. Stick that under your bed, and in a few days, you will have your gift."

Before she could ask him any more questions, he bounded down two steps and had vanished by the third.

She picked up the dead beastie by its short tail (the Wyrm could have told her it was a Japanese red-backed vole, not a mouse, but as it was dead and only a wrapping anyway, it didn't much matter) and carried it up to her bedroom, where she put it in a shoebox and slid it under her bed before searching for Phyllida.

Yes, I Will

FINN RAN SO HE COULDN'T CRY. Feet pounding first on neatly mowed turf, then on the twisting brambles that love the threshold between sun and shade, then on the thick, damp litter of decomposition in the shadowed forest, he pushed himself farther and faster. How could he sob when he needed his breath for running? That must be sweat that stung his eyes so sharply and coursed down his cheeks, not tears. He ran until his side throbbed with a stabbing pain, until a root reached up to trip him and he sprawled headlong in the dirt. His fingers dug into the soft earth, and he pulled up big handfuls, squeezing with all his strength so he wouldn't cry again.

Again. That was the worst of it. Worse than the friendlessness, worse than being scorned, worse than being struck. He could tell himself that the Morgans and Dickie Rhys were beneath him, not his sort, that he didn't want them for friends. He could tell himself, and almost believe, that their scorn came from jealousy, that they teased and shunned him because they recognized and resented his natural superiority. And as for that so-called artist, Gwidion, well, Finn consoled himself that as soon as he got back, he'd call the constable and have him locked up in a dank dungeon (is there any other kind?) for all eternity. But that they should all have seen him weep like a baby, like a girl, like . . . . Fresh tears sprung to his eyes, salty with self-pity.

"It's not fair," he said aloud to the dirt, knowing as he did so that he would never, never say that to any living being. Young as he was, he didn't believe in fair play and knew that the world wasn't a fair place. He justified many of the things he did and said by thinking that the world would do and say those same things to him if he didn't armor himself by striking first.

It wasn't fair that all of those beastly Morgans got to see fairies. He had as much right as any of them. So what if the same blood didn't flow through his veins? He was an American and (though he was also a shameless elitist) firmly believed that birth and blood were not nearly as important as determination and cunning and intelligence and an absolute refusal to stay in the place the fates tried to put you. In this last, he was a great deal like Meg, though she looked at it not so much in terms of her own situation but in circumstances around her.

Why should the stupid Morgans be entitled to something just because they happened to be related to Phyllida? Why should that beastly Rowan see all the fairies he wanted when Finn, finding fairies with his own ingenuity, was half blinded for his troubles? And Silly, the annoying little twit. Meg was okay, though. At least she didn't seem to hate him like the others. And from what he had been able to piece together about that Midsummer War business, she had acted with quite startling bravery. Still, she wasn't any better than he was, and she had both her eyes.

Thinking about his eye made his lip tremble in a new bout of self-pity. However horrible the damage, his tear ducts were still working, and it struck him as the cruelest irony that, though he was half blind and disfigured, that eye could still wound him with its weeping. He rubbed the tears away fiercely, forgetting that he still clutched dirt.

"Oh, great," he said, and to his surprise found himself laughing. A fine mess I am, he thought. Eyeless, filthy, beaten up . . . and laughing like a lunatic. He didn't realize that the tired old saying about laughter being the best medicine is true. It won't mend broken bones (or replace an eye poked out with a hazel twig), but when you can laugh, even self-deprecating laughter, you know you're on the road to recovery.

Finn wiped his palms on his jeans and carefully brushed the dirt and grit from under his black silk eyepatch. You could tell he was already feeling better because he was plotting revenge. Laughter is a good tonic; laughter mixed with anger put to constructive use can cure all but the gravest wounds.

When he heard the sound of weeping from the undergrowth nearby, he immediately thought someone was mocking him and jumped up with his dirty fists clenched, ready for battle. But no, the sobbing evidently came from a very little person, and it sounded heartbreakingly sincere.

"Who's there?" Finn asked, mostly gently but with just a little edge, in case it turned out someone was making fun of him after all.

The crying paused, then resumed with fresh passion.

"What's wrong? Can I help?"

"I bro ... bro ... broke my wagon-hun-hun!" the little voice sobbed and stuttered, and melted away into new paroxysms of suffering.

Finn looked around and saw a child-sized wooden wagon, painted blue with white lettering on the side: FENODEREE'S MOWING AND CARTING. The left rear axle was broken.

"Don't cry, kid. I think I can fix that for you." He turned the wagon on its side and fiddled with the parts. "See, I can use a branch or something, if I can find one the right size."

A hopeful little whimper rose from the wagon's unseen owner. "I love my wagon, I do," he said earnestly.

"I bet you do," Finn said pleasantly as he scoured the ground for an appropriate stick. "It's a pretty cool wagon. Here, this ought to do." He took out his pocketknife and set about shaping the stick into a makeshift axle. The blade snapped off (luckily flying clear of his remaining eye), but he managed to scrape the stick into an appropriate shape. Lost in his work, he came very close to forgetting his own troubles and resentments for almost a full minute. He fit the replacement into the wheel and gave it a trial roll. "How's that, then?" he asked. "Good as new, if not so pretty. Do you want to try it out?"

There was no answer.

"Don't be afraid. You won't come out to see it? Okay, I'll just leave it here for you." He chuckled to himself. Poor tyke. Probably so well trained by his mommy, he didn't dare meet a stranger. Or maybe she told him the strangers might be fairies in disguise. Well, it was certainly likely here. He smoothed out one last rough spot on the stick and left the wagon for its owner. Finn whistled as he walked down the lane, wanting to look back but respecting the little guy's shyness. He just smiled to himself. He felt unaccountably good, which as a rule happened only when he did something self-serving.

He had just gotten out of sight when he stumbled over a hemp bag. "Hey, kid, is this yours?" Finn shouted back over his shoulder, but there was no answer. He called out several times before he looked more closely and saw roughly scratched into the dirt the words FER YE.

"For me?" he asked. Had the little boy left him some personal treasure of marbles or chewing gum to thank him for his help? "Gee, you didn't have to do that," said Finn, warming.

He pulled the frayed and twisted cord open and felt inside the unusually heavy bag. On top was crinkling paper, and as he pulled that out, he felt something hard and knobbly beneath it. The paper turned out to be money of some sort. On one side was a pleasant-looking maternal woman in a short, spiky crown, who could be no other than Queen Elizabeth, and on the back was a bushy-bearded man who might have been the writer Anthony Trollope but you could guess from the ship, flowers, bird, and magnifying glass was more likely Charles Darwin. From the large *10* in the corners, Finn determined it must be a ten-pound note. Unless the poor dollar had fallen farther since he arrived in England, his bill was worth about twenty dollars.

There was no bank in Gladysmere, and he had no way of getting to a bigger town, so Finn had been unable to make use of the bank account and checkbook his parents had set up for him. It is even more remarkable, then, that he didn't instantly count himself lucky and pocket the money.

"Little boy!" he called out, heading back to where he'd left the wagon. "Come out! Where are you? You can't give this to me, it's too much." He waved the bill around to the empty woods. Imagine, some little child giving him twenty dollars. Even if he was well off, it had to be all his pocket money for weeks.

"I'm staying at the Rookery," he said loudly to no one. "If you change your mind, you can have it back." As soon as he said that he was sorry. He was already thinking how to spend it.

He slipped the bill in his pocket and immediately felt his hip sink. It felt like someone had strapped a bowling ball to his side. His whole body tilted, and he could hardly stand upright. He thought at first he might have dislocated his hip, but how? Then he thought maybe his foot had caught on something and was pulling him back. But no, it wasn't any pull but that of gravity—it was a weight. It had happened as soon as he put the bill in his pocket. He took it out again, and the weight vanished. The bill was as light as a hummingbird feather in his hand. He looked at it quizzically and put it back in his pocket. At once he was weighted down as if with a dangling ball and chain. He tried the experiment again and finally was forced to conclude that the flimsy piece of paper in his hand suddenly weighed a great deal more when in his pocket. It must have weighed . . . he burst out laughing even as horripilations danced on his forearms. Ten pounds. The ten-pound note weighed ten pounds!

His first instinct was to throw the unnatural thing to the ground, but a healthy respect for money (some might call it greed) made him keep it. It must be a magic bill of some kind. He looked around warily. Surely it had been a little boy he heard, not a fairy. Well, perhaps the boy had gotten the bill from a fairy. He chuckled. What had seemed incredible generosity was instead probably just getting rid of a cumbersome burden. Tiny as that chap sounded, it must have been well nigh impossible to carry around a ten-pound weight. He'd rather ditch it than carry it miles to town to spend. Finn slipped it back in his pocket and felt the same way himself. He'd carry it in his hand until he got back to the Rookery, then leave it in his bureau until he could find a way to spend it.

He took it out, expecting it to be feather-light again, but though it perched ephemerally on his hand, he could hardly lift it. Even out of his pocket, it now weighed ten pounds.

He tossed it away, and it drifted and twirled to the ground like a winged maple seed.

"Do you mean," he asked aloud, indignantly, "that if I want to spend this thing, I have to carry ten pounds around?" No one answered, but he fancied he heard a giggle in the breeze. "I mean, not that it's heavy or anything." He didn't want the kid to think he was a weakling, but ten pounds would be an annoying burden for a grown man; it was all the more difficult for Finn. He picked up the bill. He put it down again. He looked at the bill. The bill looked at him.

"Fine!" he said, almost angry at his gift. He shoved it into the hemp bag, and when his fingers hit the knobbly thing again, he remembered that he had two presents.

Something grabbed his hand, and he squealed and pulled it

out. Clutched in his hand—clutching his hand . . . in fact, shaking his hand in a cordial way—were five skeletal digits. If they'd been clean and white (or not following an enchanted ten-pound note), he might have thought they were no more than a prank, a prop left over from Halloween. But it was evident that these bones once had flesh and skin and muscle on them and that the softer tissues had mostly (but not completely) rotted away. There was even a slight stickiness to them and a stale odor somewhere between a dog bone and an unused attic.

He tried to drop the thing, but it held on, pumping his hand in so friendly a manner he could almost see the rest of the body attached to it—a man of medium build in neat but mended clothes, dark hair, a hat, a wry smile, a cunning look. . . . Finn shut his eye and shook his head, dispelling the vision, and was left only with the hand, which now skittered back into the bag and held fast. No matter how hard Finn tried to pull it out, it gripped tight, clutching the bottom of the bag in its decomposing fingers. He shut the bag and looked around him one last time. What could he do? He was afraid, but how could he not keep his presents? How could he be invited into a world of mystery and oddity and decline the invitation?

"I won't take it," he said.

He stared at the bag for a long moment.

"Yes, I will."

"There you are, child," Phyllida said when Meg found her, still in her little sitting room. There were crumpled tissues on the vanity table, which Phyllida hastily brushed into a polished wooden wastebasket before Meg noticed them. "How did the painting go?"

"Oh, fine, I guess. I'm not very good. The others liked it, though, especially Rowan and Dickie. But not Finn. He left—I don't know why."

"Oh, good, good," Phyllida said absently. "Meg, sit down if you please. Just move those things onto the floor. I need to talk with you about something, something very serious."

Meg perched on the seat, two lines deepening between her eyebrows. "Is it Moll? Have you found her?"

"No, not that. Not yet."

"I'm going out this afternoon to look for her. I was going to before Gwidion came."

"Yes, do. There's no harm in that. But what I must talk with you about, Meg . . . Meg . . ." She sighed deeply. "I am going to die."

Meg's eyes blurred and welled, and fat tears like late-summer-afternoon raindrops rolled down her cheeks. She threw her arms around Phyllida so hard she hurt the old woman.

"No, no, no! Not now, child! Not now!" She heaved a sobbing little laugh herself and pushed Meg away. "You don't understand me. I'm not dying just now, nor yet for some time, if I have anything to say about it . . . which I just might. But someday. Someday I will die, as of course we all will, but if all goes according to the plans of nature, I'll die much sooner than you. It cannot be too many years hence, perhaps a dozen if I am lucky, who can say? I have no child, Meg, no daughter. In the weeks you have been here—has it only been a matter of weeks?—you have come to seem more like my child than I would have thought possible.

"We tried, you know, Lysander and I. Seven times I was quick with life, and seven times that life melted away before it came close to seeing the sun. I couldn't carry a child. That has never happened to a Lady of the Green Hill. What will become of the Green Hill and its denizens if they have no Guardian? The people will forget. The fairies will grow bold. Wives and babies will be stolen, cattle will go dry . . . and the people will have just enough of the old lore left to remember how to retaliate. They will burn the Green Hill. They will mow the thornbushes. They will cut down the ancient trees. They will plow up the hill itself, and someday, when the truths my ancestors have held for generations are no more than fairy stories told to babes in the nursery, they will build apartments where the Seelie Court once danced. The fairies will be gone, and mankind will be diminished. I would not see that happen."

To be faced with the prospect, even theoretical, of her beloved great-great-aunt's demise was bad enough; to see practically before her very eyes the Green Hill plowed and leveled and commercialized froze Meg in an openmouthed stare. Then her jaw gaped wider. She knew what was coming next. The weight of responsibility settled on her, itchy and oppressive like a woolly winter overcoat on a summer noon, and she wanted to shrug it off immediately and run away to some cool, shady place.

Phyllida was speaking again, but Meg didn't listen. She didn't have to. Meg looked at some vague place over Phyllida's shoulder and saw her lips move. She was telling her it would all come to an end, all of it, if Phyllida didn't have an heir. And who could that heir be? Meg's mother? No, she had her life as a professor, and she'd shown no interest, no calling. Silly? Preposterous. Silly was good enough in her own way, but unless she underwent a dramatic personality shift, she would never have the serene strength and wise determination to mediate between the world of man and the world of fairies. She might study them, might, as one of Phyllida's blood, come to know practically everything there was to know about them, and she might violently and passionately defend fairy from man, man from fairy. But the position required someone steady, a diplomat, a negotiator. Silly was not the girl for the job. And yes, it must be a girl, so Rowan and James were out. It was Meg, or no one. Meg, or a strip mall on the Green Hill.

"I'm just a kid!" Meg said suddenly, interrupting Phyllida's narrative. "I can't make this kind of decision now. I don't know what I want to do with my life." It seemed like all other possibilities were flying away from her. She had wanted to be a great many things when she grew up—a paleontologist, a writer, a lawyer, a marine—her choices shifted with each book she read, each movie she saw, each field trip that inspired her. Now it felt like all of those were closed to her, and though she had to admit she probably didn't really want to be a marine, she liked the idea that it was an option, that she still had plenty of years to decide, to play with possibilities. Phyllida was trying to strip that away.

She thought Phyllida was going to say something about her destiny, tell her that she was fated to be the Guardian of the Green Hill. She thought Phyllida would try to convince her, bully her, even, and she braced herself for a struggle. She might want to be Guardian . . . but she might not, and no one was going to force her to decide her entire future on the spur of the moment. She felt in her heart that if Phyllida did pressure her, she would be compelled to say yes (and was fairly sure she wanted to say yes) but feared any decision made in haste would be repented at leisure, and she understood herself well enough to know that she would keep even a deeply regretted promise. No, she would make no promise now, and she dug her heels in and prepared to be stubborn.

But Phyllida knew her, and the world, too well for that. "It is a big decision, and one you should not make without a great deal of thought. The worst thing in the world is to bind yourself to something you hate. I think you have the ability to be Guardian . . . and I think you have the interest. But it needs unswerving dedication. It is in many ways a life of sacrifice. I have had to do unpleasant things in my day, things that, if they were not done for necessity, would mark me as a madwoman, or criminal, or worse. I ask you only one thing today, my little Meg. Will you agree to learn more? Will you let me teach you about the fairies, about the Green Hill, about what it truly means to be the Guardian? For what time we have together, let me teach you as though you were indeed to be my successor, and someday, you can decide. It needn't even be in my lifetime."

Meg felt an almost magnetic force drawing her to say yes, and for one minute more she fought it. I want to learn, she thought, all she has to teach me. She heard the Green Hill call out to her, felt it pulling her out of the life she knew, her Arcadian childhood, calling her to a wild dance in a mushroom circle. And, oh, how she wanted to join in that dance! To be as serene and wise and powerful as Phyllida, to live forever in this lovely place, to have the knowledge, the lore, of creatures who have existed for millennia, creatures so lovely and frightening she felt her breath catch to think of them.

"Will you let me teach you?" Phyllida prompted again.

Meg waited just long enough to be certain the decision was hers, then she said, "Yes, I will."

Rowan helped Gwidion carry the art supplies to the ramshackle hovel.

"Welcome to my humble abode!" Gwidion said, swinging his arms widely to display the dust and cobwebs. "A palace fit for a king, if not for a young prince like yourself. Here, find a place to sit and we'll have a nice . . . well, perhaps not a nice cup of tea, but I'll see what I can scrounge up." He flapped his handkerchief at two wicker chairs, stirring up dust-djinns, and poked around the corner of the one-room house that served as a kitchen.

"Ah, here—a tin of chocolate. And sugar. That should do. Does the tap work? Yes, but I'll let it run awhile until it's a bit less brown. Still, the chocolate will hide that, no? And cups. I'll take the one with the crack. Well, the biggest crack, anyway." He was forcefully cheerful.

"It isn't very nice, is it?" Rowan said truthfully.

"Good enough for the likes of me," Gwidion said. "Not but that I wasn't born to better things, but life hands you travails, and you take 'em and twist 'em and use 'em as you see fit. And here we are! Gwidion, master painter, and the likeliest lad I've seen in many a day. The other boy's your brother, is he? Dickie Morgan? A good lad, I'm sure, but a bit quiet, a bit *inward*, if you know what I mean." He tapped the side of his nose with a bony forefinger. "Never did trust the quiet types. Generally plotting against you, they are. Keep a man talking, and he can't be thinking of ways to harm you. But you, now . . . I could tell at a glance you're a horse of another color."

Rowan laughed at this and asked what color.

Gwidion looked him over appraisingly. "Your hair's chestnut, but your soul's piebald. Half of one color, half another, black and white, here and there, and every time someone looks at you, they don't know if they'll see one or the other. A good way to be. A useful way to be."

He pulled out a sheet of paper and started drawing as Rowan pretended to drink some rather bad lukewarm chocolate.

"Your sister, now, the older one . . ."

"Meg, you mean."

"Aye. She's a white horse if I ever saw one."

Rowan looked puzzled.

"I've never seen a white horse win a race, have you?" Gwidion asked. Rowan had never seen a horse race. "I've never seen a white horse take a high fence in a hunt. No white horse pulls a plow, or a cart, or does any real work or any great deed. But who gets in all the paintings? Who leads the parades? When you think of a king or a statesman mounted, what does he ride? A white horse. When all the time white horses are the stupidest, weakest, most useless horses imaginable, good for nothing but prancing and show. They get the credit, but it's the other horses that are more worthy."

You'd think Rowan would have bristled at this characterization of his sister, but he happened to be thinking of the Midsummer War, when he was the chosen hero of the Seelie Court. He had trained for weeks, was primed and ready for the greatest battle of his life, and what had happened? Meg put him to sleep with trickery and took his place. She got all the glory, all the honor. And she didn't even fight. There was Rowan, ready for swordplay and derring-do, and all Meg had to do was let go of an arrow string. (It didn't occur to him that the fatal blow itself is often the easiest part of killing.) Yes, he thought, Meg is a white horse. She got to lead the parade in his place. Everyone thought she was so great, when it should have been him.

Gwidion sketched away, studying Rowan's intense face, and soon, the scowl on the paper was matched by a scowl on the living lips. Gwidion added anger to the eyes, and resentment, and determination, and it was not long before the boy felt them too.

What a pleasure to practice my art on the young, thought Gwidion. They are so malleable, so pliant, so easily turned away from the things they should love.

When Rowan was in a properly receptive state, Gwidion began to lead him in earnest. "How do you like the Rookery, lad? It will all be yours someday, no? . . . No? Whose, then?"

Rowan honestly didn't know, and Gwidion made him think about it. "You children are her only heirs, aren't you? If it doesn't go to you, then who? The pensioners? The royal cat hospital? You are the eldest male heir, you know." Besides me, the rightful heir, he thought.

He went on about the beauties and the riches of the Rookery until Rowan was fairly enthralled by the idea of all that money and land, of the people who would live under the care of whoever owned it all.

"And I have heard," Gwidion added conspiratorially, "that

there is more to the estate than just the riches, the land, the title. Do you know of the Green Hill?"

"Do I ever!" Rowan said, and in his spell, he didn't know how foolish he was being. Still thinking more of Meg's usurpation of his glory than any interference in his inheritance, he told Gwidion all about the Midsummer War.

If she has done all that, Gwidion thought, she must be close to being formally accepted as Phyllida's heir. Should I focus on the old woman or shift to the child? The girl might be easier to control, but who can say how close she is to accepting her position? If Phyllida renounces her place, it is mine straightaway. If the chit is the heir and hands it to me, well, the old lady still breathes. An obstacle, but not a great one. Still, always easier not to have blood on one's hands. Better stick to the old woman and hurry, before that brat makes things more difficult.

Gwidion laid the portrait of Rowan on the dusty table before him. It scarcely looked like the Rowan we know. The face was sly, calculating, full of resentment and imagined insult. It was pinched and somehow twisted, not the handsome boy who had walked into the shack. Rowan stared lovingly down at his own image.

"It should be mine," he said softly.

"But it will not be," Gwidion hissed. "She will give it to that girl, your sister, just as they always do. It is the eldest who should inherit—the eldest male. You know that. Everyone knows that. Why should this family be any different?"

If Rowan had been in his right mind, he would have put up a pretty good argument. He hadn't thought about being rich, or a landowner, or a lord, and therefore didn't really know if it mattered to him if he was one (or all three) or not. As for primogeniture, he accepted it in books, but he didn't really think anyone was too strict about it in modern times. He certainly never thought about what he would inherit from his parents. The idea of their demise was too distant and terrible for him to even contemplate, and if they were gone, inheritance would be the least of his concerns.

If he hadn't been enchanted, he wouldn't have minded if Meg inherited the whole kit and caboodle. If it were his, he would share with all of them, and if it were hers, she would share with all of them. It wouldn't really matter who actually owned it, except that person would have to do all the dull, boring things, like taxes and rents.

But now he had no argument. Everything Gwidion said seemed to make perfect sense. Even the queen of the Seelie Court had chosen Rowan. Of course he should get the Rookery, the money, the Green Hill.

"You must fight for what is yours," Gwidion said into his ear as Rowan studied himself. "And I will help you, if you will trust me and keep my secrets."

"It should be mine," Rowan said again, absently, staring into his own flat, greedy eyes.

Gwidion took this for assent. "Then I will help you, if you will help me. I have a way with convincing people, and I think I can persuade Phyllida to leave everything to you. You'd like that, wouldn't you?"

"I *deserve* that," Rowan said.

Gwidion chuckled. The arrogance of youth, to think it deserved anything. Still, this boy could help him gain access to Phyllida and would amuse him by being a gadfly to the family.

"In return for my help, you must do as I ask . . . everything I ask, without question. Serve me, and I will serve you. I must paint Phyllida's portrait. Either get her to agree to that, or arrange it so I can observe her."

"You did a nice picture of her before. Can't you do it from snapshots?"

"No questions!" Gwidion roared, making Rowan flinch. "This portrait must be perfect, it must be real. It . . . it will be a gift, from you to her." His voice became soft and sly. "When she sees it, she will be so grateful, she will do whatever you ask. Everything will be yours. Will you do that for me?"

Rowan didn't have to think about it. It might have been his picture answering with its covetous mouth, its resentful scowl.

"Yes, I will."

Like a Pollywog, Agog

MEG'S TRAINING WOULD BEGIN TOMORROW. Today, for the rest of the afternoon, she was free, and it felt like the end of summer vacation, joyous and careless with a last bacchanalian exuberance and an undertone of trepidation.

For the first of her lessons, she, and everyone in the household, would attend the Gladysmere mowing festival. Gladysmere has more festivals than any community outside of an artists' colony, and Phyllida explained that a large part of Meg's duties (should she choose to accept them) would be chairing the organizational committees for a least two dozen holiday, seasonal, crafting, and agricultural celebrations.

"You children will have a good time at the mowing," she said to Meg before letting her scamper to freedom. "Everyone works hard, but there will be jesters and magicians and fire-eaters and such too, and every merchant for miles around will have a tent set up. You can buy yourselves souvenirs, and I'll introduce you to some of the villagers you'll have to know." She caught Meg's look, which was almost a warning, and amended, "That is, if you decide to be Guardian someday."

It might give you a hint about Meg's eventual decision to know she spent her last day before training doing a Guardian's duty on her own—looking for Moll. This time, without the magical lure of Gwidion and the bluebell woods, she set out unerringly for the Green Hill. Phyllida had said there was no point looking there, but Meg didn't know where else to start. She couldn't remember where she'd looked the night before.

The ground was still wet from the storm, and the brutal heat of afternoon made the moisture rise until it felt like a rain forest. She was slick with sweat in the heavy air, but at least it was shady. The fungi enjoyed the warm, wet conditions even if she did not, and bright-red spotted fly agarics and golden polypores stretched their caps and spread their spores, while slime molds crept their inexorable way over roots. Clusters of frail pale-brown fairy-bonnet mushrooms sprang in great profusion over and around stumps and rotting logs. Meg wouldn't learn until weeks later that there is always a diminutive fairy hidden in each bunch, and she would spend hours one afternoon peeping under every delicate bonnet until she found a sharp little face grinning back at her.

She couldn't see the Green Hill yet, only a thick ring of thorns, which she now realized, to her delight, were blackberries. She pulled off a handful of fruit, then wondered, Did berries around a fairy mound count as fairy food? On their very first day at the Rookery, Phyllida and Lysander had made sure they knew, among other things, that they were never to accept food from a stranger, lest it be fairy food. To take so much as a taste could doom you to a life of imprisonment. But no, the berries were probably safe, and she stuffed a handful of the cool, sweet fruit into her mouth. She was still chewing when Finn called her name from behind her.

"Oh, umph . . ." She gulped and hastily covered her mouth with her hand while she tried to surreptitiously pick blackberry skins out of her teeth with her tongue. "What are you doing here?" she asked from behind her fingers. "How did you find the—" she stopped. Maybe he didn't know what was hidden behind the thorn hedges.

"The Green Hill? That's it, isn't it? I don't know. I was just wandering around." He turned away suddenly and did something she couldn't see—he was making absolutely sure there were no tear trails left on his cheeks. "Maybe I paid the price and they don't mind now. Maybe they figure I can't do any harm. I wasn't trying to find it. What are you doing here? Looking for Moll?"

"Yup."

"Can I help?"

Since he was already at the Green Hill, what could it hurt? She nodded and parted the brambles.

Finn hung back. "I don't have to if you don't want me to," he said, so sourly Meg forgot her teeth and had to laugh. Seeing her berry stains, he laughed back.

"Have some berries and come on!" she said and slipped through.

Finn grabbed a fistful, and as soon as he tasted them, his sulks were dispelled. They tasted of summer, and holidays, and second helpings of dessert, and suddenly he wanted to play tag, which he hadn't done since he was five and romping with the maid's daughter Pancha. "You're it!" he cried, and tapping Meg on the shoulder and sprinting away. He flung his bag into the tall grass halfway up the hill. Meg, instantly caught in the unexpected jollity, chased after him.

The Green Hill has been host to gruesome battles and stately parades, to revelries the likes of which mere mortals cannot imagine in all their short lives . . . but never had the Green Hill seen sport to rival this. When Meg had first seen the hill, it was neat as a new-mowed lawn, with tender grass, thick and fresh and green. Now it was wild and overgrown with summer flowers, the grass as high as her waist, sprouting seed clusters. Daisies turned their bright eyes to the sun, and saucer-shaped clusters of tiny white flowers were apparently the height of floral fashion that year, since yarrow, Queen Anne's lace, wild carrots, hogweed, elder, and hemlock were all bedecked in them. Grasshoppers in brown and green frockcoats whirred and zipped away in annoyance as Meg and Finn chased each other over the Green Hill until at last they collapsed near the summit, panting, sweaty, neither knowing nor caring who won.

"I didn't know you were so much fun, Meg," Finn said after a while.

Meg didn't know she was either.

"We should look for Moll," she said about an hour later. She'd spent some of the time dozing, some watching clouds, and some trying to watch Finn peripherally without moving her head.

"Mmm-hmm," Finn said drowsily.

Very rarely, a cloud drifted by, and they talked about what they saw in it. Meg, whose imagination was usually so good, always envisioned sheep. Words grew fewer and farther between, and she said, "I'm only going to close my eyes for a minute." Not because she was going to sleep, she assured herself, just because the sky was so brilliant.

"Just for a minute," Finn echoed sleepily, as the wayward sheep clouds without their shepherds roamed free, and the benevolent sun, taking pity on them, sank lower and lower, grew dimmer and cooler, until when at last they opened their eyes again, he was gone entirely.

Meg sat up abruptly, confused. She saw Finn's dim form curled beside her and kicked him gently until he woke up. He rubbed a face that had been rubbed so many times with grubby hands it had turned a muddy brown, and sat up beside her.

"If we were home, we'd get in trouble for staying out after dark. Do you think we will here?"

"How late do you think it is?" she asked. Unlike the ancients, she didn't spend enough time in wild places at night to have any feel for reading time by the moon or the stars. It didn't feel too late . . . that was the best she could do. "We won't get in trouble, but they'll be awfully worried. Come on, we have to go. I never did look for Moll— Oh! What was that?"

It started as a moan so low it seemed more seismic than sound, like the calls of elephants or whales rumbling through the ground and up through their legs. Then it rose to an almost-human wail before climbing higher, and higher still, to a catamount scream, then an operatic soprano, and finally a keen so high it was sensible only as pain. Meg felt like she had outside Moll's house, swept away by someone else's grief, weak with pity and terror.

"It's Moll!" she said, thoughtlessly grabbing Finn's hand. "She's close. Come on, it sounds like she's right here."

They barreled down the hill and crashed painfully through the blackberries, tripping and stumbling in the darkness.

"This way!" Meg said, pulling him toward the sound.

"No, this way!" Finn said, pulling her away from it.

The keen rose again, and though it was undoubtedly close, it seemed to come from all directions at once. Still clutching hands, they pulled each other this way and that. Meg wasn't at all sure she wanted to find whoever was making that sound, but it seemed the surest way of making it stop. In the calm between cries, the rest of the forest was silent. No owl or frog dared compete with that outpouring of grief.

They came to a dark, trickling stream, a small spring that flowed through the wood until it met the river Gladys.

"Meg, look," Finn said, jerking her to an abrupt stop and nearly wrenching her shoulder out of joint. She followed his finger and saw a green-cloaked figure kneeling at the water's edge, leaning out across the flow. Her face was hidden by a deep hood, but long, wild strands of red hair fell forward into the moonlight. It might be Moll. It must be Moll. Who else could it be?

The woman didn't appear to see them, though they stood to her side and slightly behind her only a few yards away. She had something clutched in her hands. She thrust her arms into the stream and churned them among the rocks. She was washing something as she wailed, something white and red. Meg took a tentative step closer. Something about the red was awfully familiar ... red by moonlight, thick and dark with a quicksilver sheen and a taste of copper in the air. Blood! She was washing a blood-soaked shirt.

Meg squeezed Finn's hand almost hard enough to pay him back for the wrenched shoulder. She knew that shirt. The fine linen, the silver threads, splashes of other colors that were not bloodred. . . . It was the shirt Phyllida had given her to paint in. The shirt she had given to Rowan that very afternoon.

"Moll," Meg began, taking a small step forward.

The washerwoman raised her head with infinite slowness until the hood fell back just far enough to reveal eyes as bright as blood, eyes red from weeping, and redder. There were no other features, no mouth, no nose. . . . Surely they were just hidden by the hood? But the woman who stared at them, seeing and not seeing, was all eyes. What else did she require when all her life was about weeping?

Meg, wanting desperately to run, took another step toward her, but then she wasn't there.

"Was that her?" Finn asked breathlessly.

"It couldn't be."

"Then what ... who?"

Meg wished she knew more about the fairies. That poor woman must be one—how else could she vanish?—though what her unhappy purpose was Meg couldn't guess.

"Come on, we should go home," Meg said. "Phyllida will be so worried, and we have to tell her about this. She'll know what it was."

"I left something at the Green Hill," Finn said. "We have to go back."

Meg looked indecisive. This was Finn after all, and for all their sudden burst of camaraderie, she couldn't forget his fundamental nature. To meet him at the Green Hill was one thing, to lead him there quite another.

"It's important. I'll tell you about it on the way back. It's something from the fairies."

She led him through the darkness back to the hill. It seemed steeper to their tired legs, and they trudged to the summit, grunting and panting like it was any ordinary hill. Finn fumbled through the tall, coarse grasses, on the edge of panic until he found the bag, exactly where he had left it. Meg resisted the urge to ask what was inside and started back down the hill to hurry him along. Then the ground heaved under her, and as she slid to her rump, she had the impression not of an earthquake (which is rare in those parts) but of sitting atop a giant tortoise that had suddenly decided to take a stroll (which is even rarer). Finn staggered on deeply bent sailor legs to collapse beside her as the ground stopped shifting.

"What on earth?" Finn began, but Meg clapped a hand over his mouth and pointed down the hill, even as she pulled him lower behind the veil of Queen Anne's lace.

"What? I don't see anything," he said indistinctly from behind her fingers, and was piggy-pinched for his troubles.

"Be quiet!" Meg hissed fiercely. "Don't you see them?"

There was a rustle of leaves, a tinkling of silver bells, and the brambles fell aside reverently for a fine dapple-gray horse, which bore the most lovely woman in the world. When Meg had first seen her, she wore a green and silver gown speckled with jewels, but today the Seelie queen had set aside her royal raiments for hunting garb. She wore trousers and a trim green jerkin that might have been leather or might have been leathery leaves. Her hair, that ambiguously pale, shining color that shifted from platinum to gold, hung loose to her waist. A hooded hawk perched on her hand. The bells Meg heard were tied to his jesses.

Even though she knew it was only a glamour—that the Seelie queen could just as easily appear a wizened hag, or a great tusked sow, or a winged fish—Meg was so awed by her beauty that it was a full minute before she even noticed the queen's retinue. There was the prince, her friend of sorts, Gul Ghillie, in his grown-up guise, wearing a green and red doublet and puffed bombasted hose over parti-colored tights, looking rather like a jester or a slim Henry VIII. Behind him rode serried ranks of Seelie nobles, arrayed in fantastic variations of hunting garb through the ages, from foxhunting pinks to leopard pelts, and behind them capered creatures of all shapes, some dressed, some furred, some feathered, some wearing nothing but their own skins. One slate-gray sprite with stubby leathery wings played on a multiple pipe and somehow had breath enough to dance to his own lively tune. A creature that looked like a hedgehog without the spines rolled to and fro beneath prancing feet and stamping hooves. Will-o'-the-wisps hovered at the periphery, assisting the moon to light the panoply.

"What's there? What do you see?" Finn asked as low as he could.

"The court, the queen . . . Gul Ghillie . . . all of them. Hush!"

Finn clenched his jaw, mortified, angry at Meg, though it was no fault of hers. Denied again! The fairy court, the queen, within his sight, if only he could see!

They laughed and chatted and sang merry tunes as they rode directly into the hill and disappeared from sight, their voices echoing for a moment before they were absorbed into the ground. The train became intermittent after the great lords and ladies entered, as the lesser fairies, some slowed by their odd forms, followed at their own pace. They were almost gone, all but a small green piglet in a stocking cap and a manikin on a horse. It looked like Little Lord Fauntleroy, dressed beyond its years (though who knew how old a fairy might be) in midnight velvet and masses of ruffles at its wrists and throat. Its golden curls glinted in the glow of the last will-o'-the-wisp, and its face was pale as moonlight.

Why, Meg wondered, did some of the fairies choose to look like men, some like beasts, and some like nothing on this earth? Did they have their favorite forms, like the stubborn Rookery brownie, or did some change all day long? Did they reflect some aspect of their personalities? She would have to ask Phyllida when she began her formal education. That last fairy man, for example, looked remarkably like—

He turned his round little face to the sky, and Meg froze. It couldn't be.

"Oh! Do you see?"

But Finn could see nothing except the dark forest.

Her hand tightened on his again. "Finn, is it . . . is it?"

The fairy boy on the pony looked exactly like her own brother James.

He rode into the arch of the Green Hill, and the earth trembled, settled, and was still. The Green Hill had closed its earthen gates upon its treasures.

As Meg had learned once before, no amount of ranting and raving and pounding on the grass can induce the Green Hill to open against its will. The last retreat of the fairies hunkered and held its peace against Meg's commands and Finn's few baffled kicks against the turf. When Meg had expended enough of her energy to be rational again, Finn asked her what she had seen.

"James. Or . . . I thought it was James. It *looked* like James." She used to live in a world where, if something looked like a thing, it *was* that thing. Not so anymore.

"Tell me exactly what you saw," Finn said, and she did, even concealing her annoyance when he made her linger over her description of the queen, down to the moment she saw James's dear little face.

"But you can't know if it was him, can you? I don't know much about fairies"—though after weeks of quizzing Dickie on his research, Finn knew more than he thought—"but it might just be a fairy pretending to be James, right? I mean, if they knew you were watching, they might take his form just to mess with you, make you think they had stolen him. Isn't that something they'd do?"

She had to admit it was.

"That's it! I've had enough!" she yelled, not at Finn but at the Green Hill. "I won't do it! You all are crazy—you fairies, and

Phyllida, and Bran, and everyone in this village. You are horrible, mean, cruel. . . . Why doesn't everyone move away from here and fence it off with barbwire and post guards?" She collapsed into tears. "You made me kill Bran. You took James, or even if you didn't, it's just as bad to make me think so. I won't be Guardian! I won't! Phyllida can find someone else . . . or no one else! I don't care. I'm writing home tomorrow. I want to go home! I want to see my mom and dad! I hate this place!" And to Finn's dismay, she fell on his shoulder, heaving and sobbing in a wet, sticky mess.

"Uh, there, there?" *There, there?* He cursed himself. What on earth did "there, there" mean? Where, where? What good was that supposed to do Meg?

"Come on, let's go home. Phyllida can sort this out." He pushed her gently away, and as soon as the warmth of her cheek was off his shoulder, he almost wished it were back. As repulsive and confusing as it was in one way, it was also kind of nice. It made him feel important, older, different from how he usually was.

Who knows what Phyllida thought when they appeared at the door, so long after dark, coming from the woods, Meg distraught and tear-stained, Finn with obvious signs of having been struck about the head.

"Where's James?" Meg demanded before Phyllida could put any of her hypotheses into words.

"Upstairs in bed, I imagine. Meg, where were you? We were so worried."

Phyllida found herself talking to Meg's rapidly retreating back as the girl dashed up the stairs. Meg scoured the bedrooms and found no sign of James.

"Where is he?" she asked, almost hysterical.

"I don't know, dear. Tell me, one of you, what this is all about? What has James to do with it?"

Finn had to be spokesman. "We were at the Green Hill," he began.

"Meg took you to the Green Hill?" Lysander asked.

"No, I found it. We were looking for Moll." He almost told them about the weeping woman, but first things first. "Then we went back to the hill, and Meg saw the fairies, and she said she saw James with them. He went under the Green Hill, and we couldn't get in."

"Is this true?" Phyllida asked Meg as she ran by.

"Yes, yes, yes!" she said exasperatedly, making dashing forays into rooms in search of James and then coming back to the group.

Rowan, Silly, and Dickie were drifting downstairs, rubbing the sleep out of their eyes, asking what all the hubbub was about.

"James is missing," Meg said. "Have you seen him? Who saw him last?"

"Oh, don't worry, he's in the kitchen," Silly said. "I heard him go down about an hour ago, and I went down too for another piece of apple tart. You missed a good dinner, Meg. Where were you?" But Meg was already sprinting to the kitchen, with Phyllida, Lysander, and Finn following close behind her, the others coming up behind on sleep-heavy legs.

Meg peeked into the garden kitchen. There at the table was James, with a huge loaf of oat bread clutched in both his hands. His face was all but buried in one end, and he made grunting snorts like a ravenous badger as he ripped and chewed great chunks. For all that he shoveled food down his maw at an amazing rate, he looked positively gaunt. Cheeks that had been full and peachy were now sunken, and his arms looked like sticks. He got the whole loaf of bread into his gullet faster than a starving dog and turned to the remains of the apple tart, grabbing fistfuls. Between bites (or wolfings), he swigged what looked suspiciously like hard cider from a stone bottle.

Phyllida laid a hand on Meg's shoulder and drew her gently back. They gathered in the parlor.

"That's him, isn't it? He's okay? It was just a trick when I saw him go under the Green Hill, right?" Meg hoped against hope Phyllida would give her the answer she longed for.

Phyllida sighed. "It was right before my eyes, and I didn't see it."

"No . . . no!"

"He grows skinny and cold. He eats like a glutton. Has he been rude, improper?"

"Yes," Meg admitted. "He . . . yes, very rude. Not himself. I thought it was just a phase."

"I think . . . I cannot be sure until we perform the test . . . but I think that is not our James in the kitchen. That is a changeling, and you saw the real James on the hill tonight."

"We have to get him back! What do we do, Phyllida?"

"Lysander," she said, "get the eggshells from the compost pail."

"What are you going to do? You're not going to hurt him, are you?"

"You can't hurt a fairy," she said as she sorted through the eggshells, picking out the most intact ones and brushing off bits of coffee grounds and carrot peel. "But no, the test won't hurt him a bit, whether it's James or a changeling. Come, follow me into the kitchen and just watch, don't speak. Whatever happens, don't ask questions or look surprised at what I'm doing. As far as anyone is concerned, we just got out of bed for a midnight snack."

The whole group filed into the kitchen and took places around the table, trying awkwardly and unsuccessfully to look normal. Fortunately James had found a smoked ham hanging on a hook near the hearth, and he was tearing into it with teeth that looked a little sharper than usual. He made a grunting sound to acknowledge their presence, and said, "Hullo, fatty," to Dickie, who sat next to him. This wasn't exactly fair. Dickie had certainly been plump on his arrival, but since his asthma and allergies didn't seem particularly susceptible to English pollen, he'd managed to be a lot more active and had firmed up considerably. Still, both fairies and children will seize on your most sensitive point to mock, and that was always Dickie's.

As they all watched and pretended not to watch, Phyllida took another stone flagon of cider from the icebox and a pair of tongs from the drawer, then turned up the gas on the stove. Whistling a little tune as she worked, she took the largest of the eggshells gingerly in the pincers, poured in a measure of cider, and held it over the flames.

"Ginger or cinnamon?" she asked casually.

"Oh, both, if you please," Lysander answered, just as casually, as he prodded the low hearthfire into more robust flames.

She sprinkled the spices into the mulling brew and swirled the concoction around until it started to steam. James looked up from his ham haunch and stared, gobbets of meat falling from his mouth, as Phyllida handed the eggshell cup to Lysander and placidly started on another.

James slammed down his mangled hambone and sprang up onto the chair, where he craned his neck and bobbed up and down, trying to see Phyllida's handiwork from all conceivable angles. "Damme!" he said, in a grainy growl completely unlike James's dear little voice, and continued,

> Here I stand, all in a fog,
> Like a pollywog, agog!
> Flummoxed, fuddled, and hornswoggled
> Like a lummox, all boondoggled!
> I have seen the first chick pip,
> I have squeezed the first rose hip,
> But ne'er in all my unborn days
> Has cider been brewed thisaways.

"Eggshells?" James who was not James said. "Bosh!"

The adults sprang into action—Lysander tossing back his egg of cider like a shot, Phyllida dropping her second brew onto the burner, where it filled the room with burnt sugar fumes. They grabbed little James roughly by the arms and flung him headfirst, shrieking, into the flaming fireplace.

"No!" Meg screamed.

But she heard a high-pitched laugh and saw a dim shape rise up through the chimney, and when she'd shoved and elbowed her way to the hearth, there was nothing there but a charred lump of wood.

"James?" she breathed.

"The changeling has gone back to where he came from," said Phyllida, panting.

"What was all that business with the eggshells?" Rowan asked.

"To expose a changeling, you must do something so unusual it makes him forget his disguise as a human baby and speak as his true self. Brewing in eggshells is a time-honored method, though come to think of it, I'm not sure why all the fairies don't know about it by now."

"Probably too embarrassed," Finn said. "It's pretty silly if you ask me."

"No one did," Rowan said, and there might have been a fight if Meg hadn't reminded them about the more important issue.

"But where is James?"

"That," Phyllida said, "is the problem."

She explained to them that getting rid of the changeling is the easy part. After that, who knew? "Sometimes the real child appears at the doorstep as soon as the changeling disappears. Sometimes he returns to wherever he was taken from. Sometimes, though, they don't return him at all."

"What do we do then?" Meg asked.

"We'll cross that bridge when we come to it," Lysander said decisively. "Now, all of you take torches and look around the house and grounds."

Meg ran to the front door. Before she could open it she heard the *thud-thud-thump!* of something on its last legs collapsing against the door. She pulled it open, and in fell a dark, shaggy form.

"Bran! Oh, Bran, what's wrong? What are you doing up?" Though of course by now he wasn't up. She placed a hand to his chest and felt something warm and wet. She didn't need to shine her flashlight on her fingers to know they were darkened with blood. Oh, blood and more blood! I want to go home, she whimpered to herself, but with heroic effort, she cut her self-pity short and dragged Bran into the house. (Which, should you ever encounter a fellow with a barely healed arrow wound to the chest, is not the best thing to do to him, though it seemed like a good idea to Meg at the time.)

"There ye are, ye baggage," Bran said weakly. He tried to sit, coughed, and much to his frustration, sank helplessly into Meg's lap. "Where were ye, gallivanting about in the dark? Thought ye fell in th' abandoned well."

(So there *is* an abandoned well, Meg thought.)

"You went out searching for me? How could you? You're in no shape to be on your feet, certainly not to hike around looking for me. You could have killed yourself. After all the trouble I've gone to, too." She'd already killed him once. She didn't want to be responsible for his second death.

"Yer precious," he said, and coughed painfully again. "Nothing can happen to you."

"What do you mean?"

"The Green Hill . . . Lady . . . Guardian . . . without you . . ." He curled into another painful paroxysm of hacking, and Meg called, "Help!" down the hallway. Wooster came running in a stiff and dignified way.

"Call for the doctor," Meg ordered. Wooster glanced to Bran

for confirmation of his instructions, but Bran had his eyes shut tightly, keeping a firm hold on his agony. "Go! Do it!" She might have been a child, but her voice already had the Guardian's authority, and Wooster couldn't deny it. He scurried to the stables and sent a lad.

"Bran, be still," Meg told him when he tried again to rise. "You shouldn't have risked your life to look for me. I can take care of myself, and anyway, forget about that Guardian business. I've thought about it, and I won't do it. As soon as we find James, I'm going home. All of us are going home."

"Find James?"

"Stop trying to talk. Yes, find James. He was replaced by a changeling. Phyllida got the changeling to leave—now we have to get James back. Then I'm through with this place. Now, don't get upset again," she added as he struggled against her gentle but firm hands. "It's not your fault, and I love you very much, all of you, but I can't bear this anymore. First you, now James, in only a few weeks—who knows what would happen if I decided to stay? I don't know how Phyllida does it. But she chose to do it. I don't. I won't be the next Guardian. It's too much for me."

He gripped her weakly. "Then forget the doctor. You might as well have left me dead on the hill, or under it, or outside on the doorstep till dawn. If you will leave us, all is lost!" He clenched his teeth against the pain and was unconscious by the time Phyllida and the others found them. When Dr. Homunculus pulled up in his little red sports car, Meg slipped away to be alone.

She considered going to her retreat on the Rookery roof, but the thought of her small self against that vastness of stars overwhelmed her. Again, it was the kitchen, that place for schemes and comfort, that called her.

In all her years on this earth, Meg had never been so confused. She wanted to stay, and she wanted to flee. She wanted to learn, and (like the Wyrm) she wanted to forget what she had learned. She felt some mysterious pull—whether it was her blood or her curiosity or her budding sense of adventure, she could not say—telling her to stay in England forever and be a part of this strange life with the fairies. And she felt a push nearly as strong sending her toward safety and predictability and, if she was completely honest with herself, dullness.

And now Bran, she thought miserably. Just when he seemed on the verge of recovery, both physical and psychological, he sounded hopeless again, and it was all her fault. He'd pushed himself to the brink of death once again to search for her while she heedlessly stayed out late. And because she might not (might?) want to become Guardian, he seemed on the verge of despair. Couldn't she do anything right? She could, maybe, if she knew what right was.

She looked around for something to eat, but most eatables had been laid waste by the changeling. She tidied up a bit, helpfully putting things where they did not go, so that for weeks to come, Phyllida would search in vain for spatulas and whisks. Meg desperately wanted to do something useful. She could not help Bran; that was the duty of Dr. Homunculus. She could not search for James, for she did not know how. She spied the butter churn in the corner. She shook it and heard a liquid slosh. Someone, Phyllida or a maid, had started churning and had probably been interrupted. She grasped the well-worn dasher handle pressed with indentations from several generations of women's hands. Hers were a little small, but they found a comfortable place, and she set about churning.

It was harder than it looked. She had to use not just her arms but her whole upper body. After a few minutes she ached, and the cream was no thicker.

"I can't do anything right," she said in disgust, and thrust the plunger hard into the churn.

"Twist as ye churn," came a voice, mournful and low.

Twist she did as she whirled around and found the Rookery brownie regarding her glumly. And no wonder. She was about to ruin his batch of butter.

Leathery, callused hands wrapped around her own and guided her in the right kind of agitation to make the better congeal. It was with some alarm she realized she was actually being touched by a fairy. He felt decidedly unhuman, his skin the texture of a bat's wing, and cold, like James had been, now that she thought of it. He turned her hands around on the plunger as together they raised it up and forced it down until, only a moment later, it began to thicken. And she had been about to give up.

"There," the brownie said. "Keep at it, and you'll have butter ere long." He settled himself on a bench and lit a cheroot.

Meg churned away, and as the brownie puffed, she told him some of her troubles. He offered no advice about recovering James, and she turned to Phyllida's desire to train her as her successor.

"Why can't Bran take over for Phyllida?" she asked at length.

"He's young, and he knows all there is to know about fairies. He'd do it, and happily, I'd think. Or Rowan. He'd be just as good as me. Hasn't there ever been a male Guardian?"

She hadn't thought the brownie would answer. Taciturn and stubborn, he rarely spoke except about matters that concerned him directly (like his precious butter). So she paid particular attention when he said, "Aye, once. Fer a time."

"Then why can't it happen again? I don't think I want to be the Guardian."

"He were Guardian for ten minutes, no more, and he were druv out o' the county with a price on his head. No, there canna be a male Guardian. It's agin' the laws of nature." He blew a smoke circle, then a smoke square.

"But why? That makes no sense."

"The blood mun stay wi' the land. A woman knows if a child is her own, a man, never. The blood mun stay." He snuffed his cheroot and moved her aside to scoop the clotted butter and press out the buttermilk. She pestered him with questions as he kneaded the butter, rolled it in cold water, and salted it, but he was intent on his work and ignored her. She thought she understood what he meant, but wasn't quite sure.

"But what am I supposed to do?" she asked, at her wit's end, as he spread the butter into molds.

When he finished, and not before, he cocked his head at her, looking more friendly, more human, than she had ever seen him, despite his rags and square feet. He smiled and took her hand, pressing it against his cold, barrel-shaped chest.

"What d'ye feel?"

"I . . . you? Your skin?" She didn't know what he was getting at. He put her hand on her own chest.

"What d'ye feel?"

"I feel . . . my heart beating."

"How can I tell ye what to do? Ye have what I don't. That will tell ye."

"You mean my heart? Follow my heart?"

The brownie harrumphed. "Hogswallow! Heart . . . humph! That's blood in there, girl child. Ye mun follow your blood. Ye can do no other." He dropped her hand and vanished, and she was left with six neat slabs of butter and her own heart in her hands.

The Burden Is Hers, All Hers

MEG TRIED WITH ALL HER MIGHT to stay home with Phyllida and Lysander as they worked on a way to get James back, but her might was not equal to the task, and she found herself trundled off to the mowing festival along with everyone else.

"But I have to be here to help you! You need me!"

"We need no such thing, child. Among Lysander and Bran and me, we've got almost three hundred years' experience with the fairies. You never knew fairies outside of bedtime stories until a few weeks ago."

"Even if I can't really help, how do you expect me to have fun when all the while James is a prisoner?"

"I don't expect you to have fun," Phyllida said. "I expect you to be out of my hair so I can work free from pestering. I expect you to be so surrounded by diversion that you might forget your troubles for just the barest instant, smile at a jester, no more. Better that than sulking and moping in your room. And pacing.

Yes, I heard you all morning, since four o'clock, stamping with those big feet of yours. Oh, touch a nerve? See how you can forget for just an instant? Well, they are not big feet, but they certainly sound big stomping right above my head when I'm trying to get my beauty sleep." Actually, Phyllida had been up until nearly three, and the beauty sleep was only a desperate hour or two snatched so she wouldn't go absolutely insane with sleep deprivation.

"I won't forget James," Meg swore, "not for a single second!"

Phyllida took Meg's cool cheeks in her hands. "You will drive yourself mad if you stay here, helpless." And the rest of us too, she did not add. "You will be weak and fretful and headachy and no use to us at all when we really do need you."

"Need me? You'll need me?"

"Aye, we may well. Who knows what it will take to free your brother? If I can make use of you, then I surely will, and you must be in a fit state for it. Which you will not be if you mope in your room all day. Now, for the last time, for your brother's sake, get out of this house!"

Meg couldn't fight anymore. Finn could have, and if he really wanted to get his way, he would never stop arguing, would lie and sneak to achieve his ends and, truth be told, was not above a bawling, screaming, fist-pounding tantrum. But Meg wasn't like that, and what's more, she still believed that grown-ups were usually right, or in any case, couldn't be fought.

So Silly and Dickie (with the invisible Wyrm around his shoulder) and Finn (complaining of the heat and sun and dust all the while) and a very reluctant Meg set out on foot for the hay-fields on the outskirts of Gladysmere. Rowan stayed behind for his art lesson and said he would join them afterward. Apparently Phyllida didn't see any danger of Rowan getting in her way.

Meg went, but she went defiantly, first speed-walking in a huff, then dragging her feet so much that, if she was careful, she might never get there at all. Look at them, she thought as she watched Silly skipping ahead of her, stirring up dust on the roadway. She doesn't care, not one bit. Nothing really bothers her. She doesn't think what poor James might be going through, how scared he must be in that dark place without us. She thinks that everything will be all right, always. It's no different from a book for her—the world might be dull in the beginning, full of adventure in the middle, but the ending will always be happy for the main characters, and in her mind she and our family are undoubtedly the main characters. Silly might actually be worried if Dickie were in trouble, but James, to her, must be immune. That's what Meg thought about her sister, anyway.

Meg read her sister correctly in one respect—Silly never doubted for a minute that James would be recovered unharmed. What Meg didn't realize was that Silly was scheming to get him back herself.

"Dickie," she said, skipping in place so he had a chance to catch up, "I need your help."

"Sure, what's up?"

"I'm going to get James back."

"You are?"

"Yup. Wanna help?"

"Sure. Let me get Meg, and we can—"

"No! I don't want her to know."

"How come?" He didn't like keeping secrets from Meg and was pretty sure Meg wouldn't like it either.

"Well . . . I don't know if it will work, for one, and I don't want her to get all upset. And then . . ."

Dickie waited.

"Oh, don't look at me like that!" Silly said, though Dickie didn't know he had been looking any particular way. It only goes to show what a guilty conscience will make a person see. "The thing I'm planning to do, I don't think she'll think it's *nice*." She pronounced *nice* with sneering disgust, as you might say *mice* if you found them using your pantry for an outhouse.

"Then maybe we shouldn't do it."

"What are you, a goody-goody?" He was, and he knew it. "Don't you want to get James back? Well, then, I have a perfectly good idea, and it will work, and just because it's not nice doesn't mean I'm going to let James stay with the fairies. He's probably having a blast, and I wish I was there, but that's not the point. It's the principle of the thing."

"So? What are you going to do?"

"We," she said with emphasis, for if she went down, he was going with her, "are going to kidnap a fairy."

"Hisss-sss-sss," a sibilant voice said, and the Wyrm dimly materialized.

"Oh, that thing always gives me the heebie-jeebies," Silly said. "No offense, but you do tend to *appear*. Wait, were you laughing at me?" She stopped squarely in the road with her fists on her hips, ready for battle. No one better laugh at Silly unless she told a joke, and then they better laugh but good.

"Kidnap a fairy?" the Wyrm said. "How, pray, do you propose to do that?"

"I don't know!" Silly said defiantly. She'd had visions of simply grabbing one of the smaller ones around the throat, stuffing it in a backpack, and arranging an exchange. Now that the Wyrm mentioned it, though, it might be just a little bit harder than that.

"That's why I have you," she said to Dickie. "You know all there is to know about fairies."

"I wouldn't say that," he said.

"Nor would I," the Wyrm added loftily.

"But you know a lot. You're always reading about them in the Rookery library. You were able to help Meg when she had to get to the Midsummer War. You must know some way of capturing a fairy."

"Well . . ."

"And your Wyrm can help us."

"I beg your pardon!" the Wyrm hissed, furiously flapping the stubby wings behind his neck. "I am no one's Wyrm but my own, and how dare you imply . . ."

Silly, accustomed to offending people and not at all ashamed, said an automatic and insincere "sorry" and went on. "Between the three of us, we should be able to catch one, right?"

The Wyrm said, "I'm afraid—"

"Ohhh," Silly said in apparent sympathy. "If you're afraid, that's another story. I thought you just weren't as smart as you always say you are." She averted her eyes and waited for this two-fanged attack to strike home. You'd think a Wyrm so old he had learned everything there is to know and started to forget it again would be immune to such facile tricks of psychology. But perhaps among his forgotten lore were the special tactics of determined nine-year-old girls. Good thing he fell for it, or Silly would have had to whip out her heavy artillery, the dare and the double dare.

The Wyrm's shining scales stood on end, and he spat in rapid-fire patter, "Ground ivy, milkweed fluff, daisy chains, pig's bladder! So there!"

Dickie and Silly looked at him in confused amazement. The Wyrm, having proved himself, settled back down around Dickie's neck and preened his scales with his nose.

"Um, what was all that?" Dickie asked.

The Wyrm blinked (for unlike snakes, he had eyelids), sighed, and said, "I was under the impression you wanted to know how to capture a fairy. You can tie him up in ground ivy or a daisy chain, you can blow a cloud of milkweed seeds at him to immobilize him, or you can stuff him in a pig's bladder, and he can't escape. Why I have to prove my vast knowledge to a couple of chits like you is beyond me, but you weary me to no end, and I am going to sleep." With that he closed his eyes and fell into a deep and utterly fictitious slumber.

"Well," said Silly, looking sidelong at Dickie and just managing to suppress her giggles, "that certainly helps. So, Dickie, are you in?"

"I'll do my best," he said.

To keep up appearances, they opened their easels on the croquet lawn, but not a smear of charcoal nor a daub of paint violated the pristine whiteness of the paper.

"Where is she?" Gwidion whispered. "You have to bring me to her, without her knowing."

"I can't find her," Rowan said. "You're going to get it for me, aren't you? All for me? You're going to help me?" He rubbed his hands together like a fly.

"If you help me. That was the bargain. Help me complete my portrait of Phyllida Ash, and she will leave everything she possesses to whomever I say."

"I looked all over, and I can't find her. The fairies took my little brother, you know."

"That is none of my concern, nor should it be any of yours. When the Green Hill has a new master, you can order the fairies to return your brother."

"I don't think it works like that."

"Just find her," Gwidion said, clenching his teeth in exasperation. Children were easy to manipulate, but they were so dense at times it was hardly worth it.

Rowan went back into the Rookery and began a systematic search. It wasn't nearly as fun as hide-and-seek, and after poking his head into the first few dozen rooms he began to feel lonely. The house was so huge it was daunting. Who would want to live in a mansion? But to *own* a mansion! That was another thing entirely. His true nature warred with the acquisitiveness laid on him by Gwidion's spell. Every silver wall sconce with stalactites of old wax-drippings, every suit of armor dented from a bout that happened centuries ago, every peeling bit of wallpaper in forgotten guest rooms called out to him like a siren, *I am yours, take me!* Even as he got sick to death of the endless rooms, he wanted to own them all.

How lucky that Gwidion had happened to knock at their door. Otherwise he never would have known his true ambition.

He was lingering in a sort of study, looking lovingly at a vase covered in improbable dragons and ghastly peonies, a vase he would never in a million years choose or suffer to stay unbroken in any home of his but which now, for some reason, joined the ranks of things that he must own, when he heard voices from the next room. He put an ear to the wall. The voices were still too muffled to tell what they were saying, though he was pretty sure he heard Phyllida. The sound seemed to be coming from around his feet, and after a little searching, he found a mousehole in the baseboards, the same mousehole, in fact, that had once held his life-egg. It communicated directly with the adjoining room. He lay down on his belly, and sure enough, the voices came through clearly. It was Phyllida and Lysander.

"I feel so helpless," Phyllida said.

"No, you know the way of it. It happened to you, it happened to your mother, and to her mother before her. Every Guardian heir loses someone she loves to the fairies. There is always a hostage, since Angharad first stood on the Green Hill and declared herself defender of the fairies and of the people."

"But it's not right. He's so young . . . and so is she. What if she can't get him back? It took me all my life to rescue my own father. What if she spends a lifetime searching for James? Do you know the heartache of losing someone precious to you? Of knowing that they are ever near you, just through the woods, but as good as lost to you forever? Oh, Meg! I don't want her to suffer as I have suffered."

Rowan laid his cheek on the floor and found that if he held his head sideways just so, he could see into the room. It was a small, square library—at least, it must be a library because it was full of books, but also full of rolls of paper and even tablets of stone inscribed with what looked like Roman characters. Phyllida was sitting in a leather armchair cradling a vellum volume bound in kidskin.

"This is my mother's book. Her test, her hostage . . . it was not Bran, did you know? He was mine, my sorrow. My mother lost her own brother Llewellwn."

"The one who was banished?"

"Aye. He was under the Green Hill for a time. I sometimes think that's what set him off. No one is ever quite the same, you know, after they have been under the Green Hill. Maybe it's best to leave people there, once they are stolen. Like Bran. They never seem to quite fit in the world again."

"That's no excuse for what Llewellwn did," Lysander said harshly. "Bran was gone below for years, and he would never be a kin-slayer." He gulped, remembering that once they thought he *would* be. "Why was Llewellwn just banished? If the decision had been mine, I'd have cut his throat."

Which is perhaps why women are always Guardians.

"I was not born then, so I don't know all of it, and my mother did not like to speak of it, as you can imagine. She lost a brother and a mother all in one day, and became Guardian herself in pain, not rejoicing. From what I understand, Llewellwn did not kill my grandmother directly, or my mother would have ended his life with her own hand. But she died because of him, there is no doubt of that, and he was sent from this place forever."

"It is not an easy life for you, is it?" Lysander said, and the *you* stretched back hundreds of years.

"But it must be done. There must always be a Guardian. And now . . . I don't know if Meg's heart is in it. It is a broken heart now, that's for certain, until she saves James. If only I could tell her. She thinks we are trying to get him back, but the burden is hers, all hers! I am not allowed to help her—it is forbidden. The ancient law says it must be her test alone. How she would hate me if I told her. Oh, Lysander, what would I do without you?" She leaned against him, and he supported her like an old oak, strong and steady.

She rested there, and Rowan, who thought things might get mushy, took advantage of the lull to go back downstairs. He did not hear their affectionate murmuring, did not hear when Lysander said, "I wish I could take more of the weight from your shoulders, beloved. If it were allowed, I would take your place, if only for a day, and chance the consequences, just so you could get a little rest."

She kissed him. "Ah, and I think I would let you, if only for a day. I grow so weary, Lysander. So old. You are my strength. Ha! Wouldn't that be something, if you ran the Green Hill and I could lie back and eat bonbons and read Angela Thirkell novels for the rest of my days? What luxury! But no, it cannot be. Llewellwn Thomas tried to take the Guardianship, and it was almost the rack and ruin of all. But thank you, dear. As long as you are at my side I will have strength enough for anything. I hope when Meg stands in my place she has a man half as good at her side. Leave me here for a while, though. I feel like being among memories for a time." She gestured to the books that surrounded her.

ꕉ III ꕉ

"But these aren't your memories," Lysander said.

"Mine or theirs, it is all my past, all my history, all my blood. Good-bye, my love."

Rowan found Gwidion Thomas pacing the croquet lawn, with Pazhan pacing a contrary course.

"Well?"

"I found a place where you can watch her, if she stays there. A room with a peephole."

"Take me at once!" he cried, grabbing up his art supplies.

"This?" he hissed in a whisper, getting down on his hands and long, bony shanks and peering at a very uncomfortable angle through the mousehole. "You expect me to paint my masterwork looking at her from this angle? What am I, a worm, a grub?"

"If you lie down like this and press your head flat, you can see most of the room. Lysander left, and it looks like she's going to be there for a while."

Gwidion made a growling noise.

"It's the best I can do," Rowan whined.

"Then perhaps you won't care for the best I can do for you, boy! It will have to suffice, for now. Go, and don't disturb me. There's work to be done."

When Rowan left, Gwidion locked the door and silently set up his easel. He spread his spidery limbs on the floor and peered through the hole at the woman he would control, manipulate, usurp, and if necessary destroy, to claim what his grandfather Llewellwn Thomas had tried and failed to get.

He's the Little Boy

Finn walked slowly at Meg's side, though it was almost impossible for someone not mortally depressed to walk as sluggishly as she did. She kicked stones morosely, sending them skittering down the lane, and when there were no stones, she kicked up clods of dirt.

"I have to do something," she said half to herself. "What can I do?"

"Phyllida will think of something. She got Bran back, didn't she?"

"But not till years and years later. She was a girl when he went with the fairies and an old woman when she got him back. What if James is gone for fifty years? What if he doesn't escape until I'm old, or dead, and he's still a little baby and all alone?" Her voice rose in panic, and Finn was sorely tempted to there-there her again, but controlled himself. Instead, cleverly, he changed the subject.

"What did Phyllida say about that woman we saw washing the bloody clothes?"

Meg stopped short. "I completely forgot to tell her. Come on, let's go back!" She had the perfect excuse for skipping the mowing festival and checking Phyllida's progress.

"We can't," Finn said. "She needs you to be away so she can work. You know how you'd be. She wouldn't be able to concentrate. Anyway, I don't think that woman we saw is important. Probably just another fairy doing some mysterious fairy business. You're sure it wasn't Moll, right? Then it can wait. Please?"

Finn carried his drawstring hemp bag and desperately wanted to show off the contents. He'd had sense enough to realize last night that a missing brother trumped any mysterious gift of ten-pound notes and skeleton hands, but today he wanted to get his fair share of attention and admiration, and Meg, probably the only one who wouldn't find some way to make fun of him, was a perfect audience. He never stopped to think exactly why Meg didn't make fun of him, and he never bothered to wonder why so many other people did. It certainly didn't occur to him that he was a completely different person around Meg.

"I want to tell you what happened to me last night, before I met you at the Green Hill." This almost set Meg off about James again, but he leaped into his tale with such gusto that she couldn't compete.

"And you say it was a little kid?" she asked when he was finished.

"That's what it sounded like. His toy said 'Fenoderee's Mowing and Carting,' so I figured that must be his dad. Then when I left, I found this bag." He held it up with some effort.

"What's in there, a bowling ball?"

"Here, open it and see," he said, handing it over proudly.

"Oh, it's not as heavy as it looks."

He watched her in amazement as she tossed the bag lightly from hand to hand. He checked her arms for bulging biceps, found none, and was forced to conclude that it didn't weigh so much when Meg was holding it.

"Go ahead, take a look."

She yanked the twisted cord open and pulled out the bill, holding it with apparent ease. "Oh, how nice! What are you going to buy? Wooster said there are some really good pastries, and there's a man who carves—what? Why are you looking at me like that?" She turned half away and tried to remember if she'd brushed the raspberry jam seeds from her teeth that morning.

"Doesn't that bill feel . . . funny . . . to you?"

"Funny? No."

"Heavy?"

"No. What are you talking about?"

Finn took the bill and immediately his hand dropped. If he'd been wearing a beret and stripes and whiteface, she might have thought he was miming carrying something fairly heavy. She picked it up from his palm with the tips of her thumb and forefinger, and the bill wafted in the breeze. She set it down in his hand, and though the tiny balls of muscle in his arm strained to keep his hand steady, it fell several inches.

"So it's only heavy when you carry it, but not for someone else? Well, that *is* funny, and inconvenient."

"Tell me about it. I'm going to spend it as soon as I can."

They heard a happy ruckus before them. Despite Meg's best efforts, they had reached Gladysmere. A festival market was set up along High Street, the main and, for practical navigation purposes, only street in Gladysmere. Delicious smells reached them of things roasting and stewing in spices and slick with honey. Folk from all over the county gathered for the harvest days, and the streets were teeming with far more than Gladysmere's few hundred residents. They exchanged gossip with people they hadn't seen since the planting festival, ate things their diets and doctors would firmly forbid, and drove hard bargains with canny merchants for things they didn't need.

"Here," said Finn, pulling Meg to a booth selling gingerbread pigs. "Let me buy you one of these."

Meg didn't know how to swoon on command, but the thought of Finn buying her a treat made her legs go watery for some reason she couldn't quite fathom, and her neck got red and her cheeks got hot, and if she'd lived a hundred and fifty years ago, someone would have had to fetch the smelling salts. He only wants to get rid of that heavy money, she told herself, which was in fact the truth, but some tiny little voice in the back of her mind said, *It's almost a date.* She told that voice to shut up.

Finn handed over the ten-pound note to the buxom old woman behind the stall. For the gingerbread seller, the bill was as light as any.

"Well, that's taken care of," Finn said with relief, fondling his shiny one- and two-pound coins, which fortunately didn't weigh one and two pounds. They leaned against a bookshop that bore the sign CLOSED FOR MOWING and ate their pigs. Meg ate hers as though it might have a personal preference about the order in which it was eaten, starting with the feet and leaving the head with its eloquent currant eyes for last. Finn gobbled up his pig's head, then choked before he could chew it.

"Meg, it's back!"

"What is?"

"The bill, the bill! My bag just got heavy again." He peeked in and closed it quickly. "It's there, like I never spent it."

"Is your change still there?"

He felt his pockets. "No, darn it."

"Well, that's a relief."

"Why? At least it would be worth carrying this dang thing around all the time if I could make a profit on it."

"But what about that poor woman? If you have your ten pounds back, she can't have it, and since she gave you change that means she'd be out almost twenty pounds. Or wait, just the change. My head is getting muddled." Math wasn't her strong suit, and she was working on only a few hours' sleep. "In any case, I know you got the gingerbread pigs for free, and they're very good, and thank you."

"Well," he conceded, "that's something. How can I get rid of it, do you think?"

"You could just throw it away, or give it to someone," Meg suggested.

"I can't throw so much money away! Are you crazy? What if I buy something that costs exactly ten pounds? Maybe it's because I didn't spend the whole thing."

Meg had no idea, but she accompanied him on his rounds of

the stalls. There wasn't a video game or designer shirt in sight, and Finn couldn't find anything he wanted to buy. Finally he spotted a stall selling knives. "Here, how about this?" It was a little folding pocketknife with a creamy, textured deerhorn handle. He haggled the merchant down from twelve to ten pounds even.

"Ha!" Finn said, strolling down High Street with his new pocketknife open, looking for something to carve or stab or cut. People gave him a wide berth in case he was a lunatic. "I did it! I got rid of that—oh, no!" He dropped the hemp bag, for it had suddenly gotten heavy. He looked inside and pulled out the bill. "Look!" It wasn't a ten-pound note—it was a twenty-pound note, doubly valuable, doubly heavy.

"Wow." He made a mental calculation of the value in dollars. "Come on!" he said, excited. "Let's shop!"

He no longer wanted to get rid of it. Awed by the idea of free and never-ending money, he visited every stall and bought almost indiscriminately. He soon had a felt hat with a feather, a belt with small, pinched faces twisted into the leather, and a clockwork cricket in a tiny cage. Each time his bill returned to him, and after the third time, it was a fifty-pound note.

"I can hardly pick it up," Finn said, stooping to hoist the little hemp bag. "Here, help me, and I'll buy you something." Meg tried to help, but it wasn't heavy to her, and her assistance didn't seem to lighten his load. "Ugh, I can't keep this up," Finn said, dropping the bag and panting. "Will you carry it?"

"Why don't we just leave it here?"

"No, I can't throw fifty pounds away. That's about a hundred dollars." He looked around. "Here's a dress shop. Pick out something inside, and I'll buy it for you."

"Really?"

"Sure. Then I promise I'll leave the money for some other poor sucker to find. If it goes to a hundred pounds, I won't even be able to get it out of the bag."

Finn waited outside while Meg went into the store. It was very small, and the dresses were handmade, but they all had lovely needlework. The shopgirl helped her find her size, and she chose a green and cream dress with drooping sweet peas embroidered around the waist and trailing down the hips. "Oh, how lovely!" the shopgirl said, clapping her hands. Meg looked in the mirror and saw another person. It was like seeing herself in Gwidion's portrait, only this was the real her. No, she thought, it can't be. Why, that girl is beautiful. No, it's just the dress. The dress is beautiful, and I happen to be in it.

Meg peeked outside and saw a man bearing down on Finn. It was the knife vendor.

"There ye are, ye sly pickpocket. Hand it over!"

Finn scuttled backward toward the shop, dragging his precious hemp bag. A small crowd was gathering, wondering if there was going to be a play or a fight. The merchant, pleased to have an audience, hammed it up a bit and pointed dramatically at Finn. " 'E stole my knife, one of the best on me table."

"No I didn't! I paid ye—er, you—for it."

"Ah, but then ye stole the money back, didn't ye, ye rascal ye? Soon as I turned my back, that ten pounds was gone. Hand it over or hand over the knife, ye young rapscallion." He advanced on Finn menacingly. The crowd grew more interested, and a delicate matron screamed, then looked embarrassed.

"Here, take it!" Finn said, and though he tried to fling the bill at the merchant, at fifty pounds it was more of a two-handed roll. Finn grabbed his bag and slipped inside the dress shop while the knife seller, a very portly man, adjusted his legs and then his pants until he was limber enough to bend over to retrieve his bill.

"Hey, this is too much!" he called into the shop, for he was fair. The man tried to open the door, but Finn had locked it.

"Let's go. We have to find some place to run to . . . while I can still run."

"But . . . I have to change!" Finn hadn't even glanced at her lovely new dress. No, it wasn't hers, because the knife man had the money, for a while anyway.

"Now! It will be back in my bag in a minute."

"So leave the bag."

"No! Come on, I'll tell you when we're safe."

How much danger they were in was debatable. Meg was in none, having done nothing, and in a town accustomed to fairy tricks, Finn could probably merely explain that he'd been given enchanted money, and after a good laugh (and return of his ill-gotten goods), he would be released on his own recognizance. But Finn thought he would end up in jail or the pillory, or be beaten by the knife man, and for him there was nothing else but to flee.

Meg looked helplessly from Finn to the shopgirl. She desperately wanted to go with Finn, but . . .

"You're the Lady's kin, aye?" the girl said with a crooked grin.

"Go with your young man, then, and good luck to ye. You can pay later." She had a young man herself and would do anything to go with him. She showed them the way to the back door and stood laughing at the front of the shop with her hands folded as the knife merchant pounded on the door.

Finn pulled Meg along at a breakneck pace, looking for sanctuary before the weight of the bill returned to his bag. There'd be no running then.

"Here," he said, yanking her into an alleyway. There was a large sky-blue wagon with empty traces for horses. The white lettering on the side read FENODEREE'S MOWING AND CARTING. They scrambled into the wagon and covered themselves with empty sackcloth, and just in time too, for Finn's fifty pounds were back.

They lay in silence for a moment, panting, expecting sounds of pursuit. Meg, acutely aware of the mucky floor, was almost in tears to think that her beautiful dress was already ruined. Snuffling discreetly, she said, "Now, why can't you get rid of the bag?"

" 'Cause there's something else in there that won't come out."

"Won't?"

"I don't know what it is. Well, that's not really true. I know what it is, I just don't know what it does, and it must do something."

He handed her the bag. She opened it and noticed white knobby things in the bottom of the bag. She reached in and—

"Eeek!" She'd never known people really said "eeek" outside of mouse encounters in books until she herself said it. A hand just barely on the right side of decomposition (if such a thing exists) reached up to grasp hers in a perfectly friendly, manly shake. Then it dropped free and pulled itself back into the bag like a hibernating whistlepig woken too early and curled up, apparently to sleep.

"What is it?"

"Well, a hand, of course. A skeleton. But I have no idea what it does."

"It seems . . . friendly."

"I know, and when it shook my hand, I saw someone attached to it for just a second, a man. So you see, I don't really want to give up the bag until I know what that hand is all about."

There was a sudden sound of clanking metal and banging wood, and they ducked their heads back under the sackcloth, sure they were about to be pounced upon. By the time they realized horses were being hitched, they were already off. They decided it would be too awkward to announce their presence just now, but agreed that if the wagon didn't stop in a few minutes they would jump off and chance the consequences. So they lay low, their heads jostling together as they jogged to parts unknown.

They didn't go far. Hooves tramped and harnesses jangled for only a few minutes before they stopped and heard a heavy form dismount from the front. They hunkered anxiously, sure the driver would look in the back, but no, they heard him walk away immediately. Meg peeked out and caught a glimpse of a retreating hulk, a massive man covered in a hooded cloak completely at odds with the weather. His legs, bulging with mighty calves, were bare, as were his hairy feet. He carried what Meg first took to be a weapon, a wicked curved blade on a long wooden haft, but she then realized it must be a scythe for mowing. The wagon was parked outside a tavern on the outskirts of town. The cloaked man went inside.

"Okay, it's safe," Meg said, and helped Finn haul the bag out, though as before, it felt light to her and she was of dubious assistance. Grunting and sweating, Finn was dragging the bag to the tavern when he spotted a group of men on horseback riding toward them. Among them was the knife merchant. Certain it was a posse come to round him up, he cast about frantically for a hiding place. There was a door on the side of the tavern, and he pulled and twisted the knob, but it was locked. The posse rode closer. The stables were nearby (for in days of yore it was a post tavern), and the riders would no doubt leave their horses there while they refreshed themselves in preparation for fresh pursuit. Of course the knife merchant had already forgotten Finn and was only intending to have a pint with his mates before the mowing competition, but to Finn everything was about Finn, so he was sure they were out to get him.

"Open, you . . . you . . ." He couldn't think of a word cutting enough for the stubbornly locked door.

"Finn, look!"

The bag stirred, and the skeleton hand dragged itself nimbly out and scurried like a gecko up the door. It paused and seemed to look (if a hand can look) at Finn, then grasped the knob, and gave it a twist. The door swung open. Finn hardly had time to be amazed before Meg pulled him and his burden into the cool darkness inside.

The room was fragrant with hops and fermented apples, oaken casks, and honey mead. It was the taproom, which is why it was locked, for you can't leave alcohol lying around unguarded on a festival day. Meg perched on a squat barrel, brushing the dust off first, though she knew her lovely new dress was already past hope. She looked at Finn, a mischievous glint in her eyes.

"I know what it is," she said. The hand, no longer needed, returned to hibernation.

"What is it, then?"

"It's a skeleton key!"

"What?"

"You know, a key that can unlock any lock. I always thought they meant a real key, and I never knew where the skeleton part came in, but it makes sense, doesn't it?"

Finn admitted it did.

"Let's test it," Meg said, looking around. She spied a small wooden chest bound in iron with a padlock on the front. "Here, open the bag by the lock." He did, and the hand obligingly crept out and fiddled with the lock until it fell open. Then, as before, it returned to its hemp cave. The chest didn't have anything particularly interesting in it, only six simple bottles of amber liquid labeled MACALLAN FINE AND RARE, 1926. No treasure. How disappointing. They locked it up again.

"Well, I can't get rid of it now. Can you imagine what I could do with something like this?"

Meg had visions of Finn's new life of crime: housebreaking, robbing banks, emptying Fort Knox. "I think you ought to give it back."

"To the little kid? But he gave it to me!"

"Yeah, but I bet it was his father's. That must have been his wagon we got into, right? So that's him in the tavern. Let's just give it back to him."

Finn had no desire to part with his new treasures.

"Seriously, Finn, how long can you carry around a fifty-pound bag? I mean, if you can't get rid of the bill and you can't get the hand to come out unless it wants to, I don't see what else you can do."

Finn, not easily deterred, spent the next few minutes pulling with all his strength at the hand, which remained placidly affixed to the bottom of the sack like the most determined limpet.

"I give up," he said at last. "Why is it always like this for me? I mean, you get all the fun, and I get . . . this." He gestured to his dashing black eyepatch, which, when the thought of what lay beneath wasn't giving her the willies, Meg rather liked. "And now, someone gives me a magic gift, but it might as well be a curse. I can't do anything with it. I bet the little brat is laughing at me. I wish I'd kicked his toy wagon to pieces!"

It was Meg's turn to say "there, there," and though she refrained from patting him, she felt so maternal it almost brought tears to her eyes to see him so upset. He was right, it wasn't fair. She hadn't asked for any of her fantastic experiences, hadn't asked to be able to see fairies, or find the Green Hill at will, or be the heir apparent of the Guardian. She didn't want it. It all just fell into her lap. And here was poor Finn, dying to be a part of it and thwarted, often violently, at every turn. She tried to come up with some way to make amends, almost as if it were her fault, but she couldn't think of anything. She could give him the weatherstone, if Silly would let her have it back, but even though that was interesting and decidedly magical, it didn't serve any particular purpose.

So she did the best thing she could, which was offer silent sympathy, and it seemed to work, for after a while Finn's bitterness and self-pity faded. He took a surreptitious swipe at some moisture in the corner of his eye, then let go of the bag and said, "As soon as the knife guy and his friends leave, I'll give it back to Mr. Fenoderee. You're right, it's probably his anyway, and his boy just took it. Mr. Fenoderee looked strong enough to carry a hundred-pound note if he had to. I just hope the little guy doesn't get in trouble. Here, I see light coming through the wall. I bet we can see into the tavern."

All around the periphery, at the bar and in the booths, jollity reigned. Tankards clanked together in toasts, voices raised in boasts and friendly argument. The light was dim and flickering. It was a room meant to be cut off from the rest of the world, where men (and a few rougher women) could escape from their homes and sheep and fields, all the things they loved but which plagued them to death, and gradually drown their sense of responsibility and obligation.

Thus were the edges of the room, all mirth and song. But in the center there was a heavy, empty space devoid of sound and good cheer. Seated at one end of a long table with plank benches was a huge hunched form, broad and shadowed, partly obscured by a cloak. There was no one near him, and when the barmaid came to refill his cup, she moved with brisk efficiency and quickly blended back into the crowd. He might have been surrounded by a phalanx of guards, so strictly did the revelers of Gladysmere keep their distance. He raised the cup to his lips and his hood fell back.

"What is he?" Meg gasped, but of course Finn had no idea.

His size alone should have given them a clue to his unnatural origins, for his back stretched twice as broad as even the village blacksmith's, and his head might have been an oak stump. In some ways, he resembled the Rookery brownie, though on a far more massive scale—his hair was thin and lank, his skin sallow gray and leathery, his eyes huge watery pools. But his nose jutted forward in something that was almost—but not quite—a pig's snout, and small tusks curved up from his lower jaw, forcing his lips out so he drooled a little. His scythe was propped on the table beside him and might have been another reason why patrons kept their distance.

Everyone in the tavern watched him while pretending to ignore him. Meg, sensitive to the suffering of others, felt his sadness and, perhaps worse yet, his absolute acceptance of this treatment. She could see why everyone might be afraid of him, but since they weren't fleeing in terror, they must be used to his appearance. Why couldn't one single person sit with him?

"Is that Mr. Fenoderee?" Meg asked. "Is that the little boy's father?"

Finn made a few unintelligible noises. If that's the kid's father, it sure explains how the kid got hold of a bag of magic tricks, Finn thought. And here I assumed he was just some village kid. What had the boy looked like? A pink piglet?

"I'm not going to walk up to that ugly thing and hand him the bag," Finn said at last.

Meg remembered why she didn't like Finn some of the time. "He's got to be a fairy. I thought you wanted to see fairies. Anyway, I don't think there's any harm in him. He's sad. And lonely."

Before Finn could answer, they heard the subtle grating of a key sliding into the lock. They barely had time to duck behind some of the larger casks when three men came in.

"Ugh," said the first, a prosperous farmer named Smythe. "'E sure makes me lose my appetite."

"But not your thirst," said the second, also a farmer, called Jonas, as he tapped a spigot into the bunghole smartly with a mallet and caught the escaping spurt in his glass. Smythe and the third man, a tightly muscled bruiser named Tansy, shouldered forward to fill their own.

"Easy there, Tansy. Gotta be ready for the mowing. It might be in the bag, but still, you won't mow many rows if you're so befuddled you chop your own leg off."

Tansy swigged down his glass and wiped his mouth with the back of his hand.

"It is all arranged, then?" Jonas asked.

"Aye, same as last year."

"And the year before, and before that. Don't you think it's high time we thought of something else? Fenoderee's bound to catch wise by now."

"That dull lunk? He wouldn't notice a bumblebee on his own pig snout, not if it stung him. Trust me, if it worked last year, it will work this year, and we'll have most of our hay mowed for nothing. That's a fortnight's work, all done in the space of a day. How can you argue with that?"

"Ain't arguing," Tansy said. "Fenoderee'll lose and mow your fields fast as a fairy. You'll beat the others to market and get top price. Nice for you, but what if he catches us?"

"He'll never know," Smythe insisted.

"I'm the best mower in the county," Tansy said with becoming honesty, "but to look at him, I don't think I can beat him. His arms are half again as long as mine, and that scythe o' his has a blade twice as long. And he's a fairy, so he's got powers beyond me."

"It's all settled," Smythe said. "I've already put thin metal bars all through the patch he's to mow, planted 'em as it were, all through the hay. Can't see 'em while you're mowing, but he'll sure feel 'em. They'll slow him down and dull his blade, and fairy or no, you'll not have a lick of trouble beating him. He'll never know the difference, the clod. He'll just drool and grunt and swing away and make no progress and never know why."

"And if he catches onto you?"

"To us, my boy," Smythe said sharply. "He hasn't yet, and we've been deceiving him these many years, one way or another, from my grandfather's time."

"I don't know," said Tansy with more sense than any of them. "If he finds out, he'll likely do something terrible to us. You know he will. I have a little one on the way. Fine lot my woman'll like it if I'm gutted by a fairy."

"You fret like a gaffer," Smythe said. "Believe me, he'll never know. We'll get free work out of him and not see him till the next mowing festival . . . when we'll do it all again. Now, go on out there and look pleasant, and I'll see you at the fields in an hour. And you, Jonas, go make nice to your ugly mower out there. Best remind him which end of the scythe to mow with, the great lummox."

They stepped out of the taproom back into the hurly-burly of the tavern and went their separate ways so as not to attract notice. Jonas reluctantly approached Fenoderee, on the side away from his scythe, and said a few words to him, at which the fairy drained his mug, grunted, and stalked out of the tavern.

"Now!" Meg said, and started out the door to catch Fenoderee. It wasn't until she exploded into the sunlight that she realized Finn was still cowering in the taproom. Why of all the . . .

But it was too late to change her mind now. There was the bright blue wagon, and there, oh, lordy, was Fenoderee. He must have been seven feet tall.

She could run, or she could scream, or she could gather her courage and do what she must.

"P-please sir," she began, for it never hurts to be polite. "Will you come with me?" To her amazement Fenoderee obediently took her hand and let her lead him into the darkness of the taproom, where Finn, watching, had backed even farther behind the barrels.

"Who's there?" Fenoderee asked in a small voice, looking nervously at Finn's shadow in the corner. He stepped behind Meg, looking for all the world like he was afraid.

"It's okay, it's only Finn. Come out, Finn." You coward, she thought. "See? Finn won't hurt you." Can't is more like it. "He knows your son."

"Sun's in the sky," Fenoderee said. "I know the sun too. He's my friend."

"No, I meant . . ." Fenoderee was looking at her with such

childlike simplicity. Meg had a thought and immediately dismissed it, but it refused to be dismissed. Could it be? He was a fairy, and a giant, bigger than any man she'd seen.

"Come out, Finn. Let him see you." Reluctantly, he emerged. "Mr. Fenoderee, this is Finn. I think you've met him before."

If it were possible for a seven-foot creature to peer out from behind the skirts of a young girl, Fenoderee would have done so. He stood behind Meg as if she were his mother and he was safe as long as she sheltered him.

He spied Finn and cried, "You!" and swept Finn up in a crushing bear hug, tossing him in the air just before his ribs cracked and catching him in another hug just before his head hit the ceiling.

"Careful," Meg admonished, and pried the dizzy Finn loose.

"He fixed my wagon," Fenoderee said gleefully to Meg. He skipped from one foot to the other, shaking the room to its foundations, then sat down on the rush-strewn floor with his legs spread straight out in front of him. "He helped me, he did. He fixed my wagon for me ever so neat. He's my best friend, my best in the world."

"You mean he—" Finn started, wide-eyed.

"He's the little boy," Meg clarified to the astonished Finn.

"Look at my wagon," Fenoderee said proudly to Meg. "See how he fixed it ever so sweet."

Meg cracked the door and peered at the wagon, with Finn, sidling nervously past Fenoderee, looking over her shoulder. "Is that the wagon you fixed?" she asked.

"It was the same color and had the same lettering on the side, but it was just a toy, no more than a foot long. Oh, look! Look there!" He pointed to the left rear axle. "I fixed that with a stick, a piece of a branch I broke to the right size. That's it . . . but it's more like a tree now. I remember snapping off that little bit on the side there, and I scratched it down with my pocketknife. It can't be, but it must be. This is the wagon. That is the little boy. But how?"

"Fairies can change size, you know," Meg said. "Maybe his wagon can change too."

"But I never thought . . ." He wouldn't admit it, but if he'd known he was repairing this monster's toy, he would have lit out for the Rookery and tucked himself into bed.

"It's easier to be a little 'un the rest of the year," Fenoderee said. "They don't notice me so much when I'm a little 'un. But for the mowing it helps to be a big 'un. I like to mow, don't you?" And he started playing with bits of hay in the dust, making figures and shapes and looking for all the world like James when he played his self-absorbed games on the ground.

"Where do you live?" Meg asked him gently.

"Nowhere," Fenoderee said with a sniff. "Not for a long time." He brightened. "I get to go back soon, though. Only another hundred years, and I can go home again. I miss my mum and da, I do."

"You can't go home for another hundred years? Why?"

Fenoderee looked glum and scraped his heels in the dirt. "I let her go."

"Let who go?"

"The girl with the golden hair. She were took from a big stone house, and her father raged ever so, but our lord would have her, he would. He took her down below and made her stay, but she didn't want to, not one bit. She cried and cried and her gold hair went all gray, and still he wouldn't let her go, but I was sad to see the gold all gone, so I took her back up to the sunlight, and she went home to her own da and mum, and they made me go away for a thousand years and a day, and it's the day that's hardest, they do say, for it comes at the end, not the beginning."

It took Meg a while to sort through the story and all the jumbled pronouns. "Are you just a child, then?"

She wasn't sure if he'd take offense, but he nodded and said, "My mum and da were the only ones to have a baby in the last two thousand years, full fairy, that is. My mum swore something fierce when they sent me away, but there weren't nothing she could do. I've been a brave boy, just like she said, though. Haven't I?" He looked at Meg pleadingly.

"Of course you have," she assured him, and patted an arm that was bigger around than her waist. He had the same shape-shifting abilities as all fairies, but he was just a kid, after all. He should still be with his mother. How cruel to banish a mere child, even one who could look as fearsome as this. He had survived on his own for nine hundred years, alone, away from his own kind, thrust into a world that would at best ignore him, always mock him, at worst persecute him. Somehow, wandering, alone, he had put his rare abilities to use at harvests. And, oh, how horrible of those men to trick him, year after year!

"You can't mow this year," she said. "You can't mow in the contest."

"How come not? I like to mow."

Meg hesitated. As much as her dander was up at Fenoderee's

ill treatment, and for all he was no more than a little boy, he was a huge little boy with a scythe, and a fairy, to boot. What would he do if she told him he was being tricked? She wasn't sure, but she had visions of him going after his deceivers with that glinting, grinning blade. They almost deserved it, but no, not quite.

"Can't you not mow this year? For me? For Finn?"

"You're going to lose," Finn said, and Meg shushed him and made a face, which he didn't understand at all.

"You lost last year, didn't you? And the year before that?"

"I did," Fenoderee said, "but I tried. That's what's important, they always tell me. Mr. Smythe, he always wants his man to mow against me because I'm such a good sport, he says. I try my best, but the hay is always hard to mow in the beginning. Later, when I mow all Mr. Smythe's fields, it gets easier. Mr. Smythe says I just don't get limbered up until I've mowed an acre or two."

If she saw Smythe again, she vowed, she would step on his toe as hard as she could.

"I've got to go or I'll be late, and everyone will be mad at me. They all smile and laugh when I mow. That's why I like to do it." And he ran off before Meg could think of a way to tell him he was being tricked that wouldn't result in the evisceration of three men.

The Edification of the Common Man

"... Or we can find a fairy mushroom circle, and I can go in and grab one, and you'll have a rope around my waist to pull me out. Or, no, I better be on the outside, I'm stronger than you. Or we can ... oh, look, pies!" Silly's already rather squeaky voice squealed up an octave as she spied a confection shop down a little alley off High Street. Though obscurely tucked away from the bustle of the main boulevard, it did a thriving business, first because it used far more sugar and butter and chocolate and marzipan and cinnamon than can possibly be good for anyone and second because it had an industrial fan in the doorway to waft its delicious scents down the alleyway to High Street. Silly made a beeline for the inviting window with tiers of pastries on display and was soon sucked in.

Silly and Dickie emerged a few minutes later, a bit poorer and a lot stickier, gobbling the last crumbs. They were lured to a floating gossamer dragon at a kite shop a few doors down. But they couldn't afford their favorite kites, so they came out again and were immediately caught by a barker at the door of a little store selling exotic pets.

"I have here in my 'umble establishment the very last of the pigmy hooded rats, denizen of the far-off minarets of the Orient. Last of his ilk, I tell you, and a steal at five pounds."

They peered down at a perfectly ordinary dark-brown and white Norway rat washing his nose and whiskers with clever pink paws.

"Or I have the rare and exotic coracle tortoise. Most tortoises can't swim, you know, but this one lives in the flood-prone Valley of Kings, and when the river rises, he just flips on his back and floats till the water recedes. Only seven pounds, cage and swimming bowl included."

They saw a pretty little tortoise who obviously wanted nothing whatsoever to do with his water bowl.

"I see I'm dealing with a couple of savvy youngsters," the man said, tapping the side of his nose with one forefinger. "Tell you what, you head down the alley till you get to the empty lot where the orphanage used to be afore the fire. My cousin Carl from the Cotswolds is there with his wagons, having a show for the edification of the common man. Wonders you never did behold in all your many years, my kiddies. All for fifty pence at the gate, fifty pence each for the special exhibits. Even a couple of blasé kids-about-town might learn a thing or two there."

This tantalizing information was enough to send Dickie and Silly farther down the narrowing alley until they found an open paved spot sprinkled with bits of crumbled masonry as though a building had once stood there and been demolished.

A tattered banner at the makeshift gate read CARL COTTAGER'S ODDITIES AND FREAKS OF NATURE. For the first time in her life, Silly didn't know what to do or where to look. She was filled with curiosity, an overwhelming desire to just stare, but countering that were pity and embarrassment. She felt ashamed of herself for wanting to look, ashamed of her fellow man for so eagerly seeking out society's poor unfortunates, and yet, she did not walk away. She couldn't. She and Dickie handed over their fifty pence and walked into a realm that could have been filled with denizens of the Green Hill, or the creatures from a painting by Hieronymus Bosch.

A young black-and-white heifer with an extra leg growing out of her back lowed mournfully in a dirty pen. A man in striped satin pantaloons thrust a two-headed snake at any squealing girl who passed too close. He wiggled the poor beast to make it look more menacing, but the snake hung his heads and tried to hide up the man's sleeve. A headless chicken in a cage continued to scratch at bits of grain. Strange, lifeless creatures floated in jars of formaldehyde.

"Ugh! The poor things. This is terrible!" But Silly couldn't look away. And anyway, she had spent her fifty pence, and why be half shocked when she could be wholly shocked?

She didn't know which was sadder, the helpless animal entertainers or the human ones who might be thought to have a say in the matter but in point of fact had few other options. Some were merely performers—a sword swallower, a contortionist—some obvious frauds, like the bearded lady, but others had been born with deformities so grotesque that they only felt at home with other grotesqueries. They perched on stools atop raised platforms, covered with curtains so that spectators could only get limited glimpses of them.

"Some of them look like fairies, don't they?" Silly said. And it was true. A single-armed young man's legs were fused so he looked like the one-armed, one-legged creature whom Silly had seen wielding a mace in the Midsummer War. And a woman with huge, puffed and swollen feet resembled a fairy who'd lumberingly capered behind the Seelie rade on the night Silly saw her first fairies. But that big-footed fairy had almost instantly shifted to a lissome, gazellelike creature, and that monster with the mace chose his form for its frightening appearance. Fairies could be anything they liked and laughingly change when the fancy struck them. But these poor people were trapped forever in their misshapen form and had decided that the only way to survive was to let people stare at them for money.

Silly felt ashamed but justified it by telling herself that if she didn't stare, they wouldn't get paid, and they wouldn't like that much, would they? It never occurred to her to pay and not stare, and it certainly never occurred to her that Carl kept all but a modicum of the money his freaks earned for him, giving them just enough for food but not enough to leave. Carl gave them clothes, too, but only their outlandish show costumes, so that they'd have nothing normal to wear if they tried to escape. They were virtual prisoners, of their bodies, their circumstances, and their ringmaster.

"They should be in hospitals," Dickie said. "Some of them anyway. That woman must have some kind of lymph disease, and she's not getting proper treatment. And look at the fat lady. She'll be dead in a few years if she keeps that up." The Fabulous Blubberous Maybelle, as her sign identified her, lolled in a cart drawn by four hairy-legged drafthorses, a cart she no longer had the strength to leave. She was the only member of Carl Cottager's show who was well fed, though by *well* he meant sticks of butter and bowls of sugar, which she swilled down for a cheering audience. Once, when she told Carl her bones ached and she wanted to try a diet, he threatened to roll her off her cart in Piccadilly Circus and let the news crews find her. After that, she obediently ate her sticks of butter. To be carted around to provincial venues and treated like a massive sort of fertility goddess was one thing, but such public humiliation would kill her faster than her clogged arteries. And so she thought she was trapped, just like the others.

There were two tents with special exhibits at which spectators could gawk for an additional fifty pence each. One was labeled "For Adults Only," and from the comments of people leaving the tent, Silly and Dickie gathered it had something to do with Siamese twins. The other promised "A Creature So Strange It Will Haunt Your Dreams! Only 50 Pence for a Peek at the Goblin Brat!" They handed over their coins and filed in with a few other people when the last group came out.

"From the dank, dark underground fairy warrens comes this wee monster," Carl said in high melodrama. "Just a baby, yet strong as a rhino." He guided them to a dark corner where a small shrouded box sat on a table.

"Is that it?" Silly asked. "There can't be much under that." It was bigger than a bread box, but smaller than a television.

Whatever it was, she thought, at least it wasn't another poor deformed human. Or was it?

"This beastie is endowed with the magic of the ages," Carl continued, toying with the moth-eaten green velvet curtain draped over the box. "They call them the Good Folk. They call them the Neighbors. But never let your guard down around a fairy, my friends. He would kill us all, slaughter us where we stand with his thoughts alone, if not for the powerful charms we've placed on him. Observe! The cage is thrice barred with iron, deadly poison to the fairies and pixies. Around the cage we have tied the finest gossamer spiderwebs, and onto their deadly stickiness we've blown dandelion seeds, and those things together no fairy can penetrate. We've wrapped the whole in strands of ivy and bound up the wee man's powers."

He could see the crowd was getting restive, but he wanted to give them their money's worth, and he had a tale to tell. He told them something about a wedding and a funeral held at the same time, and a man in a high silk top hat who might have been the groom, might have been the chief mourner, might have been both, and how a train of little green men came through, and the last one was scooped up in that high hat and imprisoned. But Silly hardly listened. From near her ear came a hissing voice. The Wyrm, coiled around Dickie's shoulder and still invisible, woke to point something out.

"Do you remember what I told you about how to trap a fairy? All around us is flummery, but this, methinks, is real." There was a sound of shifting scales as he, invisibly, raised his head to see what was inside the covered box.

The man made a few more boastful claims about the rarity and danger of whatever hid in the box, then, pressing a lever with his foot that made a multicolored strobe light start to flash, he grasped the green curtain in the center and pulled it up with a dramatic flourish.

Silly and Dickie couldn't see anything at first. The adults in the room pressed forward and crowded the children out as they pushed their faces against the box. A moment later, though, like the tide turning, they began to drift away with little disappointed murmurs. Dickie heard someone tell his wife they should demand their money back. Silly pulled him through a gap, and he finally managed to look into the box.

Crouched in the back, as far from the invasive eyes and leering faces as it could get, was a creature no bigger than a newborn baby, naked and scrawny. Its skin, baby soft, was a very pale mottled jade, and its eyes were unnaturally big. Its twiglike arms were curled against its chest, and it trembled uncontrollably. It caught Silly's eye, and for a moment the hopeless look vanished and it started forward, but then a fat, sweaty matron, who had bargained a cheaper price for her brood of ten children, shoved Silly and Dickie aside, determined that her chicks should have their sport and she would get her money's worth.

"What is it, Mum?" a towheaded boy asked.

"It's a dirty fairy," the mum said.

"Why's he dirty, Mum?" asked a freckled girl in chestnut pigtails.

"'Cause he sucks eggs," she replied irrelevantly.

"Is this what'll get us, then, if we go in the scummy pond?" a redhead inquired.

"Or if we climb the roof?" asked a black-haired girl.

"'Cause you allus tell us the fairies'll get us if we do anything," said a tiny tot with golden wispy curls.

"If this is fairies," said the eldest boy, "then I ain't afeard of them. Mum, I'm a-gonna swim in that scummy pond when we get home, first thing. If I'da known this is all there is to fairies, I'd a-done it long ago!"

Seeing her lifelong hold over her unruly offspring quickly evaporating, Mum ushered her brood out the door and hauled Carl after her by his sleeve, giving the poor man a shrill piece of her mind for corrupting good, wholesome family life with this shocking display. Silly, Dickie, and the Wyrm were left alone with the little green fairy.

Silly, impulsive as ever, attacked the box bodily, but the iron bars wrapped all the way around and were joined by a padlock as big as her fist. She tore off the spiderwebs and dandelions and vines, and the little fairy seemed to relax a bit, as if relieved of some constant pain, but it still wasn't able to get past the iron bars.

"What do we do?" she asked Dickie helplessly. Her main resources, strength and recklessness, had failed.

I don't know, he almost answered, but he'd learned in the last few weeks that looking confident was almost as good as being confident, and certainly makes everyone around you feel better. So he said, "Go to the door and keep watch. If anyone comes, cough and do what you can to distract them."

She stood just inside the tent flap and peeked out to see Mum still haranguing Carl. As if they were another sideshow spectacle, a group was gathering round them. Silly felt a tickle in her throat, an almost unbearable desire to cough.

"What do we do?" Dickie asked the Wyrm when they were alone. "How can I get through the metal?"

"Alas, there are great gaps in my metallurgical knowledge. Once I lived a score of years with the dwarves of the Rhineland, learning all the skills of forge and bellows, but now . . . oh, look, a set of keys." The Wyrm pointed his wedge head behind the cage, but seeing Dickie look wildly around, he remembered he was still invisible and considerately changed to a ghostly, half-visible shape. Dickie took the bunch of keys from the large iron ring hanging from a hook at the back of the cage. It was a lesson he'd yet to learn: When in doubt, try the obvious.

"Silly," he called softly, "we found the keys!"

Silly snatched them out of his hand with a jangle and started trying them in the lock. In her rush she wasted a lot of time, trying keys that were obviously too big or too small and dropping them twice and losing complete track of which ones she'd already tried. If she had just let Dickie do this, a lot of what came next could have been avoided. Dickie could see almost at once which key must fit the lock, and they could have been off with the little green fairy quick as billy-o, and when Carl returned to find the fairy missing, he naturally would have suspected Mum and her multitudinous offspring, obviously using a distraction technique. No one had noticed Silly and Dickie in the crowd, and they would have gotten off scot-free. But no, thanks to Silly, who had to do everything herself, it was not to be.

Finally, when she had exhausted every other possibility (some twice or more) she lit on the right key and the lock fell open with a rusty protest. The door swung outward and Silly found herself with an armful of little green fairy—who wasn't a little green fairy for long. In a fit of shapeshifting, it changed from a giant mushroom to a tiger cub to a Psammead to an unwieldy bird that might have been a dodo. It made little mewling sounds as it changed back into a little green fairy and wrapped its skinny arms chokingly tight around Silly's neck. She hugged it back with a fierce love she'd never expected, that protective love we sometimes feel instantly and automatically for things that depend on us.

They heard a cough from the tent flap, the sign for an approaching intruder, but it wasn't one of them as sentry—it was Carl, and his face was red and fuming.

"Hand him over, you lousy little brats," he said. He actually said something much, much worse, but since neither of them quite knew what the words meant, "lousy little brats" will give you the general idea. He held a wrench in one hand and slapped it against the palm of the other.

Silly clutched her small fairy to her and felt it bury itself in her hair. "I'll never let him go! Never!" And then she did a very foolish thing—she charged straight at an angry man five times her size who was holding a bludgeon. Maybe she didn't really think he'd use it. Maybe she simply couldn't conceive of failure. Maybe she panicked. Who knows. She charged directly at his belly, tucked like a linebacker ready to tackle, and at the last instant dodged to the right. Carl raised his wrench, and even he didn't know if he would actually hit her. He had children of his own, but these brats were stealing his livelihood.

Before he could decide to strike, the tiny, helpless fairy shape-shifted again, this time into a cinnabar and gold dragon, on a small scale but with a yawning toothy mouth that roared into Carl's face. He stumbled back against the flimsy tent wall and brought the whole thing down on them all.

"Stop that girl!" he shouted, but he couldn't see if anyone heard him. By the time he flailed himself free, Silly was a distant speck, her legs flying as she ran away toward the center of town. Carl stood, brushed himself off, and spied a lump writhing under the collapsed tent.

"I caught you, you blasted accomplice!" Though again, *blasted* wasn't the word he chose. He grabbed Dickie by a handful of shirt and hauled him up so he dangled in the air. "Now take me to . . . oh, another fairy, I see. Well, I won't be fooled twice." He eyed the Wyrm, who flapped his stubby wings and hissed menacingly, his head swaying like a cobra's. "You can change shape, but you can't hurt me in that form."

He was wrong, of course, on both counts, and the Wyrm bit him on the shoulder.

"Aayyyeeee!" Carl squealed, knocking the Wyrm heavily to the ground. But he didn't let go of Dickie. He only tightened his hold and stalked through his freak show, to the amazement and amusement of his employees, dripping blood from a number of puncture wounds.

The Wyrm was a scholar, not an athlete. Though hardly hurt by the blow, he was momentarily stunned, and when he shook his head and cleared his senses, Carl and Dickie were long gone.

"Oh, for my library," the Wyrm said miserably to himself as he tried to wipe the nasty taste of Man out of his mouth. "This is the consequence of fieldwork. Theory, theory only, from now on."

"Pardon me, mate," said a voice behind him. "D'you know a sheila name of Meg Morgan?"

A Deus ex Machina Is a Shabby Device

IF YOU LIVE IN THE COUNTRY and have any idea what it is to mow vast acres of hay, you probably envision a great tractor towing whirling blades that cut through the grass and pile it neatly. Later another machine will compress the hay into small, rectangular bales or cylinders the size of a hippo's belly. Though there is a certain amount of human labor involved, the bulk of it relies on gasoline and internal combustion and mechanics.

In Gladysmere, the harvesting of hay is another animal entirely. Through long tradition, and despite the pressures of speed and profit, all harvesting is done by hand, or, more properly, by arm and back and muscle and sinew. How they were convinced to eschew modernity to such a great extent no one can say, except perhaps Phyllida Ash.

Hard labor was balanced by fun, and every harvest was an excuse for a village-wide party. Muscular swains strutted about with their scythes over their shoulders, and for once Meg was glad she hadn't reached her full height. Even so, she felt anxious with all those blades overhead—what must the tall adults feel? But no one seemed nervous. They laughed and slapped one another on the back and held tankards and mugs in hands that weren't holding scythes. The men—all of whom would be competing in the various mowing competitions—struck poses to show off their physiques, much to the pleasure of giggling girls with flowers in their hair, as well as of their grandmothers and maiden aunts.

Meg hadn't been able to persuade Finn to abandon his money and skeleton key and help her keep Fenoderee from being tricked. He said someone would steal it even if he left it hidden in the cart, but if you really must know, he didn't want to see Fenoderee again. So she helped Finn and his burden into the safety of Fenoderee's wagon and went looking for the pig-nosed fairy.

The mowing competition was set to start just after midday, and under the glaring eye of the sun, they gathered at the first plot of hay marked off from one of the communal fields planted specifically for this day's demonstration.

Whoever organized the competition had an entertainer's knack. First on the list were a very tall, fat man and a scrawny dapper little fellow barely five feet high. Obviously friends, they teased and tormented each other with good-natured enthusiasm and a malicious wit that delighted the crowd even more than their physical contrast alone would have. They were the opening act, the jesters, and they helped gather the crowd and hold their interest. Meg, still at the back of the group and focusing more on searching for Fenoderee than watching the swinging scythes, heard the lively insults but didn't get to see any of the mowing.

How could a pig-faced fairy almost seven feet tall be so elusive? She shoved her way through the press until she came to an open area, but she couldn't see the distinctive head anywhere. She didn't know that whoever was canny enough to open the show with comedy was also clever enough to save the high drama of the star act for the end. How else could he get hundreds of people to watch farmers they didn't know mow a patch of hay? Holding the audience riveted to the end meant more betting, more drinking, more spending. So the laws of entertainment decreed not only that Fenoderee must be last, but that to heighten the shock value (even among those who had seen him at past mowing festivals), he must be hidden until the moment of his grand entrance.

Finally Meg intimidated two small urchins into moving from their perch on a fork-armed lamppost and climbed up in their stead. From there she had a panoramic view of the field. Only two patches of hay remained, rippling like a dun-gold pond. From her height, she could clearly see brighter glints in the leftmost patch, thin metal bars planted among the grass to stymie the mower. Anyone on ground level couldn't see them, and trusting Fenoderee would never think to look for them. However hard his years of banishment might have been, they hadn't corrupted him so far as to make him expect treachery.

There was an excited sound running through the crowd as each turned to his neighbor and asked, *Is it time? Where is he? Will he come this year?* Meg wondered how many of them knew Fenoderee would be tricked.

Even though she knew what to expect, she caught her breath

when she saw him come out of the little shed where they'd made him hide. He stepped into the sunlight, noble for all his ugliness, so strong, so trusting that even his pig snout wasn't hideous anymore. Fenoderee wasn't aware that he looked different, that mothers pulled their babies closer and hid their eyes, that pregnant women turned from him, lest (according to the old belief) their child be born with a snout too. Where he came from, appearance was a thing of the moment, a whim of the individual, not, as with us, an almost moral quality upon which people are judged.

He towered above the heads of all present, indeed, stood almost as high as Meg in her aerie. He carried his scythe casually around the back of his neck, a thing no mortal would dare, with the finely honed cutting blade resting lightly on his bare skin. Seas of people parted before him, and if she hadn't known better, Meg might have thought it homage for a hero. But they cringed, they did not bow, and Fenoderee was alone in the crowd, a pariah.

She wanted to call out to him, to stop him before the contest could start, but she still couldn't think of any way to keep him from exacting some revenge when his childish illusions were shattered. She was on the verge of just shouting out the truth and trusting to luck to prevent bloodshed, but she had seen children in the throes of blind tantrums strike out at their own beloved mothers before, and knew there was no force she possessed that could stop Fenoderee if he was determined.

She had a sudden inspiration. Why couldn't she confront Smythe and the others? She wouldn't have to tell Fenoderee, only threaten to tell him. When they knew they were in danger of discovery, they would back out of the contest quietly, no harm done. Maybe later she could explain things to Fenoderee, when Smythe was safely home, help him understand that the world was not a safe and pretty place, make sure he didn't get fooled again. Yes, that would work.

Like trees and cliffs, lampposts are easier to get up than down, particularly ones with ornate filigreed iron scrollwork at their capitals. Meg had been sitting astride the bent arm with her bedraggled skirts carefully tucked up under her. She started to swing one leg over so she could sit sidesaddle before shinnying down the post. All very good, in theory, but in fact she tangled her skirt in the unnecessary artistic flourishes, pitched forward when her momentum was stopped, hurled her top half backward to save herself, and, after a loud ripping of material, wound up hanging upside down by one knee six feet off the ground.

To the two grubby boys she'd evicted from their prize perch it was better than seeing a fairy mow, and they hooted and giggled and soon drew everyone's attention to the filthy girl hanging with her skirts around her head and her free leg flailing wildly for purchase. For the first few seconds, she was terrified of the six-foot drop onto her face, but for the next few seconds, which felt like a lifetime, all fear was replaced by utter humiliation. She couldn't see a thing beyond the tent of her green and cream skirt, but she heard the laughter and even a few bawdy jests, and she risked her own safety to try unsuccessfully to hold her dress modestly in place. Finally Tansy, on his way to the hayfield, took her on his broad shoulder and let her down.

"Are you okay, lass?" His eyes were bloodshot, but his grin was friendly and only a little teasing. He picked up the scythe he'd set down for her rescue. "Steady!" he said as she stumbled, her knees wobbly. "Here, let me take you to the front. Have a sit-down in the shade and see the mowing." He swung her back onto his shoulder like she weighed no more than a marmoset. Still a little nauseated, she would have preferred to keep both feet on the ground, but he meant well, and it got her through the crowd to where Smythe was pacing, anxious for the start of the competition.

Tansy's kindness settled it. She couldn't let Fenoderee wreak vengeance on him, even if Smythe deserved it for orchestrating the whole thing. Tansy wasn't blameless, but at least he wasn't the ringleader, and she didn't want to see him hurt. She didn't want to see anyone hurt. As soon as he put her down, she ran up to Smythe and faced him squarely. He stared at the grimy, pathetic, daggle-tailed creature who stood with her hands on her hips and a scowl on her dirty face.

"I know what you're doing," she said, loudly enough for those nearest to hear but not so loud that Fenoderee, sharpening his scythe on a stone, could catch her words. "I know you have metal bars in the field and you're cheating Fenoderee to get him to mow all your fields for free. You'd better stop this contest now, or I'm telling him, and you know what will happen then!"

Smythe looked down at her and said the last thing she expected.

"So?"

Finn sat restlessly in Fenoderee's wagon. It was fiercely hot, and unless he crawled under the sacks there was no shade—but better sun in the open air than shade under a stifling blanket. He wanted to enjoy the festival, but he didn't dare leave his prized possessions alone. That skeleton key! If only he could figure out how to get it out of the bag, he wouldn't mind leaving the fifty-pound note behind.

From somewhere far away he heard a shout and commotion, a man's voice calling to someone else, but he couldn't see anything. He knew it was almost time for the mowing competition, and though he couldn't think of anything more boring than watching a bunch of yokels cut hay, it was better than sitting around in the glaring sun, hot and miserable and alone. He began to feel sorry for himself again, and he blamed Meg for leaving him, even though she'd tried to get him to come along. He hefted the sack morosely to remind himself how bad off he was, and to his surprise, it didn't weigh nearly fifty pounds. He pulled the drawstring open and pulled out the bill. There was the bill with the illustration of Darwin—and it weighed only ten pounds.

To save you the trouble of figuring it all out, it might be best to explain now that the fairy money shrinks and grows according to need. In the normal course of its existence, it is worth about enough for a hearty meal—until someone starts to spend it. The first time or two, it stays the same, but the more it's spent, the more it weighs, until the owner stops spending. Finn was new to the game, so it had returned to its proper weight quickly, but if he'd stayed greedy and kept spending, it would have taken longer and longer to shrink, and someday it would never shrink at all until he managed to get rid of it.

Finn dimly guessed something of this. In any case, though he had a fleeting desire to spend, spend, spend straightaway, he controlled it and counted his blessings that he would be able to walk at an almost normal pace with his reasonable burden.

Positively rejoicing in the weight he once found so troublesome, he jumped lightly out of the cart . . . and immediately hid behind the cartwheel. Gwidion, dressed in his paint-spattered clothes, was just walking into the pub. His goat tried to follow him but was shooed outside by a bouncer. The goat either gnashed his teeth or chewed on something, Finn couldn't be sure, and walked around the corner.

If Finn ever looked handsome, he looked it now. A keen, malicious glow of anticipated revenge lit up his face, his cheeks lifted, and his lips curled. He was preparing to do his worst, and it suited him. He didn't yet know what his worst was, but there was his enemy, the man who had insulted and hit him, waiting like a sheep for the slaughter.

His were the instincts of a spy and assassin, not a hero, so the first thing Finn did was creep back to the taproom and hold his hemp bag up to the door.

"Could you, um . . . please . . . ?" he said to the hand. He felt embarrassed, even though no one could see him.

The skeleton key, which had been treated far more rudely in its time, was happy just to be asked and obligingly opened the door. In a flash, Finn had his eye pressed to the chink in the wall, Pyramus to Gwidion's oblivious Thisbe.

Gwidion was in high spirits and ordered a drink. "And a round for the . . . gentleman beside me." He'd almost said *for the house*, but even though most people were at the fields for the mowing competition, the house was still packed enough to break Gwidion's meager bank.

He'd chosen a seat near Finn, and between that and the fact that his volume rose noticeably with each of the small glasses of amber liquid he tossed back, Finn could hear him quite clearly.

"Never . . . hic . . . never worked so fast in my life," he said to no one in particular. "Got the sketches done, got well into the masterwork." Already his face was flushed and a sheen of sweat shone on his brow.

Some of the patrons looked at him like he was crazy, but a few, recognizing an easy supply of drinks, sidled closer. A customer with gray stubble all over his head, cheeks, and upper lip pulled up a chair and clapped him on the back. "Bring us the bottle," the man said, with a nod toward Gwidion to indicate on whose tab it should appear.

"I've done it," Gwidion said to his new friend. "Or as good as. I thought it would take two weeks, a week at best . . . because this has to be my very masterpiece, you know." The stubbly man didn't know, but he nodded and chewed on a pickled egg. "But in one day I'm half done. Tomorrow, or the day after, she'll be mine. It will all be mine."

Stubbly, catching the feminine pronoun, assumed he was courting and said, "A looker, is she?"

"None better," Gwidion said proudly, thinking he meant the portrait. "My best yet. She's weakening, I can feel it. She was weeping today, you know."

The bottle was as good as his, so Stubbly said, "Aye, when they go over all weepy, you know they're yourn."

Finn didn't understand all of this, any more than Stubbly did, but he grasped that Gwidion was working on a masterpiece, and immediately he knew what he wanted to do. Gwidion was obviously proud of whatever he was drawing. Finn would hurt him, like the artist had hurt him yesterday.

A barmaid with dark, tumbling curls and a revealing sheer white blouse passed by with a friendly nod, and Gwidion's bony arm snaked out to grab her. "Come here, sweetheart, and give us a kiss."

Only years of experience kept her from dropping her laden tray, and she let herself be pulled down to his lap to avoid falling to the floor. Her smile broad and artificial, her eyebrows scowling, she tried to pry herself away, but Gwidion was persistent. "Come on, darling, be good to me. I've got prospects. I'm up-and-coming!" He guffawed at himself. At last he took one liberty too many, more than even a barmaid can expect from her intoxicated patrons, and she slapped him resoundingly.

His look of drunken lasciviousness turned to hatred, and he said, "You'll come to me, willing or no, wench."

She just tossed her curls and stormed off.

"Seems to me, if you got one gal, you shouldn't try for two," said Stubbly, but Gwidion ignored him.

He fumbled in his vest for a pen and snatched a paper cocktail napkin from the far end of the table.

"'T'ain't 'arf bad," Stubbly said, looking over Gwidion's shoulder as he drew. No matter how he twisted himself, though, Finn couldn't see what he was drawing.

When the barmaid passed again, giving Gwidion as wide a berth as possible, he called out to her, "I'm sorry, miss. Will you have this as a sign of my most humble contrition?" He thrust out the napkin and the woman, fascinated against her will, came closer. He held it just out of her reach until she was at his side.

She stared at it, and her whole attitude changed. Shoulders that had been rigid softened, her body inclined toward Gwidion, and though Finn couldn't see it, her once-guarded eyes dilated. She gave every indication of a girl in the first giddy flush of love. Without being pulled or prompted, she sank down on his lap, wrapped her arms around Gwidion's neck, and kissed him full on the lips.

Finn's jaw dropped. That woman had clearly despised Gwidion just a moment before. Finn had been admiring her good taste. He'd almost hoped Gwidion would try his luck again, for the girl looked like a capable scrapper and she had easy access to heavy glass bottles. How was it possible that she could change in such a short time? What was on that napkin to convince her? He had to see for himself.

While the girl cuddled on his lap, Gwidion took another napkin. He made a quick sketch under Stubbly's eyes and passed it to him. "You've got the check, eh, friend?" Gwidion asked.

Stubbly looked down at a picture of himself cheerfully handing cash to the bartender. He was dazed for a moment. It was the most outlandish thing he ever heard. He'd never paid for another man's drink in his life, not to say half the bottle. If possible, he avoided paying for his own, running up a tab at various pubs and taverns until the proprietor started discussing broken thumbs. He was therefore amazed to hear his own voice call out to the bartender, "These are on me."

Gwidion, his arm around the barmaid's waist, tipped an imaginary hat and headed for the door.

"Cover my tables, will you, Doris?" the girl said to a similarly dressed blonde. "Me and my gentleman are going out for a stroll."

Napkins in one hand, girl in the other, Gwidion walked out. Finn slipped out of the taproom and crept up unseen behind them. He heard the girl coo something about baby-cakes into Gwidion's ear, and when he thought his target was properly distracted, he snatched both napkins and danced out of arm's reach.

"What the . . . why, you little . . . I'll tan your hide! Give me those!" Reluctantly, Gwidion let the girl go and made a grab for Finn, who circled the wagon. As long as he paid attention, he could keep its blue bulk between him and Gwidion, and unless Gwidion got help, he would never catch Finn until he made a break for it. This is a useful tactic, for it also makes your opponent look ridiculous and annoys him to no end. Keeping an eye (only one, perforce) on Gwidion, who circled frantically, Finn looked at the napkins. One was the aforementioned sketch of Stubbly volunteering to pay the bill, the other, rather better, a drawing of the lush barmaid looking out at the world with her eyes half closed and her lips puckered.

"You fell for this trash?" Finn asked the girl scornfully.

She watched her new paramour chase a little boy and wondered vaguely what she was doing. She felt woozy and light-headed, almost tipsy, though having seen in her professional capacity what drink can do, she avoided it. Still, she was held under Gwidion's spell and made no move to leave.

"It's rotten," Finn said, more to Gwidion than the girl. He thought the worst thing he could do was insult the man's talent. If Finn could disillusion the girl (though he had no idea how apt that word was), so much the better. "You couldn't draw a nose to save your skin. And you made her eyes too close together." Tauntingly, he allowed Gwidion to come almost within grabbing distance, then put on some speed and raced around to the other side.

"I vow to you, if you don't give that back, I'll eviscerate you slowly with a meat hook, you . . ."

Finn paid him no mind. He was used to idle threats. "Yeah, you and what army?"

Pazhan came around the corner and stood at his master's side. So much for Finn's strategy.

"Where the devil were you?" Gwidion asked the goat. "You were supposed to be standing guard at the door." He slapped the goat across the muzzle with the back of his hand. "Now, get that boy before he ruins my plans for tonight."

Pazhan stood a moment on stiff straight legs, gazing at his master levelly, then said, "I obey," and slowly began to walk around the wagon, his hard little hooves clip-clopping on the cobblestones.

Finn gulped. The man alone he could handle, if only by running away. The goat was another story. Pazhan's yellow-brown horns curved backward a bit, but if he lowered his head enough, the deadly points faced forward. He did that now.

"Hey, call off your goat," Finn said, backing away, and held up the two napkins, the girl on top, ready to tear them. He wasn't prepared for Gwidion's reaction. Gwidion looked over his shoulder at the lovely, patiently waiting girl he'd trapped with his drawing, then back at Finn. He began to tremble, and first Finn thought it was fear that made him shake. Then Gwidion turned and stalked away so fast that Finn gave a short, mocking laugh of triumph, thinking That's it? I made him stand down by threatening to tear up his drawings? He stopped laughing when Gwidion whirled around and charged him with a pitchfork that had been leaning against the wall.

Finn tore the napkins in two and ran for his life.

The girl, blinking as if she just woke up, looked around, felt her gorge rise to see the company she was keeping, scooped up a glass bottle lying on the rubbish heap and threw it with a strength born from years of lugging trays heavy with lager. If her aim had been truer, she might have knocked Gwidion cold. As it was, she only stopped him in his tracks.

"After him!" Gwidion shouted to the goat, and whirled back to face the girl. "Sorry, pet," he said, his voice wheedling, trying to make himself appealing even through the murder in his eyes. He tossed the pitchfork to the ground, where it clattered at their feet. "Now, where were we?" He reached for her, hoping against hope that something of the spell lingered, but it had evaporated with the destruction of his drawing.

"Touch me and die, scum," the girl said, scooping up the pitchfork. She made a trial jab, shifted the weight, and stood like a Valkyrie. She looked as if she almost hoped he would try.

Gwidion, still shaking with rage and now shaking with disappointment and frustration too, took three quick, shallow breaths and managed to croak, "Another night, perhaps, sweetheart." He turned tail and staggered after Finn and Pazhan.

"Hey!" came a voice from the tavern door. Stubbly came out, rubbing his eyes. "Come back here! You owe me ten pounds!"

"So?" Smythe said again. "Tell him. I'll think of some excuse, and he'll believe it, like he believes everything. Anyway, he's started, and the rules say he can't back out now. Step aside, girlie. I've business to attend to."

Meg turned and saw it was true. A whistle sounded, and Fenoderee and Tansy honed a last fine edge on their scythes and commenced mowing.

Tansy held the end of his scythe in his left hand and the grip about a third of the way down, in his right. He was bare-chested now, and what Meg thought was sweat was actually a thin layer of oil applied to make his muscles look more defined. He didn't need the oil's help. As soon as he swung the scythe his muscles bunched and extended like dancing buffalos in a tight herd. The cut started with his body twisted to the far right, and the blade glinted in the midday sun as he unwound his torso to slice a narrow, perfect swath of hay that fell down in obedient homage at his side. He took a half step forward and swung again. The first few strokes were for showing off—appreciative squeals followed each play of his muscles—but as he found his rhythm, his speed increased and the rows of fallen hay grew. The blade sliced easily, the hay as yielding as warm butter.

Fenoderee was having a harder time. His first slice with his massive scythe was met with boos and hisses from the audience and a harsh grating sound from the hayfield itself. Miraculously, the mighty scythe with his fairy strength behind it cut through the metal bars. But it took much greater effort, and only a few strokes later, his blade was so dull that the haystalks didn't fall, they merely bent and rose halfway again, their seeded heads nodding as if to say "Good try, but you'll need better than that to fell us, sir." Fenoderee was half a row behind Tansy when he stopped to whet his blade, a full row down when his scythe was sharp again. He kept at it with dogged determination and even had a smile on his face. He felt he was doing something to be proud of, and no matter how hard it was, he enjoyed mowing.

He fell farther and farther behind, and Meg was too afraid of the flying scythes to approach. She'd have to wait until the contest was over. Then, regardless of the consequences, she'd tell him the truth, make him understand how badly he was being used.

Tansy was a fine mower, and it wasn't false pride when he said he was the best in the county. He finished in record time, the stalks lying in orderly rows. But he wasn't pleased with himself. He knew he wouldn't stand a chance against Fenoderee in a fair contest.

"Mr. Fenoderee! Mr. Fenoderee!" Meg called out, thinking the contest over. But the pig-snouted fairy wasn't satisfied with a job half done. Even though his blade would barely take an edge now, he swung on. She started forward, and a rough hand grabbed her arm. She pulled away from Smythe, and the hand tightened.

"None of that now, girlie," he said, leaning close and breathing sour ale in her face.

"I thought you weren't afraid of me telling him," she said defiantly.

"Best to take no chances," Smythe said, and started to drag her toward the shed where Fenoderee had been hidden before the contest.

"Help!" she screamed, and though there were some thirty or

forty people quite prepared to help her, for none liked Smythe and most knew who she was, several other things happened first.

Like a convergence of compass points, four forces came running to Meg at the center.

From the north, dashing at breakneck speed, calling "Meg! Help me!" came Silly, clutching something that looked like a jade-green hairless monkey.

From the east, lumbering under his burden, came Carl clasping his prisoner, Dickie, who was hanging limp like a kitten in its mother's jaws. "Stop, thief! There she is! I'll have satisfaction!" He waved his wrench over his head.

From the west, sprinting for his life, came Finn with Pazhan, foaming at the mouth, in hot pursuit. Lagging behind, with glances over his shoulder, came Gwidion.

From the south came the thing that stopped everything else.

On its shoulders perched the Wyrm. "A deus ex machina is a shabby device," he said clearly in the sudden hush. "But at times quite useful."

The Wyrm's mount was somewhat longer than a large crocodile, but built on a heftier scale. His legs turned to the side like a crocodile's, and he walked with the same swinging alternation with his belly only just off the ground. But that's where the resemblance ended. He was a mammal, or more mammalian than reptilian, and covered with short, thick hair like a lion's pelt. His tail was more like a horse's, and it swished from side to side. No one noticed his tail, though, because his head commanded all the attention.

At least two times too big for his body, it could have been a hippo's, if hippos were even meaner than they are . . . and they are very mean. His eyes were small and piggy, perfect for muddy waters, but what everyone saw first, and remembered longest, were his teeth. Or they might have been tusks. In any case they protruded upward from his lower jaw and downward from his upper jaw by about a foot and a half. They looked like they had been sharpened by a professional whittler, and their ivory was stained by something suspiciously reddish-brown. He walked deliberately through the crowd as the Wyrm whispered something in his ear and pointed to Meg with the tip of his tail.

Silly skidded to a halt and said, "Wow." As you know, Silly was not easily impressed.

Finn also skidded to a halt and said a bad word (as did many people there that day).

The goat knew he had met his match and sat down to eat a discarded cigar, wondering what would happen.

Gwidion leaned on his goat and wondered if perhaps he'd had too much to drink.

Carl dropped Dickie, who came suddenly to life and did the bravest thing anyone ever saw—he ran directly toward the creature. He reasoned that if it was friends with the Wyrm, it couldn't be all bad. He didn't go quite up to it—no one in the world is that brave—but he came close enough for the Wyrm to flap heavily over on its stubby wings, its body drooping down, and drape itself over his shoulder. It gave him a quick reassuring nuzzle, which is about as demonstrative as a Wyrm gets, and settled down to watch the play unfold.

Smythe gripped Meg by her other arm too and held her out in front of him when it became clear where the creature was headed. He as good as said, "Here's a tender morsel, consider it an offering and let me live."

"Cooee, cobber! Meg Morgan, fair dinkum? What's all this barrack, then?" It took her a moment to realize the creature was speaking English, or a version of it, and another moment to wonder how he talked with all those bloody teeth (or tusks) in the way. When he spoke, she saw row upon row of smaller, dirk-like teeth in his mouth with gobbets of flesh between them. The interloper seemed to notice Smythe for the first time and fixed him with one beady eye. "This drongo bothering you? Oi, mate, let Miss Meg go, if you please."

Meg rubbed her arms where finger-sized bruises were already purpling.

"Bonzer," he said, satisfied. "Would you like me to eat him for you?"

"Oh, no, please don't," Meg said hastily. If nothing else, it would be a mess and an embarrassment, and she was heartily sick of people staring at her.

"Or I can leave him for you to eat. Selfish of me, to think of eating him myself. But then," he added demurely, "I am very carnivorous."

"What are you?" Meg asked.

"Me? Why, I'm a bunyip." Suddenly remembering his diplomatic mission, he dropped his Australian cant and said very formally, "On behalf of the United Federation of Bunyips and Aboriginal Entities, I'd like to offer our fealty to you, Meg Morgan."

"Do you mean I woke you up too?" she asked, aghast.

Lightning spirits and odd two-tailed cats were one thing, but she didn't want to be responsible for a monster like this walking around. And if he was part of a federation, there must be more of them.

"Woke me? No, we were not sleeping, exactly, though we had returned to the Dreamtime. But now you have made this world comfortable for us again, so we have emerged. A few of us, anyway." Thank heaven for small mercies.

"I will not stay, for I hunger, and it would be rude to eat any of your friends or, apparently, your enemies." He lowered his head and glared at Smythe. "I see that many things have changed since I dreamed. But first, I bring you a gift, a token of our esteem."

The bunyip's body heaved and from one of its three stomachs (one for flesh, one for bone, and an extra one, like we all have, for dessert) it brought up a stone. It was small and brown, a pebble really, and covered in intestinal slime. Meg felt a little heave in her own stomach, but she didn't want to be rude, so she bent down and picked it up, mucus and all.

"What is it?" she asked. Her other two gifts had gone unexplained, and though she really wanted the bunyip to leave, she had to know what the stone was for.

"It is a heart's desire. Not *your* heart's desire, mind you. Wouldn't that be nice? They're very hard to come by. Someone else's heart's desire. Give it to 'em, and they get it, you see? Well, ta and hooroo, Miss Meg. Come down and see us when you've a mind."

He hauled that crocodile body around and lumbered down the lane, and there was dead silence until he turned the corner and was out of sight. As soon as he was far enough away, Silly, Dickie, and Finn crept up to stand beside Meg.

Nearly two hundred pairs of eyes stared at Meg, flabbergasted. Silly whispered a brief synopsis in her ear, and Meg came out of her daze. There were problems for her to fix.

I may not be the Guardian, she thought. I *won't* be the Guardian. I'll never be like Phyllida, commanding their respect. But after the bunyip, I think, for just a little while, they will do whatever I tell them. No one would dare gainsay the girl to whom a monster bowed.

Her posture, which, left to its own devices, was not good, straightened, and she threw her shoulders back and lifted her chin. She was normally terrified of public speaking, but these were desperate times.

"You!" she called clearly, pointing at Carl, who still held his wrench. "You kept a fairy captive, which is forbidden. I should give you to the Green Hill and let them do what they wish with you." She felt like she was acting in a play. Here was a new role for her—a powerful, confident person. Someone others would obey. It was heady stuff.

"You will trouble my sister no more, and if you try to catch another fairy, I will know about it."

The man groveled and wrung his hands. "Please, missy, I didn't mean him no harm. Someone gave him to me, and I looked after the little feller as best I could."

Silly whispered something else in her ear.

"And take better care of your employees, or I know who you'll see about it." Of course everyone thought she meant the bunyip. Carl ran off when she dismissed him with a wave of her hand.

She heard murmurs in the crowd. *The Lady? The little Lady? Herself's heir, must be. The next Guardian.*

Sotto voce, she asked Finn if he was okay. He saw Pazhan and Gwidion in the distance, the one nonchalantly chewing a discarded nosegay, the other swaying uncertainly on his feet. "For now, but I have some things to tell you later."

Good enough. She whirled to face Smythe, hands on her hips. "As for you!" She stared him down until he looked away. "You are a liar and a cheat. You tricked poor Fenoderee so he'd do all your mowing for you." She turned to see how Fenoderee would take the news, but he was still diligently mowing. Had he even noticed the bunyip?

"It's a lie!" Smythe cried. "Who are you anyway to question me, girlie? Everyone here knows me for an honest man. If there's any trickery, it's not my doing." He looked frantically around for Jonas, but whether to elicit his support or to blame him, Meg didn't know. The canny man was nowhere to be seen. "You, Tansy, tell her. It's an honest, friendly game, and my man won fair and square."

"No," Tansy said, "it's not fair, and it's not square, not a bit of it." He turned to Fenoderee, who was still mowing. "Fairy man, hear me! You've been cheated, and I'm that sorry. Will you take my help to finish your task?"

Fenoderee looked up at last. "You . . . you want to help me? No one's ever helped me afore, 'cept him over there, my best friend in the world." He pointed at Finn with his scythe. "He fixed my wagon, you know." Tansy took a position far enough away to avoid Fenoderee's blade and tried to cut a swath. He did, barely, with great effort, but his blade chipped and was too dull for a second cut. He sharpened it and swung again, and man and fairy worked side by side.

"I like this place," Fenoderee said companionably to Tansy. "I think I'll stay awhile." If anyone groaned, they did it quietly.

So much for a ferocious Fenoderee lopping off heads.

"If that will be all, miss," Smythe said, trying to slip backward into the crowd.

"That will *not* be all," Meg said. "You owe Fenoderee some compensation."

"He doesn't want anything. Look how happy he is." Then Smythe pushed his luck. "Besides, he lost, and whatever the reason, rules is rules and he has to mow my field."

Meg took a step toward him, and he backed down. She looked like a girl who could fight a Midsummer War, strong and sure. "Very well, he will mow your field," she said. "Who am I to break with custom? But he will keep all the hay he mows."

There was scattered applause from people who either sympathized with Fenoderee or disliked Smythe.

"D'you want to beggar me, girl? I've put all my profits into the hay. I've borrowed against this year's gains."

Meg thought a moment, almost weakened, then steeled herself. If she was to be Guardian—no, not she, not Guardian. Where had that thought come from? She was leaving, forever, as soon as Phyllida got James back. But she just couldn't let Smythe get away with it. And in any case, he looked prosperous enough to survive a bad year.

"Very well," she said. "You may keep one half of your crop. The rest goes to Fenoderee after he has mowed it." She kept her voice sweet and reasonable. "That's only fair."

Smythe looked as if he'd like to grumble, but he held out his hand. "Deal," he said.

She didn't take it right away. "But we decide now which half Fenoderee's to have. Deal?"

The odds were decent, Smythe thought. They didn't know which fields he'd planted, so they might pick the drier ones, or the ones interspersed with too much milkweed. He took her hand. "Deal."

Meg gave him her most charming smile. "Fenoderee will take the top half."

That year, Fenoderee carried thirteen wagonloads of hay to market.

Smythe had a bountiful harvest of roots and stubble.

Who Must Do the Hard Things?

IT'S LIKE OLD TIMES, Meg thought as they ambled home. Old times of a scant few weeks ago when they were all safe in Arcadia, traipsing through its quads, dodging college students intent on Frisbee playing or love affairs or anything but their studies, trudging up the steep hills only for the joy of running breakneck down them again. With the excitement behind them (how little Meg knew!), she felt the preternatural calm that follows unexpected action and unexpected success.

Only a pebble in her pocket remained of her adventure. Was that me, she wondered? Was it Meg Morgan to whom a monster paid homage before all those amazed eyes? She, who hated to be before a crowd, had suddenly known the power of leadership. No, she told herself, I will not be the next Guardian. But the power was intoxicating, not so much for itself but for the things she could do with it. That one distinction separates the tyrants from the good kings.

Why, she had saved her sister, and apparently a baby fairy (which she still had to get to the bottom of) and Dickie. That man turned tail when he saw her with the bunyip, and she knew it was not just the monster but her own ease with the monster that made him run. It was true: she hadn't been frightened of it, really. And Fenoderee, poor simple Fenoderee, had been saved from base trickery, his tormenter justly punished. She had done all this in a few minutes. What could she do to heal the world, or Gladysmere at least, as the Guardian? There were people and fairies who needed her help and protection.

"Where's Rowan?" Meg asked. "I hope he's not in trouble too. How is it that every single one of us had an adult who wanted to hurt us? Why was Gwidion chasing you, Finn?"

He glanced up at Silly and Dickie. Silly, as usual, was too restless to walk slowly and skipped and capered ahead. Dickie, who wanted to talk to her about the little green fairy, struggled to keep up.

"Well, after Gwidion hit me I—"

"He hit you?" Meg asked, aghast. "When? Why?"

He looked at her oddly. "Don't you remember? Didn't you see? When we were having our first art lesson?"

"There was . . . something. You got mad and left. He hit you? Really?"

Finn described the incident.

"And I was there? I swear I don't remember any of it. Gwidion kind of gives me the creeps, though, and I don't think he likes me, but I don't know why. I guess it's because I don't have any talent. Rowan does, though. They took to each other right off."

"Figures," Finn began, and was going to say some unpleasant things about Rowan until he remembered that Meg might have some soft feelings for her brother. "Anyway, after you left me in the wagon, Gwidion and his goat showed up and . . ." He told her what he'd seen, "And that's no ordinary goat. I think I heard him talk. There's something wrong about them both."

"And those pictures he drew . . . tell me about them again." Meg was getting a faint inkling.

Meg was silent and thoughtful as she listened. It seemed like a silly idea, but not any sillier than weatherstones and bunyips. "Do you think his pictures make things happen? That what he draws comes true?"

Finn chewed his lip as he thought about it. "I suppose . . . though it sounds a little far-fetched to me." Then he remembered his ten-pound note and skeleton key.

"Do you know, I remember something . . . I think I remember it anyway. Right when you ran away cry—I mean when you ran off yesterday, Gwidion drew a picture for us. I can't remember what it was of, but I believe I was angry with him before and I wasn't angry with him after I saw the picture. Do you suppose he did something to me, to us? Did he make us forget?"

"That would be a neat trick," Finn said. "I just wish I could draw. I'd do a doozy of Gwidion and his dirty goat at the bottom of a pit trap."

"Finn!"

"Well, I would. Don't look at me like that. I know you're all soft and kind and that nonsense, but I'm still going to get even with him."

"How?"

"I don't know yet." But he had an idea.

"Don't get in trouble," she said anxiously, and he snorted. "And don't hurt anyone. Please?"

"I'm not making any promises," Finn said grimly. "He hit me, and he's up to something."

"What?"

"I don't know. But why was he so upset when he found out I wasn't related to you guys? And why is he so chummy with Rowan?"

"And why," Meg added, "did Phyllida let a stranger move in? Onto the grounds anyway. You're right, it is peculiar. Ugh, let's hurry. I need to find out if Phyllida's close to getting James back. Then I swear I'm going home, even if I have to walk . . . and swim." She quickened her pace.

It was a hot and heavy midafternoon, and the air was sharp with the carrying scent of fresh-cut hay. As they approached the Rookery, they saw a quaint figure before them dressed in an odd assortment of riding breeches, gaiters, and tweeds. It carried a short walking stick and twirled it on every third step.

"Rowan?" Silly asked. She skipped up to him, lost to hilarity. "You—what in the world? You look like a . . ." He looked like an Edwardian squire, but she filled in the blank with *weirdo* instead, which was almost as accurate.

Rowan, garbed in the mismatched togs he'd found in assorted closets, scanned them over coolly. "Just surveying the estate," he said, grinding the tip of his cane into the gravel and swinging the brass knob in an arc with his palm. He looked older, more careworn, with an anxiety in his eyes that was still part greed but more a concern about business matters that wouldn't be of interest to such children. There were some drains at Gladys Gap that needed tending to. The Bungys' roof was in need of repairs. They'd been good tenants for generations and should be looked after. There were rumors that Ajax, who kept chickens, was harassing a vixen. And that foal by Fetlock out of Silversides . . . should he keep him or sell him?

Gwidion's spell had had an unexpected effect on Rowan. While the artist hoped to make him a nuisance and a thorn in his relatives' sides, someone else to harry poor Phyllida, he had instead created a conscientious lordling who took a keen and highly personal interest in the affairs of his estate. At first Rowan coveted each step of the many staircases, each worn and moldering rug, each portrait of distant ancestors on the walls. But as the hours passed, the spell evolved, keeping the core of its original intent but shaping itself to Rowan's nature. He wasn't a bad sort—quite the contrary. He had all the makings of a hero. It was just his bad luck the world kept interfering. Gwidion meant mischief, but he had accidentally created a young man who took his duties as heir very seriously.

Meg could tell from Wooster's dolorous face as he met her at the door that there wasn't any good news, but she passed him by hopefully and went to the source. She found Phyllida in her sitting room.

"Where's James?" she asked breathlessly. If she phrased it like that, as if he was just in another room, it might all be okay. If she had faith that he was safe, he would be.

"We haven't found a way to get him back yet," Phyllida said, carefully avoiding the fact that they hadn't been trying.

Meg's heart sank, but she laid a hand on Phyllida's arm. "Don't worry, you'll be able to do it. I believe in you."

It was all Phyllida could do to keep from breaking down. If only she could tell Meg, encourage her to start looking for James herself. But no—by tradition, it must come entirely from Meg, unprompted. Phyllida managed to control herself just long enough to say, "Go wait for me in the garden kitchen, there's a dear. I want to look up one more thing." Only when Meg was safely gone did the tears fall.

I'm a horrible old woman, she thought bitterly. I deserve to die alone, with no heir. It's wrong, wrong, wrong! She trusts me. She loves me. James is imprisoned under the Green Hill, waiting for us to rescue him, and because I keep to the old ways and stay mum and fool Meg, no help is coming. Can't I at least encourage Meg to look for him herself?

The whispered voice of Angharad, the first Guardian, came to her. *That is not the way. You must test her as I was tested, as you were tested. The life of a Guardian is not easy.*

Phyllida scowled at the voice in her head. Bloody right it's not easy, she thought. But because I love her, I want to smooth the way for her. Most of all, I want to keep her trust. I was lucky. I didn't find out the truth until my mother was gone. I never knew that she was forbidden to seek Bran, my father, her husband. And yes, I hated her at first for deceiving me . . . but I couldn't hate her long. She had to pretend to seek him, waiting all the while for me to realize the test was mine. She died without her love. What would I be without my Lysander? I would lay myself down and never rise again.

With heavy steps, she followed Meg downstairs.

Everyone but Rowan was gathered in the garden kitchen, that bright, cheery place where the line between growing food and eating food was blurred. Silly, with the green fairy still wrapped around her throat and refusing to look at anyone, was animatedly telling Lysander about their adventures.

"And he tried to kill me, but I got away, and then when he almost caught me again, Meg saved me. Oh, you should have seen her!"

She summarized for Phyllida's benefit, then told them both about the bunyip. "And he smelled just horrible, like rotten meat and swamp gas, but he was so polite. He even offered to eat someone for Meg."

"I didn't let him, though," Meg said hastily. She pulled the pebble out of her pocket. "He gave me this and said he had been in the Dreamtime, though I didn't wake him up exactly. Did I bring the bunyip back into the world from wherever he was? I didn't mean to do that. If he eats people, I think he should go back to the Dreamtime."

"I still don't know what it's all about," Phyllida said. "Bran said the currents run all through the world, like the Cherokee spirit, so maybe . . . I just don't know." Her head was starting to ache, and she had other, more pressing worries. The things that sought Meg out didn't want to hurt her, quite the contrary, so they could be set aside for the time being. "I'll have to ask Bran when he's feeling better."

"Where is he?" Meg asked, guilty that in the day's excitement she'd forgotten about him as well as James for a while.

"Oh, Dr. Homunculus came and gave him a sleeping draught. He wouldn't take it, of course. We had to sneak it into his drink. You know him. He said he had wood to chop and tried to get up with blood running down his chest."

"It's my fault," Meg tried to say, but Lysander hushed her.

"It's no one's fault but his own, child. If he'd be sensible and rest—"

"Sounds like someone I know," Phyllida said wryly, looking at her husband with eyes full of worry and love. "You've been working too hard of late. I should slip *you* something."

Lysander chuckled. "That's why I make my own drinks, woman! I've long suspected you of trying to drug me."

Meg saw him take Phyllida's hand under the table. It was true, he had been working too hard. Her fault as well, no doubt. She could see his other hand tremble as it brought a spoonful of mutton and barley soup to his mouth, and he looked pale and tired. They were so old, she realized, wondering why she'd never seen it before. Phyllida's skin looked paper-thin, and for all she was vigorous now, there would come a time one day when she was not. She seemed distracted, almost flighty, depressed and nervous.

They gossiped for a while about events at the festival, and Meg won high praise from the Ashes for saving Fenoderee from another year of servitude. "I should have done something about it myself," Phyllida admitted. Another failing, she thought. If I cannot pass on my responsibilities to another soon . . .

Then Meg remembered what had happened the night before, forgotten in her concern for James. "Just before we saw James at the Green Hill last night, we saw something else. It was a woman.

I thought it was Moll at first, but now I'm sure it wasn't. She wore a hooded cloak, and she knelt by a stream. Oh, she made the most terrible sounds, like wolves and wildcats and weeping. She had bright red eyes and nothing else on her face. Nothing, no nose, no mouth. And she was washing—" She heard Phyllida gasp, and Lysander went limp against his chair. "What? What's wrong? Who is she?"

Weakly, Phyllida asked, "What was she washing? Could you see?"

Meg was alarmed now. Phyllida looked terrified, Lysander like he was about to faint. "That was the strangest thing. I'm pretty sure she was washing the shirt you gave me, the pretty white one with the silver stitching. It looked like it anyway, only it had blood on it. I decided I didn't want to paint, so I gave it to Rowan. He was wearing it earlier today. I saw him in it before we went to the festival, so it couldn't be the same shirt."

Phyllida and Lysander exchanged looks and made an obvious effort to pull themselves together. But Meg could see from the tension in Phyllida's arm that her grip on her husband's hand under the table was painfully tight.

"What does it mean?" Meg asked.

"Oh, oh, nothing really," Phyllida choked out. "Just a washer-woman fairy. Not very common."

"That's it," Lysander said with the most ghastly attempt at laughter Meg had ever heard. "She probably saw all the paint splashed on it and tried to wash it off. Nothing a fairy hates more than a mess. Well, you young uns can fend for yourselves for the rest of supper, eh? My lady and I have work to do." He pushed himself up on his gnarled cane and all but dragged Phyllida to her feet.

"Come on, dear girl," he said softly. "Let's leave youth to its pleasures."

The children looked at each other, confused. All except for Dickie, who looked almost as frightened and shocked as the Ashes.

"You saw a banshee," he said when they left.

They'd all heard the term but didn't know exactly what it meant.

"They're connected to a particular family, like a brownie," Dickie went on, speaking evenly like he was giving a lesson. "Banshees are mourners. They foretell when a member of that family is going to die. They wash the clothes of the doomed. Whose shirt did you say she was washing?"

"Well, Phyllida's, I guess. She gave it to me, though, and I gave it to Rowan." Her eyes widened in understanding. "Do you mean one of us is going to die?"

Dickie nodded.

Silly gasped, and even the little fairy peeked his head out. Finn didn't know where to look. It seemed like a private family moment, and he wasn't needed. All the same, he had to be there. Meg could die? It wasn't possible.

Meg swallowed hard. "Which one of us, then? It could be any one of us three, right?" Please, not me, she thought, then realized that the alternatives were only slightly less terrible. Still, *not me, not me*, her instinct cried out.

"Well . . . ," Dickie began, then faltered. He felt like he was pronouncing a death sentence himself, as if he personally were condemning one of them. Meg, Silly, and Finn all leaned toward him anxiously. "I think . . . I'm not sure, but I think that it means whoever actually owns the shirt. Phyllida gave you the shirt to use, but it's still her shirt, right? You were borrowing it and would have returned it to her when you went back to Arcadia. I think the banshee means that Phyllida is going to die." Feeling like an executioner, he put his head down on his folded arms.

Silly, who shunned tears, burst into them now, and even Finn felt his eyes get heavy and warm in a way that didn't shame him like yesterday's tears had. Only Meg remained stone-faced. She rose and said, "If you'll excuse me," and slipped out of the room.

She had to be alone; she had to think. She headed for the wardrobe in the spare room with the secret door in the back—a passage not to Narnia but to a narrow stone staircase leading to the Rookery roof. The young birds, who hadn't seen her for a while, fluttered their sleek ebony wings when she walked out, but the wise old rooks with gray in their feathers merely eyed her cannily and turned their beaks back toward the declining sun. She perched on the parapet and let her legs dangle off the edge. She'd never been brave enough to do that before, but having just cheated death, as it were, she felt no fear in her lofty perch.

She stared unseeing at the rolling hills, the dry stone walls, the woods. "If Phyllida dies . . . when Phyllida dies . . . ," she said aloud, "I can't. I don't want to." She closed her eyes and swayed on the parapet. "I have to," she said at last, firmly. She felt trapped, desperate, like the vast and limitless life that once stretched before her had closed suddenly to a pinhole, through which she could see a tiny, ordered, predictable existence. No, not entirely predictable. Fairies can never be predictable. But every other possibility was closed to her. Career, travel, . . . love? Yes, maybe even love, for how many men would choose to be consort to the Guardian of the Green Hill? Any man she loved would be trapped, just like she was.

"But I don't have a choice," she said aloud.

"Of course you have a choice," said a voice behind her.

She almost fell off the roof. The brownie leaned against a long, stiff-bristled brush, examining her. He'd evidently been scrubbing up the crow muck, and his square bare feet were white with the powder of dried droppings.

"You could turn tail now. You could jump off the roof into the topiary. Or you could do what you want."

"What I want?"

"Do you even know what you want?"

"No." Of course not.

"Then why do you complain because someone gives you a direction? You have nothing better to do." He shoved the push-broom into a crusted pile of guano.

"But I don't want someone else to decide what I'm going to do with the rest of my life. I want to decide for myself."

"So decide."

"It's not that easy. Phyllida is . . . is going to . . ." Finally the sniffles started, but she fought them back. "Phyllida is going to die. The banshee said so."

"She did, did she?" he snorted. "Overdramatic, that one. And so we get another Lady, another Guardian."

"And it has to be me. There's no one else."

"That sister of yourn?"

"Silly?" She almost managed a smile. "No . . . maybe someday, but not yet. Oh, why does this have to happen?"

"Everyone dies."

"But why now?"

"Mighty inconvenient for you, dearie, ain't it? Powerful selfish of someone to up and die just when it suits you least."

"I didn't mean that. It's just . . ." Now she felt even more terrible. Of course it was worse for Phyllida. "And if there's no one to follow her when she goes, no next Guardian . . . I have to do it. But it's so hard! Why does it have to be me?"

"Who must do the hard things? She who can." He gave a last sweep and vanished, broom and all.

"She who can," Meg repeated in a whisper. That settled it. She changed her bedraggled clothes in her room and went downstairs to find Phyllida, to tell her unequivocally that she would accept her role as heir. If she had any misgivings, she would hide them; if she had any regrets later, she would ignore them.

Phyllida and Lysander joined them in the parlor, looking redeyed but composed. They never stopped touching each other, not for a second. When Phyllida let go of his hand to reach for her glass of cordial, the other hand automatically found a place on his knee. When Lysander lit his pipe, he leaned his shoulder into hers.

Meg had assumed the Ashes would break the news to them, the news they already knew, but no one broached the subject. Probably the sad faces they saw when they walked in the door told them it was no secret. They talked a bit more about the mowing festival and asked after Rowan, who still hadn't put in an appearance. They chuckled at his outlandish attire and wondered with the others what he was up to.

Then Meg stood. She felt as if she should make a formal speech and was more nervous even than when she had climbed the Green Hill on Midsummer Night. This was a promise to someone she loved. It was more than a night of bravery, it was a lifetime of bravery of a totally different kind.

"Phyllida, Lysander, I've decided I will be the next Guardian."

Silly, not one to allow a moment of stunned silence even when it was appropriate, shrieked, "Hooray! Now we can stay! Or I can come back to visit you, anyway. I was sure once we went home we would never be allowed back again, especially not if Mom heard what's been happening. Now you get to stay here forever and ever, Meg. You're so lucky! I almost wish it was me." Even she was wise enough to know there might be drawbacks—labor, responsibility, heartbreak. As sister of the Guardian, she would have all the privileges with none of the onerous duties.

Dickie whispered, "Congratulations," in a way that sounded more like a question and laid a hand fleetingly on her arm. Finn didn't say anything. Around them all loomed Death, mocking and imminent.

Relief now mingled with Phyllida's sorrow. "If you mean it, if you truly are sure, then you must go to the Green Hill at daybreak and declare it. But only if you are certain, my own Meg. Once you have made your intentions known to the Green Hill, there's no going back. Though you may hate it, and hate me for it, you'll be bound for all your life."

"Just by saying the words?" she asked.

"By saying them and meaning them."

"There's nothing else I have to do? No ritual, no spell?"

Phyllida laughed. "The world is not so complicated as all that, child. Magic, the best kind anyway, doesn't need all that gobbledygook. Your own oath binds you more strongly than chains of steel or magic. Your will can work more wonders than any Latin chant or dancing in a circle widdershins. If you go to the Green Hill with a certain heart and speak, it will hear, and from that time on, no one else can be Guardian of the Green Hill until such day as you pass it to your own daughter . . . or great-great-niece, though if you don't mind me saying so, I hope you'll have a bountiful clutch of chicks."

Meg blushed.

"This is not something to be entered into lightly," Phyllida continued more gravely. "It is a lifetime of work, of joy but also pain, and you know enough of the world now to understand that the joy is overlooked and forgotten all too quickly, while the pain lingers fresh. Are you sure, Meg, that you give yourself freely as the next Guardian of the Green Hill and all its inhabitants?"

She didn't let herself think. She'd decided her course and wouldn't falter. "I'm sure. Tomorrow at dawn I'll go to the hill and let them know. I just hope . . . I hope there's time." It was the closest she could get to speaking of Phyllida's fate.

"Oh, my dear, you don't know how happy you've made me. Before I even met you, I had visions of this moment. I almost gave up hope."

She was interrupted by Rowan strutting in with mud on his

boots. "You should see the kennels, Lysander," he said cheerfully, oblivious to the heavy mood. "Diana's whelped, six of the most perfect little foxhounds you've ever seen. When the Master of the Foxhounds gets a look at them, he'll dance a jig."

Silly, who had gone through both a pirate and a motorcycle-gang phase and was forgiving of other people's eccentricities, ignored his squire act and said, "Meg's decided to be the next Guardian."

"Jolly good," Rowan said, swinging his walking stick. "I ought to mind, but you're right, that sort of thing is better left to girls. You have intuition and sensitivity and all that. You attend to that part of it, and I'll take care of the rest." Imagining himself heir, he had done a lot of thinking as he surveyed his estate. Yes, the fairies were interesting, but he hadn't had very good luck with them so far, and they didn't hold his interest like the Rookery and the grounds and the tenants themselves. He was already making plans for expanding the stables and adding emergency sprinklers in case of fire. Even the greed he'd felt under the fresh effects of Gwidion's spell had vanished. Of course he must have all the money associated with the estate. How else could he keep things maintained and repaired? But his desire for the money now was only practicality, not avarice.

"Next order of business," he said, a phrase that astounded them. "James. As head of the household, I am responsible for all my siblings, and as the spare heir, as it were, James is important. Meg, what have you done so far to get him back? All very good to have a test for you, but enough's enough."

"Me? I haven't done anything. Phyllida and Lysander have

been doing it all." She turned to Phyllida, who was making desperate shushing motions to Rowan. "Now that things are . . . different . . . I really should help. I don't know how much time you'll have. Wait . . . test? What test, Rowan?"

"Oh, don't worry about them. It's all up to you. You know, the test for the new Guardian. Someone you love gets taken by the fairies, and you have to get him back all by yourself. I really think you'd have been better served working on that than going off to the fair." He turned to Phyllida, who was already starting to hyperventilate. "I know there's supposed to be secrecy and all, but I plan on running things with efficiency. It's high time Meg stepped up to her duties if she really means to take them on. I'll need the help."

Meg didn't understand half of what Rowan was saying, but she zeroed in on the other half. "James being kidnapped is a test? For me?" She looked at Phyllida, not accusing yet, though Phyllida knew with heartsickening certainty it was coming. Right now, Meg only looked confused, still trusting. "I'll help. I wanted to from the beginning, and if that's what I'm supposed to do—"

Rowan jumped in again. "Not help, you nitwit. You have to do it all yourself. They haven't been doing anything to get James back. You were supposed to figure it all out for yourself, I think, but we're wasting time. The sooner we get James back, the sooner we can get to those drains at Gladys Gap."

Meg turned to Phyllida with hurt in her eyes, though Phyllida knew the hurt would soon be drowned by something much worse.

"Is it true?" she asked in a small voice. "You . . . you lied to me?"

"My dear, we had no choice," Lysander said.

"You always have a choice," Meg said, her anger rising. "Why didn't you tell me? I could have been trying, all this time. Instead I went to a stupid festival while James is alone underground. What if they're hurting him?"

"We did what we had to do, dear, and I'm sorry, but that's the way it is always done. When someone is chosen to be the next Guardian, she is tested, and the test is always the same. Someone she cares about is stolen by the fairies, and she has to get him back without help."

"But why?"

"I don't know. Perhaps it is so the fairies have a hostage. You will always treat them squarely if they have one of yours down below."

"Bran was your test? But you didn't get him back for seventy years, and you were still the Guardian."

"It's not a test you have to pass. 'Test' isn't the right word, I suppose. More like a trial, a tribulation."

"But . . ." She was wasting time on the particulars. There was something much more important. "You lied to me. You risked James's life, and you lied to me. You both lied! You lied! You lied!" Her voice was escalating, and she couldn't control what she was saying anymore. Just those two words over and over as she stared at them both with a hatred she'd never felt before for man nor beast. They were worse than Smythe, and she was more naive and trusting than Fenoderee.

She didn't cry. She had been stony when she heard Phyllida was going to die, and now in the face of this shock she was as steel, hard and cold. Very evenly, so there could be no mistake, she said,

"I don't care if you do die. I will never, never, never be the Guardian now. Not after what you've done. I hate you. I hate you both!"

She walked out and slammed the door, and if she heard a heavy thump and a cry of anguish, let us hope she thought it was only a fallen chair and not Lysander crumpling to the ground, clutching his chest. By the time Phyllida began screaming for a doctor, Meg was already at the edge of the woods on her way to the Green Hill. Rowan was right. It was time she took care of things herself.

He'll Kill You, You Know

"Silly, get Bran . . . no, he's had his sleeping draught . . . get . . . oh!" Phyllida knelt beside Lysander, crouching over him protectively as if the very strength of her grief could help him. He was pale as death, his breathing so shallow his chest barely rose. As soon as Meg exploded and fled, he'd started to his feet as if to go after her, then he suddenly clawed at his chest and throat, and fell heavily to the floor.

Rowan, with a presence of mind befitting a young lord, found a stable lad and sent him for the doctor. After he left, the others managed to get Lysander up to the sofa. His eyes fluttered and opened.

"My love, don't try to move."

"The banshee . . . ," Lysander said, and winced as a spasm went through him.

"Hush. Don't think of it. This is nothing. A little stroke perhaps, nothing more. Why, gaffer Hudson had six of 'em, and he can still shoe a mule faster than his grandson. Just rest until the doctor comes."

"I won't leave you alone. I'll try—"

She shushed him again as the others looked on miserably. They had no idea what to do.

"First Phyllida, now Lysander too?" Silly whispered to Dickie.

"He wouldn't want to live without her," Dickie said just as quietly. "Once he heard about the banshee wailing for Phyllida, the shock of it must have made him sick."

They milled around, wretched, feeling useless and in the way, but not wanting to leave in case they were needed.

"What if they both die? And Meg said she won't be Guardian. What will happen then?"

"Maybe you'll have to do it," Dickie said.

For once, the unflappable Silly was afraid. "No! That's Meg's place, not mine. I love it here, but I can't do that. No way."

Rowan came back. "That's it, I'm putting a telephone in here," said the lordling, though no one paid any attention to him.

At last, almost an hour later, Dr. Homunculus arrived. He took one look at Lysander and shooed all the children out.

Even though they were miserable with worry, Silly and Dickie took advantage of Dr. Homunculus's preoccupation to sit in his shiny red convertible sports car. Silly took the driver's seat and gripped the wheel the way she imagined a race-car driver might. The baby fairy uncoiled its clinging arms and fell with a soft thump into her lap, where it contentedly changed first to a white kitten with a pink nose, then to a wheel of cheddar, then to a fossil ammonite before resuming its usual shape. Like a human baby babbling or grasping at imaginary bubbles in the air, the fairy was practicing the skills that would serve him for the rest of his very long life. It took Silly a while to get used to the rapid changes, but he couldn't hold any shape but his standard one for very long, and she cuddled the pigs and potted geraniums and wombats just as lovingly as her fairy baby.

Dickie sat in the passenger seat and absently pinched the leather upholstery between his fingers.

"What are we going to do with the little fairy?" he asked. It was better than worrying about Meg. Or Phyllida. Or Lysander.

"I guess the only thing we can do is go to the Green Hill and demand an exchange. I bet they'll be so happy to get this little guy back—or girl, I didn't think to check, and I'm not sure if I'd know even then. Anyway, they'll be so glad, we won't have to threaten. They'd never believe it anyhow. I'd never ever wever hurt my widdle diddleums." She squeezed the fairy until he turned into a prickly hedgehog, then she had to make do with kissing its fuzzy white forehead. Dickie looked on, amazed. How had tough little Silly been replaced by this ridiculously maternal creature who spoke the foreign language of baby talk?

"Do you think we should look for Meg? She was pretty upset."

"Nah," Silly said. "She'll calm down. She's probably in her room, crying. You know her." Dickie did, and he didn't agree. "She'll forgive them in a little while, I know it. It was a pretty shabby trick, making her think they were helping, but they're like parents, always thinking they know what they're doing, even after you point out how silly it is. But now Meg has our help, whether she wants it or not. When we get James back, she'll feel better."

"Maybe we should find her and bring her. She knows the way to the Green Hill."

"No! I want to do this myself. With you too, of course. I can get us there. Won't it be a nice surprise for the others when we show up with James?"

Dickie still thought there was safety in numbers, but he shrugged, and they talked strategy until Dr. Homunculus came outside.

"What are you two whelps about? Out!" He spoke more gently than he would have if Lysander hadn't been seriously ill.

"How is he?" Silly asked as she climbed out, leaving muddy footprints on the floor mat.

"You leave him alone to rest, and he'll be just fine," the doctor said, and despite the recent demonstration, they never thought an adult would lie to them.

Rowan strolled to the keeper's shack with his hands in his pockets, whistling "Garryowen." He knocked and entered without waiting for permission, as befits the lord of the manor on his own grounds. Gwidion was standing at a large easel with a stretched canvas upon it. He looked up in alarm and tried to throw a sheet over his masterpiece, but in his anxiety not to smear the fresh paint, he fumbled and the sheet pooled at his feet.

"Oh, it's only you," he said. "What do you want, boy?"

Rowan took his time answering. What a different creature he was from the kind, simple boy he'd been back in Arcadia, or from the disappointed, proud, resentful boy after the Midsummer War, or the greedy pig he had been earlier. There was nothing acquisitive about him now. He took it as a matter of course that he would inherit the Rookery.

Rowan was in no hurry to answer. "That's a decent-looking picture so far. I don't like her expression, though. Very like her, true, but she looks too timid and weak. Phyllida's not that way at all. Listen, I want you to wait awhile."

"Wait for what?" Gwidion asked testily. He needed to work on his portrait, but it wasn't going as well as it had earlier in the day. His frustration over losing his captured beauty might have had something to do with it, as had his encounter with Finn. He didn't trust that boy.

"For making it official. My inheritance, I mean. I want you to wait awhile before you give Phyllida the portrait and convince her to make me her heir."

One aspect that remained of the original spell was Rowan's credulity. How else could he believe this stranger who had appeared from nowhere wanted to help him? How else could he believe Phyllida would make such a decision in gratitude for a gift she'd plainly said she didn't want in the first place?

"Yes, yes, whatever you say. As you see, I'm not done yet."

"It's because of Lysander, you see. He's not well, and Phyllida's pretty upset, so I don't think she'd appreciate the picture right now. When he's better, though—"

"Her husband's sick?" Gwidion asked, suddenly interested. "How sick?"

"The doctor thinks it's a stroke. He wanted him to go to the hospital, but the nearest one's twenty miles away, and Lysander refused. He said an old plough horse always stays in his traces."

"And Phyllida is upset? Very upset?"

"Well, yes, of course."

"Take me to her at once!" The sketches made that morning were good, but there was nothing like the sight of fresh tears to lend verisimilitude to his portrait of a weak and vulnerable old woman. Just a glimpse would give him fresh inspiration, and he'd spend the night in a frenzy of labor by candlelight.

"I don't think she wants to see anyone now."

"You defy me?" Gwidion bellowed, rising to his impressive height and pointing a bony finger at Rowan. "You gave your oath to help me . . . as I have helped you. Betray me now and I leave at once, and you will never get this Rookery you desire!" He rifled through a leather portfolio and brought out the drawing that had first captured Rowan. Its power was fading, but when the boy looked at himself on the page, the thought that anything might keep him from his beloved estate was impossible to bear.

"I'll take you to her, but I doubt she'll let you stay."

"Good boy," Gwidion said, rubbing his chin with paint-stained fingers. "By the by," he added, trying to sound casual, "have you seen that Finn today?"

"He was in the room when Lysander had his stroke." It didn't occur to him that Gwidion might want to know about Meg's fight with Phyllida, and of course he didn't know about the banshee.

"Did Finn say anything about me?"

"No. I didn't talk to him. Why? What would he say?"

"Oh, never mind, never mind." That was one worry eased. It was as he thought—that hateful boy had just destroyed his pictures out of spite, not because he had any idea that they were magic.

"Now lead on!" he said, and shoved Rowan out of the room.

Neither of them saw an eye-patched face peering through the grimy window, and they certainly didn't see a handsome black-haired boy unlock the door with a skeleton key and creep into the keeper's shack as soon as they were gone.

"Well, what have we here?" Finn said aloud as he surveyed the room. He stood with his arms akimbo in front of the half-finished portrait of Phyllida. At least, he thought it was Phyllida. The features were hers, but for the rest, it might have been an unpleasant joke. Half was in featherlight pencil sketching, half in oil paint, but he could see what it would look like when complete. The portrait's eyes were bloodshot and shone with moisture, the rheum of old age and tears of despair. The figure was thinner than Phyllida, almost frail, while the Phyllida of the flesh was robust for her age. And the mouth, though just sketched in at this point, quivered almost palpably on the canvas. One hand was held out as if offering something to someone. She looked old and weak, in body and spirit. This Phyllida would fold at any danger, agree to any demand forcefully made.

Why on earth had Gwidion painted Phyllida like this? A man off the streets with a magic gift of art had shown up from nowhere and wanted to paint unflattering portraits of the lady of the house, a stranger to him, who was kind enough to let him stay? If he could make magic with his drawing, why hadn't he used his talent for riches? Finn himself had only had his magical gifts for a day, and look at what they had brought him. True, the feathered hat he had bought was, on further reflection, too outlandish to wear, and the clockwork cricket broke the third time he wound it. But he still had his leather belt with the wizened little faces twisted into it. And he had his deerhorn pocketknife.

He took it out now, unfolding it with his thumb. "I never got to test the blade," he said, smiling to himself. "I don't even know if it's sharp."

He slashed the canvas, leaving a gash across Phyllida's face.

"Hmm . . . pretty sharp, but I'm still not sure." He sliced again, and again, tearing at the portrait until it hung in ribbons.

"I don't know what you want with Phyllida and her family, but you're not going to get away with it." That's what he said out loud, because it sounded good. But to himself he said, *That's what you get for hitting me!*

He found tubes of oil paints near the tattered remains and squirted them around the room one by one until the walls were as good as (actually, better than) a Jackson Pollock painting. Cerulean, raw sienna, viridian, and carmine flew in trailing squirts until every tube was empty. At last he took a tub of chalk-white paint and a wide brush and wrote across one paint-streaked wall in giant letters, I KNOW.

He paused. He wasn't sure how to finish the sentence. What did he know? Gwidion was up to something, that much was for sure, but exactly what it was he had no idea. Probably Gwidion wanted money, some exorbitant price for his work. That was as far as Finn thought, and content that he'd foiled his nemesis, he was satisfied.

"I know" would do just fine.

He looked around one last time to see if anything had escaped his wrath. He spied the leather portfolio and carefully unzipped it. Inside was a stack of papers, sketches. Some were of people he knew—two rough drawings of Meg riding in a carriage, a few of Phyllida, one of Dickie, Rowan, Meg, and Silly looking trustingly (and, he thought, rather stupidly) off the page—and some were of strangers—a man cheerfully serving what appeared to be a gourmet meal, a constable unlocking handcuffs, a tailor measuring a suit. He folded them into quarters and tucked them under his shirt. He only wanted the pictures of Meg, but he thought the others might come in handy to annoy Gwidion further. He was pretty sure the painter would pack his kit and leave as soon as he saw the damage and the ominous I KNOW, but if he stayed, the sketches might furnish some proof, of what Finn was not sure.

He opened the door and stepped right into the horns of a dilemma. Or, rather, of Pazhan.

Finn tried to slam the door, but the huge Persian billy insinuated his broad shoulder into the threshold and blocked him. His horns were as high as Finn's chest.

Unable to flee, Finn tried his old tactic of circling—he dashed behind a table and wondered how long he could hold his pursuer off. It wasn't any use with a goat, of course, and Pazhan leaped lightly to the tabletop and looked around at the damage.

"He'll kill you, you know," the goat said.

"I knew you could talk!"

"No you didn't, or you wouldn't have said that. If you were going to live long enough to benefit from it, I'd give you a lesson on the difference between being sure and being almost sure. But, as I say, he will kill you. Or more likely, have me kill you. His hands are dirty enough from paint. I'm sure he won't want to sully them further." Pazhan shook his head, tossing the heavy manelike mantle of fur on his shoulders.

"You're going to kill me?"

"If he orders me to, I don't have any choice."

Even the brownie wouldn't have had words of wisdom here. Most people have a choice, more or less, in everything, but not Pazhan. He was bound to serve each generation of Thomas men until such time as one struck him thrice in three days. Until his bonds were thus broken, he had to do whatever his current lord said, no matter what his own personal feelings. And however phlegmatic Pazhan may have seemed, he had strong personal feelings about a great many matters.

"Of course," Pazhan said wryly, "he can't order me if he doesn't know. I have to go tell him now. That's my duty, I know that much. But a simple goat like myself can't predict exactly what my master will order me to do. So no, best not to kill you now."

Finn thought that Pazhan winked at him then, but since the goat had one amber eye on each side of his head, it was a little hard to be sure. "Why, I don't even know where my lord and master is."

"He said he was going to the—," Finn began idiotically, but the goat blandly interrupted him.

"He could be anywhere. A shame that in my search for him the culprit—if indeed you are the culprit, for the evidence is only circumstantial—will have ample time to get away. Far away. Before my lord can give me an order I can't refuse."

"Oh," said Finn, who really wasn't quite as stupid as he looked at the moment, only a little frightened. "You're letting me go?"

"No such thing!" Pazhan said sharply. "But obviously I cannot both look for my lord and hold you here."

"Will he leave when he finds out what I've done?"

"If I can goad him in that direction, I will, but wherever he goes, I follow, and whatever he orders, I obey. I don't know what will come of this, but I do know that even without proof, if he spies you again, your life is over. Find someplace safe, human." He looked around at the destruction. "You've done a good day's work here. Perhaps it will be enough to change his plans."

Finn was too distracted to ask what those plans were. Happy to be given his life, he edged along the wall past Pazhan (still not sure it wasn't all a ruse to get his guard down), and with an eye on those wickedly sharp horns, he slipped out the door.

He had to find Meg. She'd know what to do. Up until her encounter with the bunyip, he'd still thought of her as a nice little kid (though she was not more than a year younger than he) but after that, he realized, as he should have sooner, that there was steel at that girl's core and a knowledge of things that were beyond him. He understood now that he was in a foreign land, completely out of his depth. He'd once thought England was a quaint version of America. Now he knew it was alien as the deepest jungles of the Congo. Meg, who had it all in her blood, could be his guide.

He knew where she must be. When she learned that her trusted great-great-aunt and -uncle weren't doing anything to find her brother, she must have decided to get him back herself. That could mean only one place.

He gulped and looked into the darkening woods. The sun was

almost down, and the sky's molten gold would soon be replaced by velvet black and stars; the hazy glow at ground level would become dim shadows that could hide anything. When he was younger, he was afraid of the woods at night because of the unknown dangers they could hold. Now he was afraid again because he knew some of the dangers.

With the threat of death behind him and Meg and the Green Hill beckoning him on, he told himself not to be a baby and in a moment was enclosed in the woods.

I found it once, he reasoned. I can find it again, and if I don't, I'll just walk through to the next village and keep going, all the way home. At least in the woods I'm safe from Gwidion.

He didn't know that the woods around the Green Hill have a way of eating people up, and if they choose to spit them out again, it may be a hundred years later, or in quite a different shape than they started out with.

He had no idea where the Green Hill lay . . . though it didn't really matter, because once the sun went down, he had absolutely no idea which direction he was heading in. There was hushed light from the stars and moon, enough to see by, but he couldn't get his bearings at all. Oh, well, he thought. If the Green Hill wants me to find it, I will.

Which is exactly how it works.

A nightjar on silent wings alighted on a branch high above him and startled him with its rising and falling *churr*. Far away, a barn owl answered with a call like a small animal screaming, and from much too close for comfort, a small animal *did* scream when a stoat caught a vole who was watching Finn pass. He saw none of the drama, but the sounds alone were enough to make him quicken his step.

It was slow going through the woods, but eventually he came to a trail, a rough winding way worn almost clear by fallow deer and the occasional bold poacher. Common sense told him no trail would lead to the Green Hill, but he couldn't resist the lure of an easier walk and followed it, telling himself he'd turn off any minute but never quite convincing himself it was time. As the gloom settled more heavily around him and the noises of unseen wings and feet got more ominous, he began to have second thoughts. He had no doubt Gwidion meant him violence, but he'd been a fool to fear for his life. Or had he? The man had come after him with a pitchfork. Finn saw a form scurry across the path and wondered if it was better to face the human among other humans back at the Rookery or the fairies all alone in the woods.

No, not alone. He heard singing in front of him, and it surely wasn't fairy singing. It was something about keeping your hands off Red-Haired Mary, sung very sloppily, off-key and with elaborate, inappropriate flourishes and the occasional hiccup. When the song came to its punchline, it was cheered with a high-pitched giggle, rather like a young boy laughing at a bodily function.

"Give us another!" cried a familiar childish voice.

The singer had just begun another ditty about taking a tramp in the woods when two figures burst around a corner into view.

It was Fenoderee in all his snouted, tusked glory. He had a heavy arm around his companion, whom Finn recognized as

Tansy. The mower was roaring drunk and still hard at it—he had a wineskin on a strap across his chest—and when he saw Finn, he squirted a swig neatly into his mouth.

"'Struth, a pirate!" Tansy said. "We're—hic!—far off course if we've come to the sea, my friend."

"It's not a pirate, it's my best friend in the world!" Fenoderee caught himself and looked guiltily at Tansy. "My other best friend in the world, I mean."

"'Sall right, piggie. Can't have too many friends. I know this chappie. He was with the little lady as tricked that Smythe proper. Any friend of hers is a friend of his. Hic! I mean, any friend of mine is a friend of yours. I mean . . . I mean something, truly I do." He swayed and would have fallen if not for Fenoderee's arm.

"We're celebrating," said Fenoderee. (He wasn't drunk, though he had a crusty white mustache from all the celebratory buttermilk he'd imbibed.) "My friend knows the most interesting songs. What are you doing out? Most people don't like the darksome times. They hurry and scurry and creep until they're safe in bed."

"I'm looking for Meg. She went to the Green Hill."

"Oh, I can take you there, lickety-split. It's just around the bend."

"Just up there?" Finn asked, pointing into the dark.

"Wherever you are, it's just around the bend. Come on, I'll show you." He took Finn's hand in his, exuberantly crushing it, and with Tansy in tow, dragged them along.

"Are you sure you should take me? I don't want you to get into more trouble."

"No trouble," Fenoderee said. "If you're not meant to find it, you won't, no matter how close I lead you."

But the fairies evidently had something in mind for Finn, for they soon found themselves among the brambles at the foot of the Green Hill.

Once, when Finn used the seeing ointment that cost him an eye, he could see the Green Hill for what it really was, a hub of life and power, throbbing as with the hum of a thousand cicadas, singing with the trill of a thousand warblers, a place where every clover held the wisdom of life and death, where the roots of the lowliest weed sucked up an energy that would inspire a man to greatness—great goodness or great cruelty, depending on the man. But unlike men, the weeds simply grew and enjoyed themselves, and became wise and powerful in their own weedy way.

Tonight Finn could only see what the hill wanted him to see—just a pretty mound under the faint starlight, with a girl perched at its crest like the pale risen moon. While his companions feasted on blackberries, Finn climbed to her side.

"It was here I killed Bran," she said without preamble.

"I wish I could have been there," Finn said.

"No, you don't. You wouldn't, if you knew what it was like." There was silence for a moment, and Finn didn't know how to break it.

"He fell right where you're sitting," Meg continued. Finn wondered if he should move. "And there was so much blood. Not on Bran—that was the odd thing. You'd think a man with an arrow in him would lose all the blood he had, but no, there was not so much. It was the others, the fairies all around us. Their blood was strange, and when it flowed, it found other blood and pooled, just like mercury. Not Bran's. His sank into the ground and was gone. The ground was hungry for it. This is a terrible place, Finn. Every seven years, it eats someone."

"But Bran lived," he pointed out. There was something that had been bothering him for weeks. "I'm sorry, Meg. About the eggs I mean. There was a lot I didn't understand then. About you, about your family, about the fairies. I just wanted to be a part of it too. If I'd known that those eggs held Bran's life and Rowan's, I would have given 'em back."

Easy to say now that he knew the consequences of his actions. If he hadn't forced Meg to show him the way to the Green Hill, spied on the fairy court for days, they probably would have let him keep his eye.

"You're a part of it now," Meg said, and sighed. "What a place this is! My baby brother stolen. Phyllida and Lysander liars. The whole village ready to trick poor, helpless fairies. Other fairies not so helpless, gouging out your eye. Don't you wish you were back in Arcadia?"

"Almost," he said, and proceeded to tell her about his vandalism and his encounter with Gwidion's goat.

"Another time I might worry about what he's up to, but not now. Not with James down there." She thumped the hill with the flat of her hand. "I don't even care about Phyllida. I don't ever want to see her again."

"What's going to happen to all this if you don't take her place?"

"I don't know, and I don't care," Meg said as meanly as she

could, though it mostly sounded sulky. "I'm going home as soon as I get James. The others can do what they want. Let her teach Silly . . . in the time she has left. Or Lysander can teach her. Or Bran. She'll love it. Not me."

That reminded Finn about his other piece of news, but he softened it to the point where he was almost telling an untruth. "Lysander isn't well. They called the doctor in, and they're making him rest."

"I don't care!" she said so defiantly it was obvious she did. "What happened?"

"As soon as you stormed out, he fell down, and we got him on the sofa and then the doctor came. I don't know what the doctor said. I was in Gwidion's house then."

Right when I left, Meg thought. That's my fault too. And Bran pushing himself to exhaustion because of me, and now in a drugged sleep. Even James is my fault. I should have known better than to leave him alone, though the others said they'd watch him. I knew they wouldn't, not really. Everything is my fault. All the more reason to leave now. I didn't know the Ashes a few months ago, except from a card once a year or so. Now Phyllida will die, and I'll be home, and I'll forget all this.

Turn tail, the brownie had said.

"But first I have to get James," she said, continuing her thoughts aloud. "Before the Midsummer War, I tried to get in, tried to get the Green Hill to open, but nothing worked. I've called and pounded and threatened, and no one answers. I don't know what to do. Phyllida said there's always some way to get a fairy prisoner back, and it's different every time. If I could just get them to open up, just see James, I know I could get him back. I'd do anything."

"I opened the Green Hill once," Finn said.

"What? How!"

He pointed. "Right over there was a rock, looked like any other rock, but it was a little lever, and when I moved it the whole hill opened."

"Did you go inside?"

"Yes, but just a few feet. There were columns, like marble, but they looked like they were made out of giant bones. It was dark, almost completely dark, but there was a swirling mist hiding something I could almost see. Then the dogs came."

"Dogs?"

"White with red ears. They chased me away."

"Nothing will chase me away if I get in!" Meg insisted. "Now, show me the rock."

He found it easily enough, but no amount of manipulation produced any result. Finally Meg scooped it up and threw it into the brambles. It hit Fenoderee on the head, but whether because his skull was tough or because she threw like the proverbial girl, he took it as a friendly way to get his attention.

"Fenoderee, can you get inside the Green Hill?"

"Sure," he replied.

"Will you let me in? Please?"

"I have to wait another hundred years or so. And a day. I can never forget the day. Then I'd be happy to." His entire face was smeared with blackberry juice.

"Oh," she said. "Never mind. I have to get in now."

"If you had a key, you could let yourself in," Fenoderee said, doing his best to be helpful.

Gee, thanks, Meg thought, but Finn said, "Wait a minute. . . ."

Why didn't I think of it before? It's not a lock, exactly, but it wouldn't hurt to try, would it?"

"What do you mean?"

"The skeleton key," he said proudly, pulling the bag open. It was a pain to lug around, but he'd known it would be useful. "Excuse me, but would you mind opening this hill for us?" He tipped the bag over, and the hand crawled out.

It glanced over its shoulder at Finn (that is, if a hand could glance, or had a shoulder) as if to ask him, Are you he sure?

"Please. Meg has to get in. It's very important."

The hand loved a challenge, and though the stakes were high, it figured nothing much worse could happen to it. It had already been severed from its body (which was long dead). The fairies might be angry, but there wasn't much more they could do to it. It didn't even have any fingernails left to pull out, or jab bamboo slivers under. It cracked its knuckles, crept around the base of the hill looking for a likely spot, and set to work. It fiddled with some stones, bent a few leaves, then plunged itself into the soft earth and quivered. When at last it pried itself free, there was a low rumble and the dirt where it had been collapsed in on itself in a circle, exposing a low tunnel.

"But where's the arch?" Finn asked. "The columns?" He bent low and peered in, but saw only darkness and dirt. "We can't go in there. We'd hardly fit, and the thing would cave in on us. It's a trap."

But Meg's feet were already disappearing inside.

Why Are You Showing Me This?

"Do you have any idea where we are?" Dickie asked.

Silly set her jaw stubbornly and said, "We're almost there." They had been wandering the woods for three hours.

They'd set out confidently enough. "Meg can find the Green Hill whenever she likes, and I'm sure I can too," Silly assured him, and she'd blustered like a bear through the forest, not looking for trails, not paying any attention to her direction, just knocking aside vines and stepping on late violets, relying on instinct to guide her. Every animal that could move faster than a slug fled from the great crashing monster who invaded their home, and Dickie (and the Wyrm) followed sheepishly in that young juggernaut's wake.

"We certainly won't catch them by surprise," Dickie said early on, when he still had some hope and fight left in him.

Now, his legs aching and scratched by thorns, he moped silently on behind her. He'd have headed home if he'd had any idea where home was. He even asked the Wyrm, who replied that, alas, he could only navigate by the stars in the southern hemisphere.

"If it pleases you, I'll brush up on my celestial navigation when we get home. Much though I loathe adding to the store of knowledge I am so earnestly endeavoring to forget."

"Fat lot of good that'll do us. We won't ever get home," Dickie grumbled. "You might as well get used to living in the woods."

The Wyrm, alarmed, longed aloud for his comfortable library and promptly went to sleep, on the theory that when he woke up, things might be better, and if not, at least he would have missed a few hours' unpleasantness.

Silly stopped abruptly and glared at the encircling trees as if they were her mortal enemies. "Don't you have any idea where to go, you silly little thing?" she asked her baby fairy fondly.

The fairy turned into a fat pink dahlia, then a spider monkey, then a blue-tongued skink before nuzzling Silly's ear, cooing, and following the Wyrm's example. "That's all right, darling," she told it, kissing its green forehead. "I don't really want to give you back anyway." She pressed onward, hoping for the best, and Dickie followed.

In the end it was Silly who called the halt. "I'm not giving up," she said adamantly. "But it's almost midnight, and I admit I'm a little lost. Just a little. I know the Green Hill's over there some-where." She made a vague gesture into the blackness. "Still, at this point we might as well wait till morning. I'm going to sleep here. Once the sun's up, I'll be able to find our way."

Since he didn't have much choice, Dickie lay down near her in a hollow of moss and fern. It was more comfortable than that bed of pine boughs survivalists are always encouraging you to make, but just barely. Bugs, sensing their warmth, came eagerly from the moss and sought out their crevices. Dickie eventually stopped scratching long enough to fall asleep, but not before he heartily wished himself back in Arcadia.

I'm not going in there, Finn told himself as Meg's heels disappeared into the crumbling hole. No way. Nothing doing.

And so he was as surprised as anyone to find his own head plunged into the earthy den as he crawled after Meg. While his mind urged him to worm his way backward before it was too late, his arms and legs kept pulling him deeper.

There was no light past the first few feet. "Meg, wait for me!" He grabbed her by the foot and shouldn't have been surprised that she kicked like a mule—who wouldn't after being unexpectedly grabbed belowground?

"You should go back," she said.

"I know I should, but I'm not."

"This isn't your problem. James is my brother. I'll take care of it."

If he'd been gallant, he would have said, *And I'll take care of you*. But his thoughts hadn't gotten nearly that far, and he only knew he was going with her whether she or, more to the point, he liked it or not. All he said was, "If you're gonna go, then go," and gave her sneakered foot a shove.

At the mouth the tunnel was big enough that if they wanted to have very sore backs, they could have walked in a deep stoop. But as they progressed, it narrowed by almost imperceptible degrees until Finn could feel the dirt scraping his back even though he was crawling. It was warm, too, even warmer than the summer night air outside. The earth around them was just about body temperature, and humid, so they felt like they were inside a living thing.

"It's getting too narrow," Finn said, but he wasn't sure if Meg could hear him. Meg, slightly smaller than Finn, was having an easier time, and she pushed on. Finn had to drop to his elbows in a military crawl.

"This is ridiculous," he said as he wormed blindly forward. "I'm going back." But he only said it in hopes that she'd go back herself. It suddenly occurred to Finn that he might not be able to reverse course if he tried. He made an experimental wiggle and all of his bones seemed to bite like backward-curving viper teeth into the earth, holding him snugly in place.

Meg crawled on as if she were deranged. Her love and anxiety for James combined with her rage over Phyllida's lies and her own guilt about not doing something herself sooner spurred her on to bravery. Perhaps she had been brave before in the Midsummer War and when facing down Smythe, but confronting a known danger in the open air is a very different thing from plunging yourself into what is practically a tomb. Though she wasn't positively phobic, she didn't like tight spaces. And indeed, the air itself was getting tighter. Eventually she too had to drop to her elbows and squirm her way forward, and it felt like the weight of all the dirt above her was crushing down on her back, choking the life out of her. The air was dank and rotten; the hole got tighter and tighter. She heard Finn say something behind her, and though his words were muffled, she knew he was saying exactly what any half-sensible person would say at that moment: "Let's get out of here before it's too late!"

At last she could go no farther. Her questing hands and then her forehead bumped solid dirt. They'd reached the end of the tunnel.

Panic filled her. She was held so tightly in the earth's embrace that she could barely move, otherwise she would have flailed and kicked her feet. She felt she couldn't even scream. Her face was pressed against a wall of dirt, and every exhalation echoed back to her. There wasn't any air! She was breathing her own air over and over again, and the tunnel would collapse behind them, and they would die suffocated and crushed and alone so far beneath the hill that no one would find them, and worms would eat them!

Then a hand wrapped itself around her ankle. If he said anything, she couldn't hear it, but that simple human touch reassured her just enough that she discovered she could breathe after all.

Who must do the hard things? She who can. Meg made mole-paw scoops with her hands and started to claw at the wall of earth. Madness, she told herself. You'll pull the whole thing down on our heads. But still she dug. This was the Green Hill, *her* Green Hill, her heritage and birthright. It might make the way hard, but it would let her inside in the end.

She scratched and scraped until a piece of the wall crumbled. Behind, the earth was softer and she squirmed her way through. There wasn't a tunnel anymore, just the hole made by Meg's body. Dirt forced its way into her mouth and even into her eyes, which against all reason she couldn't help but open periodically to check for light. And then there *was* light, tiny pinpricks like Finn had seen when she kicked him in the head. Winking diamonds whirled around her as she forced her way forward one last foot. Then she was free—or her head was—and she pulled the rest of her body out and shook herself like a dog. She gulped several deep, relieved breaths before she remembered Finn. She threw herself back on her belly and thrust her hands into the dirt. Fingers twined around hers, and between her strength and Finn's frantic kicks, he was hauled out of the ground.

He lay stunned, weakly wiping the dirt from his good eye and from behind his eyepatch. When he could see, he said, "This isn't the Green Hill I saw."

"Me neither," said Meg, who had only glimpsed it from the outside.

They were in a cave of sorts, lit by twinkling rocks in the walls and the soft reflection of glowing grubs that clung to the stalactites. Nothing in it looked man- or fairy-made . . . and yet it wasn't quite natural either. It was like a movie set: not a real cave but an almost-too-perfect representation of a cave created just for them. The rock walls were molded to look perfectly natural, the glowworms placed with careful randomness. Even the steady drip-drip of mineral-rich water from stalactite to stalagmite sounded with artificial precision.

"Hello!" Meg called, and her voice came back in ever fainter echoes, *hello-hello-hello.* . . . Where was Gul Ghillie? Where was the Seelie queen? The fairy kingdom was supposed to lie beneath the Green Hill. Bran had told her about the feasts, the dancing, the lovely fairy woman who had held him seventy years away from his family. Where were they all? More important, where was James?

"Let's go," Meg said.

"Go where?"

They were in a large cavern that branched out into various passageways. They couldn't see very far down any of them.

Meg shrugged. "I don't think it matters. We found this place. We're bound to find something."

Again, the impossibility of going back propelled Finn forward, and he followed Meg as she chose a corridor.

"There are bats, so there must be another entrance," Meg said, pointing to dim flying shapes above their heads. That was a momentary relief . . . until one of the bats swooped closer and they saw it was dark bloody purple and slimy, with a frog's face and a long, trailing tadpole tail. Like many cave dwellers, it had no eyes, so it flapped along with its mouth gaping open, tasting the air to find its direction. It bumped against Meg then swooped back to lick her on the arm, its tongue leaving a slime trail. It flew up to its cavemates, and they all touched tongues to talk about the new creature in their lair.

Meg and Finn were walking downhill, and before long they heard the trickle of water. Meg fell on her backside and was sliding down the chute before she'd quite placed the sound. Finn, finally deciding that he absolutely, positively wouldn't follow her this time, lost his footing as he scrambled back and tumbled down the chute. He landed on top of her in a pool of frigid water, and they both went under.

On the downside, the water was just a little above freezing.

On the plus side, the pool was lit from within by a strong glow that illuminated the whole cavern, and when they sputtered to the surface, they could clearly see each other's teeth chattering and their skin turning blue and goosefleshy. The pool was waist deep, shimmering silver. They couldn't see their own legs, but there were other things swirling in the water that Meg desperately hoped weren't alive.

They weren't, at least not yet.

Looking down, Meg saw people dressed in styles she had never seen. They walked in tight packs through a cityscape, and though it wasn't a place Meg recognized, it didn't immediately strike her as odd or ominous. Skyscrapers reflected each other grayly in polished windows, and cars—again, just a little different from any she'd ever seen—flew by. First she thought she was looking through the water to some realm beneath it, but when she moved and the ripples distorted the image, she realized it was a picture in the water itself. More people and different cities appeared, and it was a long while before she realized what disturbed her about the scenes: there was nothing green in them, nothing living besides the people. Every metropolis she'd ever seen had a tree or shrub planted in a preserved square of soil, clinging to life amid the smog. There should be rooftop gardens, flowerpots on windowsills. And pigeons—is there a city in the world without pigeons? In these places there was nothing but teeming humanity. She touched the icy surface with her hand, and the scene changed.

Now she saw men in military dress, soldiers with straps around their waists and thighs and chests, all holding weapons. They were running in loose formation toward... "Oh! Look!" She pointed, and the second her fingertip touched the water, the scene changed again, but she knew what she'd seen. The soldiers were about to engage an army of half-man, half-horse warriors wielding bows and lances. Men were fighting centaurs.

Another image rose from the silvery depths, a hairy, child-sized creature on two legs running for the safety of a forest while teenage boys chased it with rocks and chains. His legs were too short, they were gaining on him . . . a rock struck his head—

"No!" she cried, and touched the water again.

It was a seashore under moonlight, calm at high tide, and Meg let out the breath she'd been holding. She let the peace of the scene soothe her . . . then the tide started to ebb, revealing the mangled corpses of mermaids and mermen on the shore, their long hair flowing back and forth in the bloody waves.

Meg slammed the pool with both her fists. "Why are you showing me this?" she yelled. In answer, the water started to drain. With a whine and then a great sucking sound, it turned into a whirlpool, and Meg and Finn searched the cavern for any means of escape. But the chute that had brought them there was too steep and slippery with mud for them to climb, and the walls had no handholds. They watched, helpless, as the whirlpool widened, felt the sucking against their legs. At the end, they clung to each other as they were pulled under in a swirling mass of pressure and bubbles.

I'm dying, Meg thought as the freezing water enveloped her. *Maybe the banshee wail was for me. Maybe . . .*

But then the vortex spit them out, and they were warm and dry and standing in the middle of a massive, ring-shaped banquet table. Members of the Seelie Court were seated around the table, dining on savory delicacies from plates of gilded porcelain. At one end of the table, Meg saw a whole cooked peacock with its feathers cleverly reattached; a roasted black swan with its wings spread was at the other. A piglet lounged on a silver tray with a pomegranate in its mouth, and a crispy duck led a clutch of equally crispy ducklings around a jellied orange pond. There were cakes and sweets, marzipan mushrooms and chocolate forget-me-nots on spun-sugar stems.

All around was the gay, lively chatter of the diners at the table, and in the center with Meg and Finn, dancers moved in light, precise steps and servants (as finely dressed as their masters) carried trays laden with yet more exotic comestibles. She heard piping and fiddling and, beneath it all, a mournful bass continuo from something that sounded like a cross between a bagpipe and a harpsichord. Someone was singing a song that didn't seem to go with any of the three or four distinct melodies floating through the air.

No one noticed Meg and Finn, or if they did, they were so accustomed to people appearing from nowhere that they took it for granted. A saffron sash floated across Meg's face, and the owner, a willowy dancer in orange and gold gauze, murmured an apology but kept dancing. When the veil lifted, Meg spied the Seelie queen and dodged between the dancers and servers to reach her.

She gathered her courage and drew a deep breath to demand her brother back, but before she could say anything, her words, then her thoughts, then her feelings themselves seemed to slip out of her grasp. Her white-hot fury toward Phyllida vanished. She hardly remembered who Phyllida was. Her fears about James diminished. Of course he was fine. Weren't they all among friends?

She stared into the queen's soft gray eyes and knew there was something terribly important she'd meant to say. Remarkable, she thought, how much the Seelie queen looks like my mother, though when she'd seen the queen last time, she'd had fair hair. *Illusion!* some voice in the back of her mind chimed. *Glamour! Fight it!* But the resemblance made her feel so safe that she didn't want to fight. Mother and home were all she was longing for, and now that she was looking into her mother's kind eyes, she forgot why she wanted them in the first place. Everything was going to be all right, she thought. No, everything already was all right.

She turned, feeling a tap on her shoulder. A lissome young man with auburn curls offered her his arm, and before she could protest that she didn't know the steps and had no coordination anyway, he led her into a quadrille.

The first thing she noticed was that her nails were clean. She followed the line of her arm from her escort's shoulder to her own and found no trace of her journey through mud and worms and water. Instead she found a flowing dress in shell pink, studded with carved coral, skirts and overskirts and underskirts and petticoats in such profusion that she wondered with a giggle if her legs were still under there.

"I'm so glad we make you happy," her partner said wistfully, and as the music changed, he whirled her to another man, who took her hands and bowed before turning her back over. They formed a line, men on one side, women on the other, and partners danced between them to cheers. Meg saw (with the only twinge of real feeling since meeting the queen's eyes) Finn leading a pretty milk-white creature clad in emerald silk in sashaying steps down the gauntlet, and he didn't even look at Meg. Then she was back in her handsome partner's arms, held close as her feet magically followed the intricate steps.

All was color, all was sound, blending so the dark violet of her partner's eyes hummed a cello baseline to the tinkling of the ruby jewels at his throat, and the piper's melody floated across her eyes like bluebirds. She felt weightless, tireless, but so parched. When the music ended, she would have to get a drink. But the music never ended, and she whirled first with her partner, then another, an older dashing fellow in black, then someone she thought was the prince himself, her friend Gul Ghillie in his other form, laughing, panting, joking along with the fairy court.

At last at the end of the wild dance, someone whirled her into another man's arms. She leaned against his chest for a moment, resting and laughing to herself at nothing in particular, and when the music resumed—a slow waltz—she looked up to find it was Finn.

Perhaps they heard different music from those around them, for they moved as if they were underwater, while everyone else twirled in a frenzy. Meg tried to say something to him, but her voice sounded very far away, and he just smiled and shook his head. When the tune changed again, he would have pulled her deeper into the heart of the dancers, but her dry throat cried out for relief and she signaled to one of the servants, a handsome, sturdy woman in dark red. She took a jeweled goblet and handed one to Finn. They pledged each other with their eyes and raised the glasses, secret smiles on their lips. Then a hand shot between them, the goblets fell with a clatter, the burgundy nectar inside splashing oblivious dancers, and the servant said, "Are ye daft? Din't yer ma teach ye better than that?"

It all came rushing back to her: James, Phyllida, the Green Hill, her journey below. Her hand flew to her mouth as she remembered what would happen if she tasted one drop of fairy food. She peered around her. The dancers were still whirling, but they were different. If she didn't look too closely, they were still lords and ladies of the Seelie Court. But if she managed to focus on one of the dervish figures, she saw a hoof, or a tail, or a withered hand, or a face like a fish with one round eye. The colors changed too. At the edges of her vision, they were still shining metals and flashing jewel tones, bright silks and deep brocades, but there was a gray tinge to everything now, a misty haze as if the whole scene was polluted somehow.

Finn tried to snatch another glass from the tray—he was more susceptible to the glamour than Meg—and she had to dig her nails into his wrist to make him stop.

"Hey, what do you think you're doing?" He jerked his hand away, and he was a grubby little boy once more. She looked down at herself and was a little dismayed to find she was muddy and sodden again too.

"Come with me," the servant said.

"I have to see the queen!" Meg insisted.

"Fool, do ye think ye can look at her again and not be ensorcelled? Ye're lucky I was the one serving drinks, or ye'd be stuck here like me. Not that it's been such a bad lot."

"You're human?" Meg asked.

"Aye. Now come. We have no time for this folderol. There's a lady as wishes to see you. Another human," she added with a wink.

They ducked under the round table. Beyond the gaudy hub-bub of the feast, the air was a smoky lavender. The festivities died away, and they entered a glade of fireflies and clover. Meg looked up but couldn't see a ceiling, only shifting constellations of lights that might have been stars or more fireflies.

The servant led them on again through a corridor that pulsed with a red heartbeat. They came to an arch with an obsidian keystone.

"My Lady Angharad, I have brought the children," their guide said, and bowed low before retreating.

The First Guardian

ANGHARAD...? WHERE HAD MEG HEARD that name before? They stepped tentatively under the arch and found a woman sitting cross-legged in an alcove that was draped in soft, spotted lynx furs. She wore a gown of rough green wool and had amber beads in her hair. She looked both young and old, and it was only after studying her for some time that Meg guessed she might be forty, though her cheeks were sunken with missing back teeth and her hair was thin.

She suddenly remembered who Angharad was. "You're the first Guardian!" she blurted out.

"Not the first," Angharad said, gesturing for them to sit. The pelt purred when Meg settled on it. "Though I do believe I am the first Guardian to be known by that name, to write down her memories, and so they honor me as the beginning of a long line. The first, if such she was, came thousands of years before my time."

"When was your time?" Meg asked.

"By your reckoning, a bit more than two thousand years ago." She moved a buff spotted fur aside and revealed that they sat on a darkly shining obsidian platform. "Look you here, daughter of my daughters, and also you, son who is not my son, and I will show you where you come from."

Two pale faces leaned over the volcanic rock and saw nothing more than their own reflections. Then shadows appeared and resolved into other faces, not theirs. It was murkier than the ice-cold pool, but overall more comfortable.

Meg saw forests, thick as the forests of Gladysmere but stretching from one end of the isle to the other, and in the forest were people, small, clad in skins, painted and tattooed. They hunted, they dug in the earth, they foraged for larvae and frogs, and they in their turn were killed by beasts and disease and starvation and other people.

"There was no Guardian then." Angharad's voice came from far away. "They took what they needed from the land, and the land took them back. Their lives were short and brutish, but they did not interfere with the Good Folk, and the earth loved them."

They vanished, replaced by other taller people clad in both leather and cloth decorated with quills and beads. They hacked at trees with broad stone axes, set fire to vast fields, planted, reaped, and ate the things they grew. Disease didn't touch them quite as frequently, and the children did not starve in the winter. Beasts killed them less often; other men killed them more often.

"When the first seed was planted by the hand of man, the ties that bind humans to the earth began to fray. Man became a separate thing, and the earth something to be controlled, dominated. The fairies drew apart from man. It was at this time that the conflicts began, when men harried the fairy folk and the fairies first made their mischief and took their revenge. There were people, those who stayed closer to the earth, who felt things others could not, who mediated between humans and the Good Folk. They kept the peace for thousands of years, though man grew farther and farther from his earthly roots."

The farmers vanished, replaced by others, also farmers, but with metal swords and armor, chariots, faces painted blue. They fought with men who arrived on ships.

"Then there came a time of great pain, when the magical creatures—nymphs and fauns, half-beasts and strange spirits and all the rest—were crushed and cast aside. They disappeared, killed or vanished, stolen or sleeping, neglected or unneeded, who can say? But the world became quiet and empty without them, silent save for the constant clamoring of man. Fairies were not quite like the other creatures. They were here first, of the earth, not from it. But I saw . . . my people saw . . . that the fairies would soon disappear like the others. I was a little girl then, four or five, youngest in a family of seers and shamans, those who walked with both fairies and humans."

Meg saw four women gathered in the heart of a deep forest. There was a woman, old and young like Angharad, standing with a younger woman and two girls, one about twelve, the other a small child. Around them stood the two fairy courts.

"We made a sanctuary for them," Angharad said. "A place where they could be safe among us, so we humans would not suffer from their loss. And we made a place where the fairies would be bound, so they could not smite poor, foolish man for the wrongs he has done. We cannot live without each other, you know, though we would fain destroy each other."

The old woman in the stone raised her arms, and the earth rose with them, the trees falling away as the tumulus climbed high and verdant above the woods.

"The Green Hill!" Meg breathed. She was witnessing its very creation.

The fairies sank into the soil as if it were quicksand, and then three of the women did too, leaving the girl-child alone on the hill.

A teardrop fell onto the obsidian, quickly wiped away by a bronze-ringed hand.

"I lost them that day—my mother, my grandmother, and my sister. They gave all their power to raise the Green Hill, to lay charms upon it to keep man and fairy safe."

She sighed, the pain of two thousand years past still fresh as a knife slice. "And so I was left alone. I became the Guardian, and I taught the people about the fairies for thirty years. I bore nine children. Four survived their first year. One lass was killed fighting the Romans. My youngest girl died in childbed, but my other two daughters learned all I knew, and the eldest succeeded me, as her child followed her, daughter to daughter, until it came to Phyllida. And then you. This I foresaw while I lived, and then when death was near, I entered the Green Hill to find my kin. They are not here, though I feel them all around me. I think they are part of the earth now, though that is small comfort for an old woman who still feels like a little girl and longs to have her mother's arms around her just one more time."

She sniffed, then composed herself. "This is your heritage, Meg. Now you have seen into your past. And you have seen what may be in the pool of possibilities."

"Possibilities? Do you mean that those things may not happen? I saw terrible things, cities that made me feel like I was choking, people being attacked, killed . . . only they weren't people. I don't want it to be like that."

Angharad pointed to the arched entrance of her alcove. "Look to the stones on the left. They are the past, the deeds that cannot be undone. Look to the stones on the right. They are the days to come, unknown, unknowable. Now look to the stone in the middle. That is the keystone, without which all other stones would tumble. You are that stone, Meg Morgan. All the past was waiting for you, all the future is depending on you. You have already wrought such change to this world that people will be astonished for generations to come. But what next, little one? Do you take up this sword you have forged, though it may cut your hand, though it may smite those you love? Or do you lay it down for some other to pick up and use as he will? The world is changing, Meg. The world *has* changed, because of you. You would like to undo what you have done, but you cannot. You would like to run from what you have done . . . and that you certainly may do. But would it be wise? Would it be fair?"

With those two words—*wise* and *fair*—she appealed to the keystones of Meg's nature.

"But I'm young. I don't understand all this. There must be someone who can do a better job."

"And many who would do worse. Will you take that chance?

If you are not Guardian, some usurper will take your place, and what will happen then? Remember what the pool showed you.

"You are so young, Meg," Angharad said, stroking her head. "Though I was but five when I took up the mantle of Guardian. Don't decide now. You shouldn't agree out of guilt and dread. Wait until you are sure . . . but don't wait too long."

"Phyllida is dying, isn't she? I heard the banshee wail for her."

Angharad looked at her in a way she couldn't interpret. "Indeed, the banshee weeps for Phyllida in a way. But do not think overmuch on that. It is yet another thing you cannot change, and why dwell on those when there is so much you *can* change?"

Meg took a deep breath, and the brownie's words came back to her again. Who must do the hard things? She who can. Once before she had taken a heavy duty on her own shoulders because she thought someone else wasn't suited for it. No matter how terrible the consequences, she'd had to fight in the Midsummer War to keep her brother from harm. Or was that really her reason? Was it because she knew she would do a better job, do the things he could not? The hard things?

"Phyllida has been a fine Guardian, one of the best, all things considered, but her time is passing. You have ushered in a new era, and your world will never be the same. Go now, and find your brother. He is safe . . . safer than you would be, if not for my handmaiden. To think the fate of the world turned for a moment on your dry throat!" Angharad laughed and covered her obsidian bier with the lynx furs. "You'll find him seated at the banquet table next to the queen."

"But I was there. I looked right at her and didn't see him."

"You looked at the queen and saw nothing else—as she willed it. All of this is glamour, all illusion. Don't forget that. Don't let yourself fall under their spell. Your bloodline—our bloodline— has the power to see things as they truly are. Thank you for seeing me. When I forget who I am, where I am, this place is a paradise. But when I fight the mist and mirage and am only my tired, old self again, it is lonely."

"I'll come back to visit you," Meg said.

"Oh, no, don't do that! You might not escape again. If the loneliness gets too hard to bear, I'll just go to the surface and have one last glimpse of sunshine before I turn to dust. But not quite yet. There are still a few more things I must do."

She shooed them out of her alcove to where her human servant was waiting. As they headed to the banquet hall, though, Angharad called Finn back.

"Poor Finn, you'll need as much courage as Meg. In times to come, you will do a great evil, for a good cause, and the world will despise you for it, though you are their salvation. You will be reviled as a traitor, a criminal. But Meg will know the truth of it. That must be your comfort. You will have no other."

And with these cheering words of farewell, she sent him to join Meg.

"What did she say?" Meg asked, to which Finn wisely replied, "Nothing."

This time when Meg regarded the merriment in the feast hall, she forced herself to see the truth (which then, as in most cases, was simply a matter of will). The table was there, with some people seated and others dancing, but the entire character of the scene had altered. There was a deathly pallor about the place now, in the mist that once glowed silver but was now an ugly gray, in the faces of the revelers, once so blithe and rosy, now wan and desperate. There were humans among them too, scrawny, sickly specimens who nonetheless whirled and danced as if they couldn't stop themselves. Meg saw now that the splendid food was no more than bark and toadstools, the cordial that had sorely tempted her was merely green stagnant water with a scum of slime on its surface. It turned her stomach to think how she had longed for just one taste of that nectar. And it frightened her, because if she let her attention wander just a little bit, the glamour fought to return.

It would be so easy just to let herself see the things they wanted her to see . . . or was it the things *she* wanted to see? A moment of weakness, and all her troubles could be behind her forever. No pressure to be the Guardian, no fears of the future. She would be young and beautiful forever, have the finest things, courtiers admiring her. *Just let yourself stay, Meg,* said a sweet voice outside her.

When she blinked, her vision blurred for a moment and she saw her first charming, handsome dance partner beckon to her, his clothes perfect, his face a delight. She took a step toward him, but at the next blink, her sight cleared and his face was waxy and artificial, his clothes ragged remnants of finer things, his enticing grin a lascivious leer. She backed away in horror.

To Finn it all looked the same as it ever had. The pretty girl in green (whom Meg, to her secret amusement, now saw as a little brown wrinkled creature with a face like a walnut) called his name, and the only reason Finn didn't fly to her side was that he was dwelling on Angharad's parting prophesy. He walked in a daze through the spectacle, oblivious to the food, the jewels, the music, under the glamour of his own fate, until they stood once again before the Seelie queen.

This time Meg saw James quite plainly perched on a tall embroidered tuffet at the queen's side. And he apparently saw her.

"Meggie!" he cried, and scrambled over the tabletop to throw himself in her arms. "Did you bring me any food? I'm starving! All these people eat is slime and dirt."

She laughed and whirled him around, squeezing him as tightly as she could to prove to herself he was real.

"Oh, my dear heart, I came as soon as I could. Are you all right? Did they hurt you? Were you scared? I'm sorry I didn't come sooner."

"I've only been here a few minutes. No time to get scared. Meggie, why are they all wearing leaves and rags?"

"You mean you don't see all the pretty clothes and good food?"

He looked at her like she was daft.

"Maybe you should be the Guardian," Meg said. He was apparently immune to fairy glamour. "But you've been here almost two days."

"Nah," he said. "I know it's just a few minutes 'cause when I got here I started singing 'Ninety-nine Bottles of Beer,' and I'm only down to seventy-three."

Which tells you something about time under the Green Hill.

"Now we just have to find a way to get you out of here." Meg glanced anxiously at the Seelie queen, who for some reason looked as lovely as ever. But the queen stared through them as if they did not exist. Apparently they wouldn't meet with any resistance from that quarter.

"We can just go out that door," James said, pointing. Meg saw that where there had been bare rock there was now a simple wooden door with a brass knob. "And can you hear? Someone is knocking."

Meg was a bit distrustful. She half expected to have to tunnel her way out, or fight a dragon, or answer an impossible riddle. A door? That's it? Well, she thought, perhaps I've done all I need to do down here. History lesson of the past fifty thousand years—check. Terrifying premonitions about the world's future—check. A reminder to not feel sorry for myself—check. James—check. That, she thought, about covered it.

She opened the door to gold-white afternoon sunlight, and as soon as they'd passed through it, the door was gone.

They were attacked by a young panther, which after a baffling moment resolved itself into a joyous Silly, who knocked them to the ground with her fierce hugs.

"I knew it I knew it I knew it!" she said, letting them go to do a little dance. "The piggie fairy told us you went inside and I said to Dickie well we'll just wait 'cause she's bound to come out eventually and I know she'll have James with her or she'd never come out and here you are!"

"What are you doing here?" Meg asked, scarcely able to see now that she was in harsh real light, feeling as if she might crumble to dust at any moment like Angharad.

"We had the baby fairy and Dickie wanted to tell you but I

didn't and I made him so it's not his fault and we came here last night only not really till this morning and we were going to trade our fairy for James but now we don't have to and I'm so glad 'cause look at him isn't he the most perfect little thing you ever saw?"

She might have been thrifty with her punctuation marks, but Silly could tell a complete story in a single sentence.

"It's afternoon?" Meg asked, though the position of the sun made it rather obvious. "It didn't feel like we were in there for more than an hour. I was going to declare myself as Guardian at sunrise. I missed it."

"Oh, you changed your mind *again*?" Silly rolled her eyes. "Are you still mad at Phyllida? 'Cause you shouldn't be if it's not really her fault, since everyone did it before her and she didn't know what else she could do."

When Meg sorted that one out, she said, "No, I'm not mad anymore. Not very much, anyway. James is back, so it doesn't really matter, and since I'm going to be the Guardian after all, I can't be mad at her, can I? But I swear, if I ever have a daughter, I won't put her through that. I will always tell her the truth, and I'll always help her, no matter what!" She stomped her foot and had no idea she would one day break her oath.

"Tomorrow, then," Meg said. "Tomorrow at dawn, I'll make it official. Right now I want to go home." And this time, when she said "home," she meant the Rookery.

As they started down the hill, they heard a low moan that rose to a keening wail. Meg grabbed the first hand she could find, which unfortunately was Finn's. She released it immediately.

"The banshee," Silly said. "We heard that last night when we fell asleep in the woods."

"No, it's not the banshee," Meg said, though the sound was, if anything, more mournful.

A ragged figure came into view, her clothes torn by thorns, her hair in matted locks. With her red hair loose around her face and her eyes crimson with weeping, she looked a great deal like the banshee.

"It's Moll," Meg said.

Moll looked at her without recognition. "Lady? Fairy lady? Do you have my Colin? I've come for my boy."

Meg felt her eyes grow heavy. Moll was insane with the grief of her loss. I have to do something for her, Meg thought. I'm not the Guardian yet, not officially, but this is what it's all about. What do I do now? I can't change the past, and I can't heal her. There's nothing for her but—

She had an idea. She whispered something to Silly, who pulled away, eyes wide, and said, "No! Please, Meg, don't make me! I love him."

"You know where he belongs, Silly. You can't give him what he needs. And you know she'll love him too." Meg held out her arms, and the little fairy crawled into them. She spoke softly for a moment, and when he understood, he changed. He grew bigger, to about the size of a one-year-old boy. His skin went from pale jade to pale tan. She set him down, and he tottered a few uncertain steps.

"Mama?"

Moll's hands went to her mouth, and she fell to her knees. The fairy, who now looked exactly like Colin, ran to his mother, stumbling over his pigeon toes, only to be caught in the most grateful and loving arms he'd ever known. "I knew I would get you back. I knew the Good Folk would keep you safe and return you to me."

"But you have to go under the Green Hill," Meg said. "There's no place for you here, but if you go below, you can be with your little boy forever."

She got to her feet and nodded. "Anything you say, little Lady, so long as we can be together. How do I go?"

Meg didn't know, but the Green Hill opened of its own accord, and without a farewell or a backward glance, Moll disappeared forever from this world with her baby at her breast.

She Can't Give You What You Want

MEG WALKED HOMEWARD with the others in autumnal peace. She felt older—perhaps she'd been longer under the Green Hill than she realized—and a bit sad, as if she'd set aside something she loved very much but could do without. You might call it her childhood, but despite the heavy times before her, she would be a child for years to come. It was the carelessness of childhood she'd left behind, the idea that no matter what happened, there was always someone she could run to who would make it all better. She felt very strong now that she'd completely made up her mind and the dreads and uncertainties had ceased warring with her duties and secret desires—for despite everything, she had always wanted to be the Guardian, even when she'd wanted to run away at the same time. What was once strife and opposition was now balance, and (she thought) the path before her was clear. Not easy, perhaps, but clear. There would be no more doubts.

Silly, irrepressible even in her sorrow at losing her little charge, skipped and cavorted in the afternoon haze, and Dickie kept up an animated conversation about Gothic architecture with the Wyrm. To Meg they seemed impossibly young and removed from the real world, Silly for her lively immaturity, Dickie for his immersion in the purity of knowledge. Only Finn, darkly brooding and abstracted, walking slowly at her side, seemed a fit companion for her mood. She felt very alone.

"I wanted to stay," Meg confessed. "Even after I'd seen through the glamour. Do you know, even when I was about to drink that wine or whatever it was, I knew in the back of my mind what would happen, but I didn't care. I wanted us to stay there. We wouldn't have had to worry about anything, ever again, because nothing would be real, nothing would matter."

"The easy way out," Finn said.

"Exactly. Because I think things are coming that I won't like. But I have to do them. *Someone* has to do them, and I'd rather it was me than anyone else."

Finn, understandably, didn't feel quite the same way. Better anyone else, he thought, than me. *You will do a great evil, for a good cause, and the world will despise you for it, though you are their salvation. But Meg will know the truth of it. That must be your comfort. You will have no other.*

He shook his head irritably and pretended to tie his shoe. What does she know, the old witch. Probably batty from spending two thousand years underground on a pile of rocks and old moth-eaten pelts. But he felt a chill through the blaze of afternoon sun, and hastened to catch up with Meg.

"Silly! I just remembered Finn told me Lysander isn't well. Is that true?" Meg asked.

"Doctor said he'd be fine," Silly said, saying what she believed.

"Okay, then I'm sure Phyllida can start to train me, before . . . Oh, do you think it's really true, about the banshee?" She had a quavering moment of self-doubt. "I don't know if I can do this without Phyllida."

"Oh, she'll be around for ages," Silly said. They were just in sight of the Rookery. "That banshee doesn't know what it's talking about, and even if it's true, I'm sure it won't be for years and years."

Meg was reassured because she desperately wanted to be.

They had grown accustomed to a certain bustle about the Rookery, for it is impossible to run such a large estate without a great many servants. Phyllida's and Lysander's personal needs were few, but the garden and grounds had a veritable army of caretakers, several gamekeepers looked after the pheasants and foxes, four capable men looked to the horses, and a slew of household staff kept everything presentable. It was therefore odd that no one was about. Meg didn't know that Phyllida had given the entire staff the day off.

Dr. Homunculus's red convertible was pulling away as the children came up the drive. He honked his horn, and they gathered around.

"Will you please talk some sense into that relation of yours?" he said. "This is the second time I've come today and the second time I've been turned away. Mr. Ash should be in a hospital, but I made allowances—he's old, there's not much more we can do, and he wants to be comfortable in his home at the end. But he still needs my care! Ye gods and little fishes!" He slapped his forehead. "I begged her, practically on bended knee, to let me see him, just to give him something to ease his discomfort, and she refused. Will you lot let me in? If I could just see Mr. Ash."

"Of course," Meg said. "I can't guarantee anything, and I have to respect her wishes—and Lysander's—but you can come in." In her newly accepted role, she knew she must handle things with grave calm, but inside she was quaking. Lysander's case was that serious? She might lose Phyllida and Lysander both, at once? How would she manage without them?

"I'm surprised Rowan didn't let you in," Meg said as she fumbled with the front door. It was locked. Where was Wooster? She saw Finn about to open his hemp sack for the skeleton key but shook her head, nodding to the doctor, and they went around back to one of the servants' entrances.

"That's the oldest of you lot? Didn't see him. There was a chappie in the window upstairs looked at me, a long fellow. Did Mrs. Ash hire a nurse?"

"I don't think so," Meg said. She felt a tug on her arm.

"I'm *hungry*," James said with emphasis.

"Okay, go to the garden kitchen and get yourself a snack—but no bowls of butter and no whole hams! Doctor, come this way up the back stairs. Careful, they're a little rickety." She led, with the doctor right behind her, Silly and Dickie behind him keeping up a chatter about the baby fairy, and Finn bringing up the rear. Meg took them directly to Phyllida and Lysander's bedroom, assuming they would be gathered there.

She walked in the door and froze, giving everyone behind her time to file obliviously in and be trapped in their own paralysis. Everyone but Finn. The doorway was too crowded, and he was out of sight just outside. Meg saw the scene in bits and pieces: the knife before anything else, double-edged, almost long enough to be a short sword, with a heavy golden split pommel of two outward-facing stylized goats. It was an akinakes, a Persian dagger, acquired at the same time as Gwidion's magical art. Then she saw Phyllida's throat, thin and pale with faint tracings of thick blue veins at its side.

Meg took a step forward, and the knife and throat came closer together, the point making a dent in Phyllida's skin.

"Hail, hail, the gang's all here," Gwidion said. "Close the door, or I cut her throat." Dickie, closest to the door, did so, casting a meaningful look at Finn, who'd gotten only a glimpse of what was going on inside—Lysander unmoving, eyes closed, on the bed, Phyllida in a chair beside him, Gwidion standing over her with a knife, the goat Pazhan at his side. Finn was sure Pazhan had met his eye, and he expected to be gored from behind at any moment as he crept back down the creaky stairs.

Gwidion glared at Dr. Homunculus. "Who are you?" he snarled.

"What the blue blazes is going on in here? Is this a joke?"

"That's the doctor," Phyllida said, her voice low and shaking. "Let him go, please. He's no part of this."

"And let him tell the world? First things first, old girl. Now that I have a few more bargaining chips at my disposal, shall we resume negotiations? I've been at 'er all day, Doctor—knife and fists and threats—but she's a tough old nut." Meg could see bruises on Phyllida's face and along her arms. Gwidion leered at Meg, like her fairy dance partner unglamoured. "Perhaps the sight of her pretty little Meg all sliced up will persuade her to see things my way."

"This is absurd," said the doctor, starting forward with more courage than good sense, but Meg intercepted him.

"Please, doctor. She's right. You're no part of this." She addressed Gwidion. "What is it you want?"

"The little snippet speaks? The heir presumptive? Well, I have a thing or two to say about that. Tell your aunt, or whatever she is, to name me her heir. If she doesn't, I'll kill her."

Meg, now preternaturally calm, saw through his bluff at once. If Phyllida was dead, she couldn't make Gwidion her heir. He must be after her money, and he's trying to convince her to change her will, she thought. It was a foolish plan. Obviously a will made under coercion wouldn't hold in any court.

So she bought time. Humans are strangely limited creatures— they can't fight, or do anything else really, when they're talking. (Except eat, which is rude.) And humans love to talk. They will take any opportunity to do so, even when it is not in their best interest. Meg took advantage of that now.

"What right do you have to get anything from Phyllida?"

"Who has more right than I, the lawful heir, Gwidion son of Llyr son of Llewellwn? Tell her, old lady, what right I have." When Phyllida didn't speak, he gave her a buffet on the side of the head.

"Now, see here!" the doctor said, but was silenced by Meg.

"Llewellwn Thomas was my mother's brother," said Phyllida.

Meg was already a little confused. She wasn't very good at family trees unless she drew them out.

"He thought he should be the next Guardian, inherit the estate in my mother's stead. He tried to take it by force and was banished. This fellow is presumably his descendant. Your cousin, of sorts."

Gwidion dug the knife a shade deeper into Phyllida's neck. "A sly way to put it, old hag. My grandfather thought he should be the next Guardian, eh? And why was that?"

Bitterly he told the tale of Llewellwn Thomas, eldest child and only son of Mahald and Bel Thomas, petted and pampered by a couple who thought they may never have the daughter they longed for. Not knowing what else to do, fearing the line of Guardians might be broken, his mother, Mahald, taught him all she knew about fairies, about the care of the land and the tenants. She led him to expect, naturally enough, that it would all be his . . . and he took to it, communing with the fairies as if it were the most natural thing in the world.

"Then the girl child came," Gwidion spat. "That urchin stood on the hill and told the world she would be the next Guardian. My grandfather strode up the hill, slapped her, and told her not to be such a disrespectful chit and go back to her governess. He was told he'd inherit nothing more than an annuity that would keep him from absolute poverty. All the lands, the money, and the amazing adventure and power that go hand in hand with the fairies would go to his sister, Agnes."

"My mother," Phyllida whispered weakly, and Gwidion cuffed her into silence.

"He was betrayed by his own family! He turned to the fairies, went under the Green Hill, and received his first taste of the dark ways, from the Host."

Heedless of the knife, Phyllida burst in again. "He was my mother's test. She should have left him there! She went after him, right into the hands of the Black Prince. Llewellwn emerged, Agnes was trapped under the Green Hill, and her mother was killed getting her back. It was all his fault!"

"That minx banished my grandfather, and all the villagers stood behind her, curse them. He was driven from his own home, his own birthright. All he had was his father's brownie. He never saw his home again. My home.

"But he planned his revenge," Gwidion said with the suppressed rage of three generations. "Though he never lived to carry it out. He went to the land between the rivers, and there met with a mystic who taught him to control the minds of men. He had my father, Llyr, by a dancing girl, and took him farther east to the high plateaus. Before he died, he told my father of his birthright, making him swear to return one day and take back what was his. And my father told me."

He bent close to Phyllida's face. "I would have done this the easy way. I have no taste for blood." He laughed at the lie as he pricked her skin and Phyllida whimpered. Lysander, in his sickbed, moaned and fluttered his eyes. "But someone thwarted me, and if I catch him, I'll peel the skin from his body. If I had finished my portrait of you, you would have agreed to anything, humbly and gladly. You would have offered me that girl's head on a pike if I'd asked for it. You are old and feeble—you long to turn the reins over to someone else. To me! Not that weakling of a girl. Make me the Guardian, and you will see how real power can be used. Give me control of the fairies, and no one on earth will naysay me ever again!"

Was he mad? Meg wondered. Well, yes, he was that. But more important at the moment, he seemed to have no real grasp what the fairies were like—or what it meant to be their Guardian. He thought he could dominate the fairies? Meg knew that to be Guardian was to be one of the most powerless people on earth, someone whose own wishes never came first, who was always struggling to stay one step ahead of events that were beyond her control. And this idiot *wanted* that?

But she could see that in the right hands (or more accurately, the wrong hands), the Guardianship could bring sinister rewards. If Gwidion became Guardian and allied himself with the Host, all that malice could flood the country, unchecked. And those other horrors she'd seen in the pool of possibilities—if Gwidion triumphed, would those things come about?

All this time, Finn had not been idle. First he ran to save his own hide (always his top priority), then he looked for help. Bran was his first choice, but though he shook him and slapped his face smartly, Bran only mumbled as he slowly emerged from his drugged stupor. All the same, Finn told his catatonic body what was happening before he went in search of other assistance.

He ran into Rowan just outside the front door. Rowan, dressed in hunting pinks, was dismounting from a fine bay gelding. "Here, take him," he said, tossing Finn the reins. "The local lads and I flushed a fox, a hefty dog-fox, but of course it's too early. Still, the puppies had a fine time wallowing in the scent. What *are* you going on about?" he asked at last, realizing Finn had been trying to tell him something urgent. "Gwidion stirring things up? That man's more trouble than he's worth. Don't worry, I'll take care of it."

"You don't understand! He's crazy. He has a knife, and Phyllida, and they're all up there. . . . We need the police!"

But if Rowan heard, he did not understand. He was still under Gwidion's spell, convinced he was the next lord of the manor, and acted accordingly.

Finn raced back to the house to look for servants, a telegraph, semaphores, any means of summoning help. He ran smack into a slovenly brown little man in rags.

"Damme, sir!" the brownie said. "If I'da had toes you'da trod upon 'em."

"Whoever you are, I need help. There's trouble upstairs in Phyllida's bedroom. There's a man with a knife, and a goat, and—" But the brownie was already gone. Finn scoured the servants' quarters, and when he found no one, at last decided he'd have to do something himself. He took an antique sword from one of the decorative suits of armor scattered around the house and headed back upstairs.

The important thing was to get that blade away from Phyllida's throat. Meg reasoned the easiest way to do that was get it pointing at herself. "You don't understand how it works, do you?" Meg asked softly. "There's no point in threatening Phyllida. She can't give you what you want."

"What are you talking about, girl?"

"You want the Green Hill. You want the fairies. She can't give you that. She already gave it to me."

"That's not true!" Gwidion looked nervous. "You told me so yourself, under my spell, and the hag confirmed it under torture. You aren't declared the heir. Only the current Guardian can do that, and she hasn't declared anyone yet."

Rowan walked in, cool and calm. "What's all this? I'm afraid . . ." He was about to tell Gwidion his services would no longer be required, but he was ignored.

Gwidion went on. "All she has to do is say it, say the words, and this will all be mine! The land, the title, the money, and most important, the fairies. She has withstood a great deal of pain this day, but once I go to work on you, girl, she'll cave quick enough. A few strokes of my knife and—"

A boy stood in his face, chest to chest, man to man, and slapped him with his open hand. "The Rookery, yours? How dare you, peasant! Remove yourself at once." Gwidion back-handed him with the butt of his Persian dagger, and Rowan crumpled in a heap. Silly rushed to him wailing, but Meg only used the distraction to edge closer to the door.

"Stupid boy! Another of my pawns, not so useful as I'd hoped. Now, where were we? Ah, yes, persuasion." He started toward Meg with the knife raised.

"You're wrong!" she cried. "I *am* her heir, the next Guardian, rightly declared. Phyllida can't undo that. There's only one way you can get what you want. Stop me from going to the Green Hill right now. Once I stand on the hill at dawn and accept my place, no one can take it from me, not even you with all your threats." She put a hand on the doorknob. "It's me you have to stop. Me you have to kill . . . if you can."

Gwidion lunged for Meg with a strangled roar. Then the lion couchant became the lion rampant—Lysander, nearly dead, half paralyzed by stroke and so weak he was barely conscious, threw himself at Gwidion. There was a flash of metal, a strange thud, a groan, and Lysander slipped on his own blood and fell to the floor. Still he tried to rise and held on to Gwidion's leg when the man went again for Meg.

Gwidion shook off the weak grip in annoyance. "Pazhan, kill him!" he ordered. The goat just looked at him. Gwidion punched him in the muzzle. "Do as I say, slave!" Pazhan lowered his great curving horns and charged.

Meg knew Lysander had done this so she would have a chance at escape, but she couldn't move. The goat capered backward on his pointed little feet, his horns dark with blood, and awaited further orders.

"The banshee! The banshee!" Phyllida moaned.

Meg stood paralyzed, staring at Lysander. Dead, he's dead. He died protecting me. It's my fault. Everything's my fault. In her mind, his body joined the dead mermaids in the surf, the little hairy creature hit with a stone, the centaurs with primitive weapons facing guns . . . all the images she had seen in the pool of possibilities.

Nothing else will be my fault, she decided. At the last second, she finally found the will for flight and ran out the door. Chase me, she begged silently. Leave Phyllida and the others alone and come after me. She didn't know if what she had said was true, if all she had to do was declare her acceptance on the hill at dawn. The important thing was that Gwidion believe it and come after her.

He was faster than she thought, and her head went back with a jerk as he grabbed her by her long, mahogany hair and pulled her off her feet. She saw the knife above her and closed her eyes.

"Fiddle with my family, will ye!" came a furious voice, and Gwidion was thrown off her. She was straddled by squared-off feet. "Go, lassie, and do what ye have to do. I'll see to the Lady." The brownie raised his fists like a bare-knuckle boxer.

"Pazhan, I don't have time for this. Take care of this pest, then kill the others—except for Phyllida, I may need her yet—and help me catch the girl."

Gwidion ran after Meg, just a few steps behind her, and the goat lowered his horns to the brownie.

"'Tis you!" the brownie said. "Ye always were a foul piece, goat, even in Bel Thomas's day. Get yer stinkin' bulk awa' and trouble us nae more." Goat and brownie closed together in a tangle of horns and fists bellowing and slamming from side to side against the walls as they fought. They bounced down the hall, one writhing, pummeling ball of fury, and tumbled down the narrow back stairs.

Meg came at a dead run to the broad, curving main stairs and skidded on a Turkish carpet. That moment was all Gwidion needed to gain on her. She tried to get up, but the carpet bunched under her feet and she only slid on her back.

"So much for you!" he said, and again the knife rose above her.

Finn, with wild bravery, closed his eyes and charged with his sword swinging. Alas, he had no practical experience in swords;

he only hit Gwidion across the shins, and unfortunately the sword was only a cheap decorative replica, so it snapped in two without doing much more than bruising Gwidion.

He slashed and cursed at Finn, who through no skill of his own, dodged the blow by fainting. Gwidion growled, torn between his two foes, and to Meg's relief, finally started back after her.

Meg raced out the front door, leaped the hedgerow and ha-ha like a horse in a steeplechase, and lit out for the woods with Gwidion, limping slightly from his bruised shins, hounding her.

In the Rookery, the brownie and Pazhan bellowed and walloped each other and finally tumbled down the stairs to the first-floor hall. The goat skittered on the marble and backed to the door.

"My orders were to deal with the pest, that being you," the goat said, rather more invigorated than put out by his battle. "Since I find myself unable to deal with said pest, I can't proceed to the rest of his orders—to kill the others. I therefore take my leave of you." He bent one leg and stuck the other forward in a sort of bow. "Mind the Lady," he told the brownie. "He may return, if your girl isn't as swift as she seems." He backed out of the door and was gone, following his master.

"I nivver liked that one," the brownie said, dusting himself off, "but 'taint his fault he's bound to a lousy master. It may be he don't care for it much himself."

Finn, now conscious but really wishing he weren't, came down the stairs. "What do we do?"

"I've done all I mean to do. The butter shan't churn itself." And the brownie disappeared.

With a heavy heart, Finn crept back to Phyllida's room . . .

where he was promptly knocked down by a very groggy and unsteady Bran.

"Whu . . . oh, it's you. Sorry, boy. Up with you!" He took Finn by the forearm and hauled him up, then sat down heavily himself.

Finn tried his question on Bran. "What do we do?"

"I stay here and guard my daughter," he said, "and help her mourn my son-in-law."

"Shouldn't we go after them? Can't we help Meg?"

"I may have the strength to guard a doorway, but I'll be no good running through the woods. Meg's on her own. She's a smart girl, and favored by the fairies. She'll make it to the hill."

"And then what? She won't be able to stop him just because she's officially Phyllida's heir."

"Then she'll make her way back here. She knows the woods, she knows the fairies. He doesn't. The fairies are on her side, as much as they're on anyone's side."

Finn couldn't believe that no one was going to help Meg. Silly was beside herself, crying over Lysander's body more loudly than the strangely calm Phyllida, while the doctor tried ineffectually to revive him. Dickie was no use, of course. Much as he hated to, Finn turned to Rowan.

"What do we do?"

"Well, first we call in the carpenter to check the supports, then the walls must be patched and repapered. And the funeral arrangements. The whole town must be invited, and—"

Finn did what he had always wanted to—he hit Rowan (not

too hard) in the jaw. "What's wrong with you? You're acting like some stupid lord when Lysander has been murdered and your own sister is about to be murdered too! You're acting like you're—"

Under a spell. Of course. He pulled the roll of sketches from under his shirt and found the one depicting Rowan. "There. Take that!" he said, and tore it to bits, breaking the spell.

Rowan looked like he was in physical pain. As the shreds of paper floated to the floor, he leaned forward, clutching himself as if he had a bellyache and moaning. He fell to his knees and pounded the floor.

Finn grabbed him by the shoulders. "Snap out of it! We have to help her. What can we do?"

But Rowan didn't know. He was disoriented and thoroughly demoralized, and some small part of him, a part that existed before the spell, perhaps, was still trying to calculate costs and timetables of repairs and funeral arrangements. He shook his head and turned away, back to the pitiful carnage in the room.

Finn paced angrily up and down the hall. He was on his own, and he had no idea what to do. What good am I? he thought. She's out there all alone with a lunatic and a goat after her, and I'm just scratching my head. Except she wasn't alone. The woods were full of fairies, and as Bran said, they had to be on her side. But did they know to help her? Did they know what had happened in the Rookery?

There was one thing he could do, though it nauseated him to even think about it, and he didn't know if it would help. He went to his room and groped under his mattress until he found a small glass jar. He held it tightly in his hand, almost as if he wished it would shatter and be useless. Then he walked to the oval mirror over his dresser and peered at his face. He thought it was a handsome face, even with the eyepatch. The pain of his half blinding was still fresh, and though the injury was mostly healed, his eye, or the place it had been, still ached at times, as if the absent eye were straining to see.

"Good-bye," he said to his reflection, and went downstairs to the part of the garden nearest the woods.

He took one last look around, at the vibrancy of the sky, bright blue to the east, clouds tinged with rose where the sun settled in the west. The foxgloves depended pinkly from their stalks, petal tongues sticking out at him from gaping petal mouths. He'd never thought much about pink before, dismissing it as a girl's color. Now that he might never see it again, he clutched it to him like a precious thing. Then he looked to the dark woods. Somewhere out there, the girl who had been a friend to him was in terrible danger. With a sigh, he unscrewed the lid and scooped out a dab of the seeing ointment Dickie had made for him when he was illicitly spying on the fairies. He'd stuck it away as a keepsake with no intent to use it—having lost one eye to the fairies' wrath, why would he risk the other? Now he resigned himself to the fact that he would be completely blinded for his crimes. His hand shook, but not enough to keep him from dabbing the ointment in his left eye.

He knew there were fairies everywhere in the region. When he'd used the ointment before, he had only to stroll in the woods to find all sorts of fairies going about their daily business, secure in the knowledge that they were invisible. He had to get their attention, and he could only do that if he could see them.

At first his eye blurred, and for a sickening instant, he was sure the ointment was cursed and he'd lose his sight immediately without even being able to do something for Meg. Then his vision cleared and he saw the world as it always was . . . except that where there'd been an inconspicuous dun-colored moth, he now saw a diminutive fairy painstakingly gathering buckets of pollen. She had a paintbrush and dabbed some of the flowers with the pollen she'd collected. (And you probably thought bugs took care of pollination.)

"Hey, you!" he said, squatting down to get to her level. She ignored him.

"Hey, I'm talking to you." He gave her a very gentle jab with his finger, though he miscalculated and sent her tumbling toes over wings into the mulch.

"You can see me?" the tiny fairy squeaked, fluttering herself upright on dusty brown wings.

"Yes . . . no, don't go!" For the pixie had tried to flit away into the foxgloves. Finn caught her in his cupped hands and felt her batting her wings inside, a ticklish sensation, and then one not so pleasant when she bit him on the palm. "Don't do that. I'm not going to hurt you. I need your help." He opened his hands a bit for a peek, and she tried to squeeze through. "Can't you change into something a little bigger? I don't want to hurt you." She wanted to hurt him, though, and bit him again, this time holding on.

"I'm going to let you go, I promise," he said, wincing and focusing all his concentration on not squishing his hands shut. "Just listen to me first. Meg Morgan, the girl who's going to be the next Guardian, is in danger. There's a man chasing her with a knife, and a goat, and I think they want to kill her. The man wants to be Guardian instead of her. You have to help her." He considered the wee fairy's size. "Or you have to find someone to help her." He thought for a moment. That nasty little boy who put his right eye out—Meg had told him Gul Ghillie was really a prince or something. Surely he could help Meg. "You have to find Gul Ghillie, or whatever he calls himself today. Or Fenoderee. Someone who can help Meg. Please." He opened his cupped hands, and she flitted just out of his reach, thumbed her tiny retroussé nose at him, and fled into the woods.

"Wait, will you do it? Are you gonna find him?" But she was gone, and he had no idea if she would deliver the message. Judging from her tiny fury and the swelling bites on his palm, he didn't think she would.

He crossed into the woods and looked for some other source of help, but the only other unnatural creature he saw was the lumbering Gooseberry Wife heading into the deep forest to spin her cocoon. He hailed her, but she just gnashed her teeth at him and heaved herself onward.

There was a slithering sound like a snake on dry leaves, and Gul Ghillie came into view rolling his hoop with that sharpened hazel stick whose point was the last thing Finn's right eye ever saw.

Finn backed away and held his hands up to his one remaining eye. "Please, I know what you have to do, but don't do it yet. Let me tell you something."

Gul Ghillie stopped, swinging the hoop hypnotically on his stick. "Well?" he said when Finn was silent.

"It's just . . . I wouldn't have done it if not for . . . I didn't mean any harm this time, honestly."

"Folk who say 'honestly' are generally being dishonest," Gul said, and twirled the hoop faster. "Out with it. I haven't got all day. What's important enough to lose your other eye over? Dying for another glimpse of the queen? Got a bet on with your mates?"

"No, nothing like that," Finn said, peeping out from behind his hands. "It's Meg. She's in trouble."

Gul cocked his head to the side like an intelligent robin. "Thought you hated all them Morgans. Heard you cursing the lot of 'em a time or two."

"Not Meg. Not the others either, really, I guess, but Meg . . . she's okay."

" 'Okay' won't save yer eye, boy."

"She's nice. She's nice to me."

"She's nice to everyone," Gul said.

What Finn wanted to say, if he looked into the dark chambers of his heart, was that Meg made him a better person. When he was with Meg, he didn't hate the world half so much, didn't think it was against him . . . and if it was, he knew Meg would stand between him and the world. He wanted to tell Gul that Meg was brave, that he needed her because he wasn't brave, except just a little bit, when she was there. He wanted to tell Gul about Angharad's prophesy, but he didn't dare. He even, had he but known it, wanted to tell Gul how Meg looked in the sweet-pea dress at the festival in the two minutes before it was ruined.

But all he said, sulkily and defiantly, was, "Just help her, would you? Take my eye. I knew what would happen. I just needed you to know that someone's trying to kill Meg so you can save her."

"And what makes you think we would save her?"

"She's the next Guardian. She's going to devote her life to keeping you safe."

The air around Gul Ghillie shimmered, and he was no longer a boy but a manticore, a portmanteau beast with the body of a red lion, a scorpion's tail, and the head of a man with a curled Assyrian beard and three rows of teeth. "What makes you think the fairies need a little girl to keep them safe?" he roared, then became Gul Ghillie again.

"Child," he said, and it galled him, coming from a boy his own age. "Your Meg, if I may call her that, can take care of herself. We knew of her danger. We have known it since Gwidion Thomas first set foot on this isle. We have known it since the first vine sprouted and climbed toward the sun."

"And you're not going to do anything?"

"What we will do has already been done," he replied, which made no sense to Finn and dashed the last of his hopes. It had all been in vain, then. He would be blind for the rest of his life, disfigured and alone, and Meg would die at the hands of a madman. There was one small consolation, though, Finn thought grimly: when Gwidion had finished with Meg, he'd return and put Finn out of his misery. That was something.

"Okay, then," Finn said with false bravado. "Get it over with."

Gul tossed the hoop high into the air. Finn squeezed his eye tightly shut. He couldn't help it, though he knew it wouldn't do any good.

The terrible piercing pain never came. Just to be sure, he kept his eye closed for about five minutes. That horrid Gul Ghillie was probably just waiting for him to open his eye. This is getting ridiculous, he thought at last, and opened it just a hair, then all the way.

Gul Ghillie was gone, and the sky was brilliant with the full pink of sunset.

Thrice in Three Days

YOU WOULD THINK THAT IN ANY RACE a healthy girl fleeing for her life with a sizeable head start would have no trouble eluding an almost middle-aged gaunt fellow whose only exercise is lifting his brush. But young legs are made for sprints, not marathons, and though Meg was fast enough, she was used to the mad dashes and frequent stops of tag and hide-and-seek and soccer. Then too, she hadn't slept the night before, and though her mind believed she had been under the Green Hill for only an hour or two, her sensible body knew she'd missed a whole night of sleep. Between that and her terror, she was nearly done in. She easily outpaced him at first, but she couldn't shake him. He kept after her with the same tireless, ground-eating half trot wolves use to cover vast miles of tundra.

It wasn't just a matter of beating him to the Green Hill. Now that Meg had a moment to think clearly, she realized that she had to keep Gwidion occupied until dawn. She couldn't lose him—if she did, he might make his way back to the Rookery and harm her family. But she had to stay out of his reach until daybreak. Only when she had officially declared herself the next Guardian would Phyllida truly be safe. Then Meg would be Gwidion's sole target.

It was just nightfall. That meant she had to keep Gwidion in the woods until about five o'clock in the morning. Already she was panting, and a painful stitch throbbed under her right ribs. She risked a glance behind her. He was just within sight. At least his goat wasn't with him. Meg stumbled to a stop for a blessed few seconds' rest against an oak tree.

She began to trot again, then suddenly there wasn't ground beneath her feet, and muddy water was creeping up her nose. Until she actually stepped in it, she'd had no idea that it was a pond. Flat coins of green weed floated at the surface, creating a solid-looking carpet that yielded and sucked her under as soon as her foot hit it. Slimy tendrils wrapped caressingly around her legs, and she sputtered to the surface, snorting out the foul water.

As she kicked toward the far bank, slick fingers grabbed her ankle. She thrashed hard with her other foot and struck some-thing fleshy and yielding. She turned, floating on her back and still kicking, and saw an almost-human face with a toothy mouth a foot across, framed by black algae-filled hair.

Jenny Greenteeth would eat anything that came near her stagnant pool, but her favorite food was flesh of the very young. Even Meg was a bit too old and tough for her gourmet tastes, but good meals were few and far between. She pulled the tempting morsel closer, hand over hand, the girl's panic adding relish to

Jenny Greenteeth's hunger. She faced her perpetual dilemma—little bites first, to make them scream, or one devouring coup de grâce to make the waters churn red?

Which is why there are far more alligators than there are Jenny Greenteeths. Alligators eat first and ask philosophical and epicurean questions later, so their prey rarely escapes. Gwidion, charging up to the pond, didn't see that his job was about to be done for him, only that his prey was in his reach. His long, sinewy arm reached down and plucked Meg out of danger. Jenny Greenteeth lunged and raked at the interloper with a clawed hand, catching him on the forearm, but was left with no more than a faint taste of blood. Swearing foul fairy oaths, she sank beneath the waterweeds, and in a moment, you couldn't tell either she or the pond was there.

Gwidion dragged Meg away from the bank and threw her down.

"I've worked my whole life for this, girl, and I won't let you thwart me." He stabbed downward but slipped on the dripping algae and sprawled on top of her. For a moment no one knew where the knife was or whose arm was whose, then Meg was on her feet again, squelching away in her waterlogged sneakers, with Gwidion close on her heels.

She'd half expected fairies to spring to her defense. Wasn't she going to be their Guardian, their protector, their advocate? The least they could do was turn her pursuer around on a stray sod or befuddle him with some glamour or trap him in a—

"That's it!" she said aloud with the last spare breath she'd have for some time. Now if only she could find it. She set off running again with new purpose, if not with renewed speed.

She shed her metal as she ran. First a little silver chain with a mother-of-pearl butterfly pendant, then her watch. It was very like Meg that even with a murderous man behind her she tried to toss them in conspicuous shrubs so, should she survive, she could recover them later. She did a mental inventory as she ran in what she fervently hoped was the right direction. She felt her pockets for any unknown coins and was relieved to recall her pants were a loose pale linen with drawstrings instead of buttons and zippers. It would have been awkward to shed her pants, but she would have done it. Otherwise, the oak coppice would tear her to pieces.

The old oak of Gladysmere Forest had been wise and happy . . . until one day two drunken men had a bet to see who could chop through the mighty tree first. It took them three days, and in the end the oak got its revenge. One man fell to his friend's ax, then the tree crashed down on them both.

But old oaks are hard to kill. In spite and gall, new shoots sprouted from the roots, and the oak was reborn a monster thicket of saplings with a hatred for man and the metal that had been its doom. Meg and Dickie had been stuck in it once, and it was only when they shed all metal that the vengeful coppice let them go. If Meg could get Gwidion to follow her into the coppice, he wouldn't be able to escape.

Meg had been through the forest on a number of occasions, both day and night, but navigating through darkness at a run is difficult, particularly when the price of slowing down or getting lost could be death. She jogged by a jagged alder stump that looked familiar and veered to the right past a cluster of faintly glowing mushrooms.

Ahead, she heard a sound like the wind through a stand of

bamboo, a grinding and cracking of wood on wood. There was no wind. The coppice, sensing their presence, was rubbing its arboreal hands together in anticipation.

"Oh-ho," Gwidion said from much too close for comfort. "So the vixen thinks she can go to ground. Well, my pretty, I'll find you, and when I do . . ."

She didn't hear his threat, because a voice rasped in her ear, *Hard metal on my bones, cruel metal in my heart. Cold metal severed me, and I will sever you.* Woody hands grasped her roughly by the arms and started to tear her in opposite directions. For the first second or two, it was actually pleasant (as is the rack, they say), loosening her ligaments and stretching her muscles like a good warm-up. *I cut you. I fell you*, the coppice snarled, and pulled harder. She strained against it for all she was worth, but what is the strength of a girl to that of an oak?

Why was it attacking her? Before, once she was free of metal, it had let her go at once. *Metal, metal, biting my flesh*, the oak whispered, and began to slowly separate her arms from her body. She heard a crunch nearby—at least Gwidion had followed her. At least he'd be torn apart too. She had saved her family.

"Come out, come out, wherever you are," Gwidion taunted in schoolyard cadence. "Ready or not, here I come."

Her shoes! There was metal on the tips of her shoelaces. Just before serious damage was done, she kicked her shoes off and the tree released its deadly hold.

"Thank you," she said, patting one of the slender new saplings rising from the roots before squeezing through the tight cane-brake to freedom. "Olley olley oxen free," she said to herself.

Gwidion was a pathetic sight, but she tried very hard not to feel sorry for him. He had several pieces of metal that she could see and obviously had no idea why the tree was attacking him. He stabbed at the grappling saplings with his dagger, enraging the tree further. It had hold of his arms and legs and was doing its best to quarter him, all the while lashing at his face with its most supple switches.

"That," said a voice beside her, "is why he should never be the Guardian." Pazhan eyed his master with a detached insouciance.

Meg jumped and ran behind a tree—a quite friendly little hickory. Pazhan's horns were still dark with Lysander's blood. But the goat didn't seem at all threatening now.

"You're . . . you're not going to help him?"

"If he tells me to help him, I must." Pazhan watched his master fight being torn into pieces until Gwidion happened to see him.

"Help me, you blasted goat!" he screamed as he pulled against the gripping branches. With something like a shrug, the goat waded into the fray and began biting through wood. He tossed aside branches with his powerful horns until Gwidion could struggle through the coppice. The tree whacked him one last parting shot to the rump and rasped, *No metal, never metal. He wants to fell the sapling, but the sapling is strong. Unroot yourself, sprout!*

Taking this (rightly) as a message to herself, Meg ran again, slowly, jarring with each stride.

"I can't keep up. Stay with her!" Gwidion ordered his goat, and Meg heard the thud of hooves in the dirt grow closer.

"He doesn't think about what he says," Pazhan pointed out when they were beyond Gwidion's sight. He trotted easily beside her, and after a while without violence, Meg gave up trying to elude him. "Another reason he oughtn't be Guardian. If he tells me to kill you, I must. Be ready for that."

She slowed to a walk. "Whose side are you on?"

"Side? Are there sides in this? I am a fairy, but I have served Thomas men for seventeen generations."

"You're a fairy?"

"Do goats you know talk?"

"Well . . . I thought . . ."

"A brownie, like your own family brownie, and bound to serve Thomas men until the day one sets me free."

"Which he won't do, I suppose."

"Don't be so sure about that," said the goat with a canny wink. "Now, follow me."

"Why should I?"

"I serve now because I must, but when my servitude ends, I will be a free fairy once more . . . and mayhap I am tired of being ruled by Thomas men. I wouldn't wish it on others of my kind. Look here. Step in that."

Meg skidded to a halt before a ring of pale mushrooms. "Are you kidding? You *are* on his side! I know what will happen if I step inside a fairy circle."

"Aye, good, then you also know what will happen when he steps in to follow you. He'll be trapped—"

"Along with me, and he'll kill me."

"He'll certainly try, but I've led the wild dances in a fairy circle, I've captured mortal girls to be my partner, and I tell you that anyone'd be hard-pressed to catch their breath or collect their thoughts once inside. One fairy will grab your hands, another will take hold of his, and you'll be whirled into madness until they release you."

"Which might not be for a hundred years," she said. "No thanks."

"I give you my oath, when the sun is about to rise, I will free you both, and you can run to the Green Hill to make your declaration. It will feel like just a few moments to you, lost in your dance."

I can't run anymore, Meg thought. I have to trust him. If I can see my way to dawn, anything might happen.

She crouched just outside the mushroom ring, rubbing her ankle as though she'd twisted it. This, she thought, is the stupidest thing I've ever done.

Gwidion crashed through the trees, emerging like the wild man of Borneo, with his hair disheveled and bloody welts across his face and arms.

"Got you!" he said, and lunged at her. Meg let herself fall backward, expecting at any moment to feel the knife.

But cool hands gathered her up and draped her with garlands, laughing and exclaiming at her free hair and bare feet, the waterweeds on her skin and the wild look in her eyes. "You're one of us already," said a girl her own age with flowing brown locks and bare feet beneath short skirts that appeared to be made of lacy leaf skeletons.

"Dance with us and be free," said another, whose own skin seemed to be dappled with duckweed.

"But there's someone after me," she said, or tried to say, as the surprisingly strong hands pulled her into what looked like a grassy meadow, as close-cropped as a croquet lawn and lit with will-o'-the-wisps. She couldn't see any distinct edges. Was all of this inside the mushroom circle, then? Fairy space must work as strangely as fairy time.

And look there—Gwidion, caught by three other little girls, who pulled at his hands and clothes until he was trotting in an awkward hopping dance. One of them plucked his knife and tossed it away. It promptly disappeared outside the ring . . . though Meg couldn't see the mushrooms anymore.

Tiny butterfly fairies, just a bit bigger than the moth pixie Finn had seen, cavorted on the turf under Gwidion's feet. "Unhand me!" he said, and tried to stomp on the little fairies. They shrilled screaming giggles of delight and danced just out of reach.

With the last of his strength and free will, Gwidion lurched across the meadow toward Meg, dragging the laughing fairy girls behind him. "This is your doing, vixen. When I catch you . . ." But their partners pulled them apart, and some unseen piper struck up a lively air.

This was entirely different from the court ball under the Green Hill. These girls were wild maenads, stomping their bare feet and flinging their locks about with abandon. Meg fought them at first on general principle, but it wasn't long before she forgot Gwidion, forgot the terrible danger before her, the terrible tragedy behind her, and gave herself up to the dance. It was delicious to be moving her limbs and tossing her head. Even when Gwidion passed close by, burdened by his lively fairy partners, she wasn't afraid. She knew dimly, like a childhood memory, that her legs were aching and sore, that she was so sleepy she was about to drop, but she danced on.

Then, worse than the pain and shock and confusion of a newborn drawing his first breath to yowl his protest at all the world, Meg was dragged out of that happy dream. Hard goat horns butted her backside, shoving her from that merry musical place of ecstatic peace to the dark, dangerous real world. No, not utterly dark. To the east rose the faintest glow that presages dawn. She gasped, then flinched at the rawness of the air, so unlike the fairy air that had floated over her lungs like soothing balm.

"Go, at once. You just have time," Pazhan said, giving her another butt. "I have to get my master out now, but I'll delay him long enough for you to get to the hill."

She didn't stop to wonder why Pazhan had to get Gwidion out . . . after all, Gwidion hadn't had time to issue an order. Perhaps the goat had a scheme of his own.

Her legs were rubbery, her mind a jelly. Part of her was still stuck in that wild whirling dance, and as for the rest of her, it moved leadenly. She staggered a step or two before she got her bearings, then ran off with a strange gait that consisted of falling forward and catching herself just in time with one leg, then repeating the process with the other.

She crashed through the blackberry thorns, and when she emerged on the other side, her skin was a mess of her own blood and sweet blackberry blood. She snapped off a handful of canes, pricking her palms deeply.

"Stop her!" came a voice from the woods as she laboriously climbed and staggered and fell her way up the hill.

"Fool," said the goat, trotting to her side. "He didn't say when to stop you, or where." Meg ignored him, saving all her concentration for putting one foot, then one knee, in front of the other. "Will right here do for you? A little higher?" Meg was locomoting by grabbing handfuls of sod and hauling herself up to the summit inches at a time. "Here, then? Okay, consider yourself stopped." And the goat sat down on his haunches to see what would unfold.

Meg was struck with an unaccountable stage fright. She was tongue-tied. Why hadn't Phyllida told her what to say? Declare her intentions, she'd said, no magic spell or ritual words needed... but this was a moment of such gravity, Meg didn't want to bungle it, and she was suddenly sure she would.

"I ...," she began, then used the excuse that it wasn't quite precisely sunrise to buy herself a bit more time to think what to say.

Then Gwidion pushed his way through the thorns, and it was too late for more thought.

"I am the ...," she started to say, forcing herself to sound confident, then the knife flew point over hilt and hit Meg in the chest. Luckily she was struck only with the heavy double-goat pommel, but still it hurt enough to silence her momentarily. She turned to run again, but Gwidion tackled her from behind, knocking the wind out of her as she fell. She rolled to her back and kicked out at him, but he caught her ankles in one hand, as easily as you'd catch a baby's to change its diaper, and pinned her to the ground with his body. That alone was almost as unpleasant as her fear of imminent death, for he smelled nastily of sweat and turpentine and goat, though in all fairness Meg herself smelled of sweat and fear and stagnant water. She thrashed at him with the blackberry brambles but he just laughed and tore them out of her hands.

He stretched for the dagger and held it high above her head.

"You'll never be Guardian," Pazhan said, walking calmly to stand beside them.

"Shut up, goat!" Gwidion said. "I kill this one, then force Phyllida to give me everything."

"Force her? How? You've taken away her beloved. If you take away this girl too, what do you have to threaten her with? There's nothing else she loves, except perhaps the Green Hill. Methinks she's not one to value her own life or comfort so highly she'd violate her beliefs by turning the Green Hill over to you."

"Shut up!" he said again, but didn't stab.

"The portrait might have worked, I'll own that much. You have a certain talent for persuasion, and had that boy not destroyed your painting, you might have gotten Phyllida to quite calmly and naturally make you her heir." The goat chuckled to himself. "A fine mess he made of things, too. When I found him there with the paintbrush in his hand—"

The first touch of gold peeked over the horizon.

"You saw him? You actually saw that brat destroy my painting, my dreams, and you did nothing! You should have killed him where he stood!"

"I had no orders," Pazhan said softly, glancing at the sun that heralded a new day.

"Orders be damned!" Gwidion said, and smashed the butt of his bronze knife over Pazhan's skull.

The goat sank to one knee under the blow, but rose smiling.

"Thrice in three days you have struck me, former master, and my bond to your family is broken." He tossed his head and ruffled his mane. "Stand aside, man."

"Then you're next, goat," Gwidion said, and plunged the dagger down toward Meg's exposed throat.

Thick, curving horns came up and caught the dagger, tossing it into a high arc. It fell, burying itself to the hilt in the summit of the hill. Pazhan swung his head around and stabbed upward again through Gwidion's belly until the points emerged from his back. He paraded Gwidion's body until the screaming subsided to a whimper, then tossed aside the silent corpse.

"Say your words, Meg Morgan. Tell all who live under the Green Hill what you are."

Shaking but strong, Meg hauled herself to her feet and faced the rising sun.

"I am Guardian of the Green Hill!" she shouted to the dawning splendor.

Then, as she had the last time she saw someone killed at dawn on the Green Hill, she fainted, and the earth drank up Gwidion's blood ravenously while the Rookery crows circled and dropped to the treetops.

My Heart's Desire

FINN SPENT THE NIGHT on the croquet lawn, stretched out among the earwigs and beetles. He hadn't the heart to go back inside the Rookery. He knew he was a coward, but there it was. Lysander was dead, Phyllida might be dead too, for all he knew, if the banshee was right. Seeing her husband slain before her eyes would be enough to kill a much younger person, and watching Meg run off to an unknown fate with a madman behind her would finish the job. He didn't want to know, not till he had to. Eventually someone would find him and break the news, but until then it was better to hide, if lying spread-eagle on an open lawn was hiding, until someone remembered him.

It's all over, he thought. The Ashes are gone, or soon will be, and Meg. . . . He didn't have any hopes for Meg. I should have gone after her, he thought. I should have called the police. Someone should have, anyway, for to his surprise, lights and sirens never materialized. The house stayed closed and eerily silent.

For a while, he stared at the stars. Under the ointment's influence, they seemed brighter, and he thought he could see the play of distant gases and combustion in their twinkle. Moths fluttered across his vista, some real, some fairies, but he didn't try to talk to them. If the Seelie prince wouldn't help, what could a tiny moth fairy do?

He slept eventually, more soundly than he would like to admit. People aren't supposed to sleep well when their worlds are crumbling. His sleep was so deep he didn't hear any of the feet, or hooves, or claws, or wings, or flippers that passed near him. He didn't wake until after sunrise.

The first few somnolent moments between true sleep and true consciousness are the most delicious of the day. You are awake enough to shape your dreams into thoughts, but not quite awake enough that all the troublesome realities have rudely made their presence known.

It was just in those precious moments that Finn saw a fairy who looked very like Meg. The ointment must not have worn off yet, he thought blearily, and indeed there was very little glamour about this figure striding slowly toward him. Its dark brown hair hung in muddy locks. Its feet were bare and dirty. It was covered in grime and dried algae and thorn scratches and blackberry juice. But for all the filth, there was something otherworldly about its aspect that convinced Finn it was a fairy. Perhaps it was the way the figure seemed to glow, even beneath the dirt . . . or was that only a trick of the morning light? Finn sat up, bringing his face directly into the glaring rays of daybreak, and was dazzled into blindness. Then the sun kindly ducked behind a cloud, and he could see it was only a very disheveled, tired, and scruffy Meg stumbling toward him.

"Meg!" he cried, and threw his arms around her so hard he almost knocked them both over, then, embarrassed, released her so abruptly she actually did fall down. "You're alive!"

Pazhan ambled into view behind her, and though Finn initially ducked behind Meg, he very quickly realized what he was doing and jumped between her and the goat.

"It's all right," Meg said. "He's no threat now. He's free." Which Finn didn't understand at all.

"Where is everyone?" Meg asked.

Finn didn't answer.

"Inside?" They couldn't see the house from where they were; a line of tall privet hedges obscured their view. She started walking, and he followed her.

"Gwidion?" he asked.

"Dead," she said, leaving Finn with the astounding impression that she'd killed Gwidion single-handedly and then tamed his goat.

Meg stopped suddenly. "Is . . . I don't remember all of what happened last night. At least, it doesn't quite feel real. Is Lysander really . . . really dead?"

Finn could only nod.

"And the others? Are they okay?"

"I don't know."

"Don't know?"

"I've been out here all night."

"Why?"

"I didn't think they'd want me."

"Oh, Finn," she chided in her Mother voice. "You're as much a part of this as any of us. Come on. I know where they'll be."

She led Finn around the side of the house to the garden kitchen and thus didn't see the delegation that awaited her at the front of the Rookery. She slipped inside the house and took the shortcut to the main dining hall. It was rarely used by the family, for they weren't given to grand entertainments. Its last use had been as a temporary mausoleum for Bran during the brief and terrible time when he was dead.

Now it held another fallen member of the family. Rowan and the doctor had carried Lysander's body to the grand banquet table and then retreated discreetly, leaving Phyllida to keep watch overnight. Now Rowan, Dickie, Silly, Dr. Homunculus, and Bran waited awkwardly outside the door, wondering if they dared break in upon Phyllida's grief. James lay curled across two armchairs that had been pushed together, sleeping soundly.

Bran saw Meg first. "Heavens be thanked!" he said, and tried to pick her up in a hug, but she evaded him.

"Don't you dare hurt yourself again for my sake," she admonished. The others crowded around her, gently patting her shoulders and back, as if she were particularly fragile. They asked what had happened, of course, but she said she'd tell them later.

"We don't have to worry about that painter chap anymore, I warrant," Bran said, looking at her with grandfatherly pride.

Meg smiled wanly and let herself into the dining hall. Silly made an attempt to follow her. Meg politely but firmly closed the door in her face.

Phyllida looked up at the sound of the door.

"Isn't there anything we can do?" Meg asked, standing beside her over Lysander's body. "If we cut his ash tree, like we did with Bran..."

"No, child. This is different. When a person has lived a long and vital life and dies of natural causes, there is no way to undo it." Meg would have argued with the phrase *natural causes*. Gwidion was as unnatural as they come.

"He gave his life to save me," Meg said softly.

"To save all of us. To save the Green Hill. To help ensure the future of our line. My line, that is. He leaves no children in this world. All there was of him is gone."

She had to be silent for a while. Floods of tears can sometimes be dammed by a levy of silence, where a single word would send them surging.

Meg looked down at Lysander. Phyllida was right. She'd never thought of it before—relations are so hard to keep straight—but he was no blood kin of hers. He felt like a grandfather, though, far more than the unlikely Bran, and she'd loved him as she loved Phyllida. She cringed inwardly at that past tense. Loved? No, I love him still, she thought fiercely, as I will love Phyllida when she is gone. The banshee heralded her death. How much longer do I have, does she have? A day? A week?

Lysander had been cleaned and dressed in an old-fashioned black suit. Had Phyllida done all that? No, Meg saw now. Crouched in the corner was the rookery brownie. He must have helped her with that age-old task of laying out the body.

Meg put her hands in her pockets and rocked back and forth.

She desperately wished there were something she could do to ease Phyllida's suffering. Her fingers curled upon a stone in her pocket. Of course—the heart's desire stone.

"Here," she said unceremoniously, thrusting it into her great-great-aunt's hand. She half expected Lysander to rise up from the table, look around, and demand his breakfast and his pipe. Surely that must be Phyllida's heart's desire. Maybe there was more to it than that. Maybe there was a spell. Or maybe Phyllida just had to speak her wish aloud.

"That's for you," Meg explained. "It will give you the thing you desire most."

Phyllida looked at Meg, then the stone in her cupped hand. She closed her other hand around it and murmured words Meg couldn't quite catch, though she heard "my great thanks" among them.

"Will it work? Will it bring him back to life?"

"Back to life? Why, child, I told you it cannot be. This day has been long in coming. Lysander's heart has been failing for many years now, though he tried to hide it and mend himself with foxglove. When the banshee wailed, we knew it was only a matter of time."

"You mean you knew he would die of grief from losing you?"

"Losing me? Whatever do you mean?"

"The banshee was washing your shirt, the one you gave me. At first I thought it meant Rowan was going to die, because I gave the shirt to him, or that I would. But we figured out you really owned the shirt so it must mean you. Oh, Phyllida, I know I'm being selfish, but what in the world will I do when you're not here? I don't know anything. I need you to teach me. Bran can help, but it's not the same. I need you, Phyllida. Please, please, please don't die!" She wept hot, bitter tears onto Phyllida's cheeks.

"Here, child, take back your pebble, and we'll both have our hearts' desires, then." She sighed deeply. "The shirt wasn't mine. It was Lysander's. I took it to paint in, but really because I liked to wear something that smelled like him." She laughed to herself, a secret, loving laugh of shared intimacies that baffled Meg. Will I ever know something like that? she wondered. "When you told me what you saw, well, there was no mistaking that shirt. I made it for him myself, back in my younger days, when my eyes were good enough for fine stitching and I had more patience. And time." She stared out at something Meg couldn't see—her own mortality.

"You mean you're not going to die? You'll still be here to teach me?" Phyllida nodded. "But I want you to have your heart's desire. Doesn't the stone work? I'll ask Dickie or the Wyrm. They'll know how to make it work. We can bring Lysander back."

"Child, no," she said, restraining Meg as she headed for the door. "It *has* worked. I have gotten my heart's desire."

"What do you mean?"

"I always knew that Lysander would die someday, as we all will. And lately, knowing his heart, I've assumed he would beat me in this last great race. Tell me, what did you say when you stood on the Green Hill at dawn?"

"I told it I would be the next Guardian," Meg said.

"No, you didn't. Think. What did you say?"

"I said . . . oh, I said, 'I am Guardian of the Green Hill.' Oh, Phyllida, did I do it wrong? What are you laughing at? Did I ruin it?"

"Meg, Meg, my own, you *have* given me my heart's desire. That was the only pain of my life, the only real sorrow. Lysander's death, though it has torn out a piece of my soul, is after all only the lot that awaits all of us. And he's not really gone, you know. You'll understand that someday." But she already did, a little. "The only thing I feared was that without a daughter of my own to carry on, my life, however well lived, would be wasted. If there was no Guardian, the link between fairies and man would grow weak, and both would diminish, fairies until they were gone, I suppose, shrunk to emmets or memories, and man until he was like the cold iron the Good Folk fear, dead inside, without the pulse of the earth in his veins.

"Now in the twilight of my life you come along, the daughter I couldn't have, and you change the world. My world and, I have reason to suspect, the rest of the world too."

Meg's eyes were huge.

"Don't look so frightened. I will be here to help you, as will Bran. And don't discount your siblings and your friends. I didn't understand it at first, this great change you have wrought, but when my burden was lifted, it became clear. You will see, very soon."

There was a solemn and dignified knock on the door, a knock such as only an experienced butler can make, and after a suitable pause, Wooster stuck in his head.

"My Lady, the wake."

"Very well. Tell them we will be out presently." She turned back to Meg. "Now you must assume your duties as Guardian. I am sorry your first task will be seeing off the spirit of one we both loved so well, but—"

"Wait . . . what? I'm not the Guardian yet. I don't know what to do."

"My dear, you're the one who said it, who willed it, before all, on the top of the Green Hill. You relieved me of my burden, my dear child. You took away both my fears of what comes when my life is over . . . and the duties left to me in this life. Not that I won't have any duties, with you and the others to teach. But the real work now falls to you."

"Me?" she asked stupidly. She felt like she was a few steps behind Phyllida, like there was a very important point that somehow escaped her.

"You, girl, you! You are the Guardian of the Green Hill."

"The *next* Guardian," Meg tried to say. *No, no, no! I can't! I won't! I want to go home!* Those panicked desires returned, and her confidence vanished.

"Didn't you know? Didn't you realize? You took it away from me—for which I am heartily thankful, might I add—and took it all on yourself. I admit I was surprised, but so grateful. You don't know what it is to serve for a lifetime, though you will. I don't mean to make it sound miserable, it is anything but. It is like having a child who never grows up, a joy, but a weighty responsibility you can never, never take your eyes off of. Now it is yours, to love and care for."

Phyllida beamed, but Meg wanted to run.

"Do you mean . . . when I said 'I am the Guardian of the Green Hill,' I actually took over for you? You mean you're not the Guardian anymore? I am?"

It was just a slip of the tongue—wasn't it? Because she hadn't rehearsed an acceptance speech, as it were, because she was weary and harried and terrified after her ordeal, and she'd said the first thing that popped into her head, she was now the Guardian, for life? It had been a serious undertaking and frightening duty, certainly, but bearable when she thought she wouldn't have to assume her role for years. Anything that can be put off indefinitely isn't real. But this—this was far too real for her.

Then she looked at Phyllida, serene for the first time in weeks. Why, even the lines on her brow, which Meg had assumed were from age, had smoothed, all overnight. It occurred to her that it might have worked out the same either way. If Phyllida had kept the burdens of being the Guardian, they might have killed her. Then Meg would have been Guardian almost as soon, but alone, without her help. This way at least she still had Phyllida's guidance, her wisdom, while taking the work on her own young shoulders.

Meg felt ashamed of herself. Phyllida had just lost her husband. Worse than that, she'd seen him killed before her eyes. She'd been held prisoner, hurt by a madman who wanted to ruin everything she had worked for. She's been serving faithfully all of her life, Meg thought, and now she has a chance to rest. Can I begrudge her that?

She could, but she'd never let Phyllida know it.

She hugged her great-great-aunt and said, "I'll try to do my best."

"I know you will, child. Now come. They are here for the wake. We must forget the sorrow of his passing and recall only the vitality and joy that was his life."

Phyllida flung open the door and invited the others in. They wept, though lightly, but soon they were joking about Lysander's fondness for sardine sandwiches and the way he always mangled songs and his manner of looking sternest when he was feeling most kindly. Silly remembered jokes he'd told, Dickie mentioned the time Lysander translated a naughty bit of Catullus for him, not realizing till the end how inappropriate it was for young ears. James took one look at Lysander's body and said, "Don't worry. He'll talk to us soon," which everyone thought was an endearing bit of childish prattle.

Rowan stood guard solemnly over Lysander. "If I hadn't been such a fool, I might have saved him," he said. Then, more softly, "I would have been a good heir, Lysander. I didn't mean anything wrong by it, honestly I didn't. I just wanted to take care of things. I didn't mean harm."

Phyllida came up behind him and put an arm over his shoulder. "He knows it, lad, and so do I. Don't worry, Rowan. You have a place here, just as Meg does."

And where was Finn in all this? Whatever Meg said about him being as much a part of it as the rest of them, he knew he wasn't. They didn't want him, really. He was an outsider, an interloper, and though they might accept him, some more grudgingly than others, he had no real business being there any longer.

"I didn't from the start," he said to himself as he went to his room upstairs. "They didn't want me. My father made them take me. I hate them, and they hate me. Now I'm going home, fever or no fever." The occasional letter and news clipping from the States told them the illness, their original reason for fleeing to England, was still rampaging. Finn packed his bags but found they were too heavy to manage by himself, and he had no intention of telling anyone he was going. He rearranged things until his most important possessions were in one small satchel. With the ten-pound note inside (and the skeleton key, of course), he could just manage it. He snuck out of the house through the garden kitchen.

"Where ye off to, lad?" Bran was sitting by himself on a hickory chair just outside the door.

"None of your business," he snapped automatically. He felt like the old disagreeable Finn, and though it was in many ways more comfortable, he already hated himself for it.

"No, perhaps 'tisn't. 'Tis Meggie's business, though. She may need you."

"No one needs me. I'm going home."

"Suit yerself," he said. "But that Meg, she has a hard road ahead of her. She could use a friend. 'Specially one like you."

"What do you mean?" Against his will, Finn set his bag down.

"Yer a regular rotter, you are," Bran said. "Now don't get yerself in a huff. I didn't mean it as a slight, not exactly. But yer no better than you ought to be, times, and there's something to be said for that, if your heart's in the right place, that is. Where's yer heart, boy, eh?"

Finn didn't answer.

"Yer young yet, but no answer's answer enough for the time being. Stay awhile, lad, and see what happens. Is there so much at home that's calling you back?"

Finn thought of his pale, distant mother, his overbearing, distant father, the maids and cook who might actually miss him a bit, but not, he imagined, very much. Again, no answer was answer enough. "Oh, all right," he said as though he was doing everyone a big favor. "I'll stay for a little while." And he trudged back upstairs with his satchel.

"Sometimes it's good to have a rotter about," Bran said to no one in particular. "You can count on them to do the things others won't. Meg'll shy from dirty dealings, but that Finn won't. And necessary deeds can get powerful dirty, times."

Back in the dining hall, Meg wished she could shy away from her duties now. "I need to wash, Phyllida. I need to change." She was barefoot and filthy—a grubby, scruffy, unprepossessing specimen of Guardian. "They'll laugh at me. They'll think I can't do the job." And they'll be right, Meg thought miserably.

"No, Meg, stay as you are. All the Good Folk are talking about what happened last night, and by now most of the villagers will know too. For a place with hardly any telephones, news has a way of spreading. They'll be pleased to see you fresh from the fight, as it were. You'll do fine."

But I don't feel fine, Meg wanted to say. She wanted to curl up in a little ball and think about everything that had happened—or better yet, not think at all. Fortunately she soon learned her only duty was to stand by the door and, like a hostess at a ball, greet each visitor with a nod or handshake or word of thanks for condolences offered.

And such visitors! Hobs and bogarts, bwcas and pwcas, pixies and nixies, Cait Sith and Cu Sith, all in a trailing line come to pay their respects to the departed, and incidentally to the new little Guardian. Meg had had no idea her new kingdom was so diverse, and so numerous. They filed in seemingly without end as she wavered on her feet and tried to keep all their names straight.

Even the Host came, the Black Prince making a fleeting visit to bow curtly, sneer at her appearance, and depart, followed by his train of nobles. Bloody redcaps, a shapeless brollachan, and even the Nuckelavee eyed her up and down before passing on to bow over Lysander's body. Though he wasn't the Guardian, he had meant a great deal to man and fairy alike.

Humans came too. Not all of them, for even in fairy-steeped Gladysmere, there were plenty who either didn't believe (or tried not to) or were so mistrustful they wouldn't have any truck with them. But those who by profession had the closest ties to fairies—the bakers and the weavers, the cobblers and the midwives, among others—were there. The mayor, who went to everything with a ceremonial sash over his shoulder, made a brief speech and gave Meg the key to the city. The chief constable was there, as were most of the farmers and the girl in the dress shop with her own ne'er-do-well lad.

Tansy, looking a bit red and tired but otherwise cheerful, gave Meg a shy kiss on the forehead, introduced his vastly pregnant wife, and went outside to join the festivities—for what is a wake without drinking, singing, and dancing?

"Oh . . . hi, Fenoderee," Meg said, waking up a bit when her hand was vigorously pumped. He had something flung over his shoulder.

"I found a wee manikin out in yer garden," he said brightly. "I hailed him, and he toppled over. Is he yours?" Fenoderee produced a very limp, unconscious Dr. Homunculus.

Meg couldn't help smiling. "Not mine, exactly—"

"Tell you what he needs," Silly said, sidling up to them. "A spot of dancing to wake him up. Why don't you take him off to the fairy circle and show him a good time?"

Fenoderee, happy to oblige, dragged the doctor off under his arm to the impromptu mushroom ring the fairies had created on the lawn.

"Well," Meg said uncertainly, already thinking she wasn't making good decisions as the new Guardian, "just remember to get him out. We don't want him stuck there for a century. He probably doesn't even believe in fairies. I didn't believe in them myself a few weeks ago."

"And now look at you!" Silly said blithely.

Meg did look at herself, and saw a dirty, scared girl putting on the best face she could. She envied Dr. Homunculus. He would be lost to time and trouble in the fairy circle for a while at least. She'd give anything for a bath and a bed.

There was a lull in mourners and well-wishers, so she drifted closer to the door and looked outside. The grounds had turned into a carnival. Villagers drank ale from a barrel in the back of a dray, and fairies drank tiny cups of something squeezed directly from the udders of a small red cow, and each was very careful to not drink the disgusting beverage of the other. But though their drinks didn't mingle, they did, dancing and reminiscing about eighty years and more of a life well-lived. The two tribes of folk got together to honor a man both had loved and respected in the best way of all, through merriment, not tears. But the tears would come again through the years, in the quiet moments of loneliness when the guidance of a wise friend is needed, when a strong arm is missed and, for Phyllida, every night and every morning when the bed beside her was empty. There was no weeping in her dreams, though. In her dreams, he would sleep by her side.

Wooster approached respectfully. "There is a . . . ahem . . . small gentleman who would like a word with you, miss. On the lawn by the tennis courts." This was on the far side of the house, away from the human and fairy merrymaking.

Phyllida suppressed a look of mischief and said, "Yes, let us go and see what he wants." Meg, along with Rowan, Silly, James, and Dickie, followed Wooster away from the revelers to the relative quiet of the courts. Finn, watching everything from his room, ran to a window on the other side of the house to follow them.

"Oh, Phyllida, look!" Meg said when they came into sight. "Is it safe?"

"I shouldn't imagine it is," Phyllida said cheerfully.

There, stomping and stamping, howling and growling on the tennis lawn, was every creature she could imagine, every creature she had read about from her earliest days with Bulfinch and the D'Aulaires' books of myths, and some that were beyond both study and imagination. They huddled in a chaotic bundle, too cautious to venture far from their fellow outlandish creatures, but they didn't seem to trust one another much either.

Things that looked suspiciously like centaurs stomped their hooves at tiny, hissing basilisks. A one-horned, elegant deerlike fellow with silver-tipped blue-green scales along his body—a Chinese Ki-Lin—tried to make peace between a minotaur and a lamia, and got butted by each for his troubles. Overhead a thunderbird was torn between maintaining his lofty dignity and dropping down to eat a fat indigo bull. She saw unicorns and sky-blue Mongolian wolves.

There were griffins in all their variety—the standard winged, lion-rumped, eagle-headed; the wingless keythong; the opinicus, with a lion's forelegs; and the hippogriff, with its horse parts thrown in for good measure. They all looked more or less the same to Meg, and she was surprised to see each kind grouped in its own offish little clique, the keythongs eyeing the hippogriffs with dark suspicion, who in turn raised their hackles at the traditional griffins.

Among them all were almost-human women—exquisite peris; tall, buxom, apple-cheeked women with long blond braids hanging over their metal breastplates; the four heavenly dancers of India whose job is to distract annoying do-gooders from being so good they rival the benevolence of the gods. And men: astoundingly beautiful warriors with blue-black hair; compact brown men with curved bows small enough to be a child's toy and legs bent like their bows from a lifetime on horseback; golden godlike men crowned in laurel.

One separated himself from the horde, evidently the small gentleman Wooster had mentioned. He was a head shorter than Meg, with the torso of a diminutive, perfectly proportioned human male and legs coated in woolly curling hair with flowers woven into it. His feet were pointed goat's hooves. Horn buds peeked from the brown curls of his head. He crept up to Meg and the others, looking frequently over his shoulder at a pack of commingled satyrs and centaurs who urged him on with encouraging gestures.

"Um . . . ahem . . . I . . . that is to say we . . ."

With great difficulty, Meg suppressed a smile. It was a relief to encounter someone more nervous than she was.

"Go on," she said gently.

"You spoke to me!" He looked over his shoulder. "She spoke to me!" There was a smattering of applause and a few hoots.

"Of course I did. May I help you?"

The faun—for indeed that's what he was—closed his eyes, turned his head heavenward for a moment, and exploded into what was evidently a rehearsed speech.

"Oh, most gracious and benevolent benefactress, we hail you and honor you and thank you for doing the great deed that freed us from our assorted prisons. You have awakened the sleeping, unchained the bound, welcomed the banished. You have brought us back into this world! Ever after, you will be honored among us. We come to offer you our fealty and obedience. At least"—and this part was evidently not rehearsed, and was said in an undertone too low for the crowd to hear—"I will be obedient, though there's more than one in this motley assembly would be better left in irons. Don't turn your back on them's my advice." His voice rose once again. "Before we scatter to the four corners of our earth, though I am told now that the earth is round, or rather spherical, which it wasn't in our day, we would make our obeisance and genuflections before you and tell you this: from today forward, we consider you our Guardian and guide in this strange new world that has gone on so long without us. Already we see things to astound and dismay us, and we will need your help to find our place." To Meg's own astonishment and dismay, he lowered himself to groveling prostration at her feet, and behind him all the others bowed or curtseyed or kowtowed or salaamed or made some other form of courteous submission.

They held their awkward positions, waiting.

"Say something," Phyllida prompted.

Meg took a step forward, almost treading on the faun's out-stretched hands. She looked over the assembly. What had she done? Centaurs loose upon the world? Minotaurs? Valkyries? They certainly didn't look safe. Even the unicorns weren't quite what she'd imagined. They looked like they would rather gore a knight than lay their heads quietly in a maiden's lap.

Who must do the hard things? Well, I guess that would be me, she thought with resignation.

She saw the faun rolling his eyes up at her from the ground at her feet. "Psst . . . the Nemean lion is hungry, and the minotaurs have short attention spans."

She took a deep breath, let it out, tried again, and said as loudly as she could, "Thank you."

Luckily she didn't have anything else to say, because the tennis courts erupted in cheers and yowls and roars and bellows and hisses and a clanging of swords on shields. The spell of reticence was broken, and they swarmed around Meg and the others. There were so many beasts and half beasts and quarter beasts that Dickie started to sneeze. Meg scooped up James lest he be trampled. They crowded and pressed and nuzzled the family and pumped their hands and rubbed against their legs and gave them gifts. Meg accumulated a great store of innocuous-looking pebbles that were said to do wonders, but by the time the day was over, she'd forgotten what most of them did. They wound up in a cigar box.

Near evening most of the creatures were gone. The fairies

too had packed up their kits and trooped back to the Green Hill. The lawn had been torn to pieces by the revelers, and there was a fine mess of centaur dung for the gardeners to clean up the following day (though they found it made excellent fertilizer).

Lysander was lowered into the earth at sunset, calmly and without further ceremony, with only villagers and servants in attendance, and Phyllida retired to her room to be alone with her memories. Rowan took up Lysander's ax and set to work chopping down his ash tree.

At long last, Meg could drag herself upstairs to the blessed solitude of her room. As soon as the door was shut, she peeled off her clothes, tossing them into a careless pile. They were too dirty to salvage. She wanted to bathe but was too sleepy, and after a moment's hesitation, flung her grimy self into bed, telling herself she'd personally wash the sheets tomorrow to save the maids any trouble.

But she couldn't sleep. There was a smell.

She tried to ignore it. Whatever it is, I'll deal with it in the morning, she thought, and put the sheet over her nose. But the smell easily filtered through the fine linen. She covered her head with the pillow and still couldn't escape it.

At last, with an exasperated groan, she dragged herself out of bed and sniffed around until she found the source—not the drains, as she'd suspected, but under the bed.

"Oh, of course, the Bake-Neko present. I guess the wrapping is rotting nicely." She got on her hands and knees and pulled the box from under the bed. A wave of bluebottles rose and settled irritably against the window, and blackbeetles fled in rustling scurries.

"Ugh," she said. "Whatever's in here can wait." She took it to the window and was about to balance it on the outside sill, not really caring if it fell to the rosebushes below, when the desiccated and mostly consumed remains fell open, revealing what looked like a small nut inside. She crouched down on her knees and held the box to the moonlight.

It was a walnut, carved like an ivory puzzle ball with intricate layers of dragons and chrysanthemums in miniature. Inside she could just see something moving. She pressed one eye to the nut. It was a pale, translucent maggot.

"Ew," she said, though she didn't really mind maggots. She tried to shake it out onto the carcass. "Go back and finish eating."

"The maggot is your present, ignorant infant," purred a voice from across the room. The Bake-Neko strolled out of her closet, his twin tails swishing.

Meg stood quickly and pulled a sheet off her bed.

"The protuberances and declivities of your species don't interest me. Or perhaps you hide your ungainly hairless body in natural shame, for beside lovely me, what an unsightly creature you are. Still, as there must be admirers and admirees, I do not begrudge you your existence."

"I thought you were going back to Japan . . . I mean, Nippon."

"I was, but a fit of weariness overcame me and I settled down for a nap in your antechamber." He yawned, covering his mouth with a velvet paw. "That treasure you hold so carelessly, barbarian, is a grub of Izanami, our lady of the underworld."

"What does he do?"

"Do? Must a gift of the gods do anything? That's like asking if precious I do anything. I exist. It is sufficient."

Meg peered at her grub again suspiciously.

"Well, I suppose it does *something*, though why anyone would want to talk to the dead is beyond me. Still, to each his tastes. Farewell, oh, blissfully ignorant child. When you compose songs and sagas in my honor, please try to mention my otherworldly beauty. And my softness. And the piquant curl of my whiskers." He sauntered out the door, popping his head back in once to add, "And of course the luxurious symphony of my purr."

As soon as he left, Meg ran to Phyllida's room. She pounded on the door until Phyllida emerged in a white wrapper and pink cashmere shawl with curling papers in her hair.

"Here," Meg said, placing nut and grub into her hand.

"What is it?"

"Put it to your ear. His voice is very low."

Puzzled, Phyllida listened, while Meg watched her expectantly, almost dancing on her tiptoes.

"Hello, my love," Lysander's voice said through the grub's mouth.

"Oh!" was all Phyllida could say, and she gently closed the door on Meg.

Now, of course, Meg still couldn't sleep. There was one thing left to do, the hardest of them all. Mommy, I'm not coming back. Mommy, I've released things into the world, terrible, wonderful things, and I'm responsible for them, and for the

fairies too. Mommy, I'm scared. I need your help. Mommy...
Mommy...

She took out an ivory sheet of parchment and an old-fashioned fountain pen from the escritoire at her bedside.

Dear Mommy, she wrote, but the rest was all inkblots and teardrops.

Acknowledgments

All of my thanks to my first editor, the gracious, supportive, fiendishly clever Reka Simonsen, and to my second marvelous editor, Noa Wheeler, who fearlessly stepped into the breach. Like most writers it took me a while to warm up to the idea of editing, but these pros made it a pleasure. Thanks also to publisher Laura Godwin, who read the Omnibus and survived, and to Sarah Dotts Barley for all her help and good cheer.

Since you *do* judge a book by its cover, I would like to express my admiration for the two artists who have contributed to the Green Hill books. David Wyatt did the cover of *Under the Green Hill*, and line illustrations for both books, and Jon Foster did the incredible cover you now hold in your hand. Some people think storytellers are magicians; well, artists are just as magical, and I'm pretty sure the fairies have whispered a few secrets to these two gentlemen.

Thanks to Babaloo for being my first reader and best friend, and to Marla for being my second reader and other best friend. And deepest appreciation to The Boy With Many Names for taking long naps, without which this book would not have been possible.

Love and respect to E.N., G.M.F., A.T., J.A., M.W., and the gang. I couldn't have done it without you.

But most of all, thank you. I wrote this for you. I hope you enjoy it.